BOY CUDDLE

BOY
CUDDLE

STEVIE WHITE

ANDRE DEUTSCH

First published 1992 by
André Deutsch Limited
105–106 Great Russell Street
London WC1B 3LJ

C.I.P data for this title is available
from the British Library

ISBN 0 233 98744 4

Printed and bound in Great Britain by
Billings Book Plan Limited, Worcester

For Sean
and the six years

CONTENTS

1 THE SECOND SNEEZE

Anyway. This is now.

I'm Joseph Dean Tortois and this is a Joseph Dean Tortois evening. It's gonna be a long one cos I'm gonna tell you a few things and at first they might not make a lot of sense.

I ain't been back from the pub long. And I popped up to have a last look at Sean's place before I came home.

I tell you who I was in the pub with. Jenny called me and told me what had happened so I said look, I'll meet you down the Bunch and we'll talk about it, OK?

I never seen her look so pale and shocked and empty.

And now I'm here. Back home by the big window and it's dark outside. I can see the lamp on the mantelpiece reflected off the glass – just a hanging image of the bulb inside that boring beige shade – it looks like it's sitting on the roof across the road. And the stars are out. Faint paper cups twinkling in the black sky.

Three days into January, the light dies too soon. Doesn't everything?

And I think I'm gonna be here all night cos I've got to get all this straightened out in my mind. I've gotta go through it step by step, blow by blow.

So listen. They say listen, you might learn something, you know.

It's funny how after all this, all this time – about three years – I still think more about Jenny than about Sean.

Funny cos Sean was always there, with me. But Jen. She was miles away. At first.

The first time Jenny called round Sean was out. I remember that. The first time she'd ever come to see him an' he was out.

But I wasn't. There I stood, a strange half-caste guy yawning at the door frame. And for a second she could have been at the wrong place but when it sank in – that I'd just crawled from Sean's bed – I could hear *Oh God* in her mind and see tears of hurt and anger in her eyes.

'No, Sean's out,' I said.

She looked round. 'So, who else lives here?'

'Well, just Sean really. I stay round some nights.'

Oops, you mean you sleep in the same *bed!* I hadn't really felt it before but I found myself becoming itchingly embarrassed.

What could I say? *No, I'm not* technically *gay. Only with Sean. D'you want me to prove it? The bed's still warm!*

Christ, it sounded so stupid. *Only with Sean.* Who're you kidding? No, it's true! What is it about him? OK, I can see Marco's attractive but sleep with him? No ta!

So I looked at her, trying not to show up too uncomfortable. I was only a kid then. If it was now I'd probably say something flash or ask her out.

And the Peckham sunlight wandered in the dusty polluted windows and lounged in her hair like a halo, she was a January blonde and her pretty lips were pale.

I rubbed at my face in the mirror, asking if she wanted a cuppa, but I knew all she wanted was to demand who was this skinny black guy intruding on her girly dreams. Well, half black, anyway.

But instead she just stood awkwardly, embarrassed, as I gawked about in my boxer shorts.

So, ages later I heard she'd left her mother in St Helens.

'I *thought* you had a funny northern accent,' I told her in my funny Canvey Island accent. 'My Mum came from Northumberland,' I said but she wasn't impressed.

Anyway back to that day. She went and I was left alone with this hot prickly day burning a hole in my plans.

Outside I could see the narrow streets, shining with the sweat of brick walls. And already a haze rose like a St Tropez mirage. Faint and far off, the birds seemed to gasp as they crossed the cloudless sky.

It was a lovely day, the kind I really felt ready for the gym. I wanted to bash my gloves hard against the leather speedball and hear the mean rapid drumming of sharp cracks against the pine surround.

Smell the burning hot air and the sun streaming in from high windows and the tiny specs of skin in the light shafts, turning over and flickering like old movies.

So I went, bouncing along uneven flags in my Nike Air trainers.

And saw Marco's red face, puffing, spitting, decking his partner and then the gleam in his little Italian eye. A gleam of victory. Decking Big Jim back down for another bite of canvas.

Terry stepped in, his arm across Marco. 'Take it easy!'

Marco nodded at the ref.

The tall guy would climb back up to stare over Marco's head and go dancing away backpedalling, his brow creased and sweating, confused. Thump! Another visit to the canvas.

But he's up like Dempsey at the Polo Grounds in '23, fresh from the fall into the typewriters and those fists swing like a kid skipping double dutch back at Marco.

I was up against this new kid at the gym one time, sparring. Anyway, he comes up at me with this Mike Tyson mean look on his face, trying to psyche me out.

I looked at Terry as if to say *Who is this twat?* and Terry smiled back.

I said to this kid, 'What's the matter, you got piles or something?'

I cracked up later. I'd love to have that written on a cardboard sign and hung round my neck before my fights.

But when I was fighting foreigners it'd have to be translated. I'd have *What's the matter, you got piles or something* written in Mexican or Finnish!

An albino rode the tube one morning years ago. And I stood with Sean.

It was a young child with bleak, staring eyes yet full of joy. An innocent, naive joy of imagined fates that only a child can hope for. Held in his mother's arms, his skin seemed icing-sugar dusted and translucent, his eyes now half-closed and lidding the white and pink blossom moisture beneath.

And shocking pure white hair blending with the delicate cellophane skin which showed every flesh and underskin working.

Sean was swaying, dangling from one of them springy handle things. His eyes were closed. I didn't know if he'd been drinking.

'Are you pissed?' I said. He shook his head but didn't open his eyes.

'I went up to see you yesterday afternoon,' I told him. 'But you weren't in.'

His face looked pained and the lines on his brow bunched up.

'Anyway,' I said. 'As I was coming out a little girl was there, on the street, like, an' she said *Hello*. Well, I didn't say anything, I just locked the door and when I turned round she said *Hello* again, y'know. So I said *Hello*, all nice like, an' the little bleeder says *Get stuffed!* Just like that! I couldn't believe it! Then her mother came out so I couldn't say anything. I just walked off.'

It's always noisy on the tubes, innit? It really drives me spare sometimes. I hate having to shout to be heard. I love to shout to make a point, though.

No amount of shouting would have got through to Sean. Let me tell you about him. There was something wrong with the boy. Something not natural. I tell you, sometimes I thought he was fucking brain dead!

I remember that time.

What's the matter with him? Christ, he's just not – is he retarded or something?

Sean, are you retarded? I could've cried with frustration.

And I'd walk away from him in a blinding rage. Yeh, just leave him standing lifeless, emptyheaded, his meek, made-up face still dripping and the baggy-faced old girl cackling away from a high-above window in the wintry clouds of mist. Her yellow bucket still steaming. She'd poured her piss over him.

I can't believe it! Why does he *do* that? He gets like this sometimes. Usually he's just quiet. But sometimes he flips. He stands outside his door like some demented camp sentry in an ancient floral print dress. In a fucking dress! And make-up.

The kids and neighbours just laugh incredulously and the old dears throw things at him and now they're pissing on him and I feel sick in my stomach with frustration and I feel the tears rising.

And when, even through the pain (because I love him), I embrace him and take his hand 'Come on, let's go inside', he won't move. He won't speak. And I explode in anger and disappointment because how can I accept this? *You fucking spastic!*

And I shout it close to his face. 'You fucking spastic! What the Christ are you doing? I don't understand what's going on in your empty bastard head!'

That's it! I'm off!

There was this, er, I knew this woman once.

She was older than me. A lot older. Anyway this was when I was sort of straight. Well, I'm straight now, but I mean. . .

Anyway, she wasn't married or nothing. She was over forty but she still looked good.

She was a really smart bird, dead sophisticated and everything. Anyway I met her and started seeing her and that – I met her on a bus, actually – and we got talking. She wanted her fridge lugging up some stairs or something, anyway *I* didn't do it.

No, but she was great, you know, really good in bed and dead sexy and everything. But she was always on about getting married. Like Jenny and Sean. But I didn't want to know and I kept avoiding the subject cos, er, well she was alright, and I thought well there's no point chucking her away. I weren't about to fucking marry her though!

So I was seeing her for about three months. I was really happy with her, y'know. She was about forty but she was really nice and everything. Knew all the tricks, between the sheets. She was great but she was, er. . . she kept. . .

She said, one time, she said *I wanna have a kid. A baby!* I said *What!* I said *Why?* And she said she needed someone to look after her when she was old and she couldn't see me sticking around that long and she was fucking right about that! I mean she was good at the time but I wasn't going to look after her until she – y'know, forever, like. Fuck that!

So I said No, I'm not bringing a kid into the world just so the poor cunt can look after you! What kind of a life is that? And she took the huff and fucked off and that's the last I saw of her.

It was Sean who started calling me *Toys* first. Joseph Dean Tortois. *Toys.* Make sense?

I didn't see him for ages after we left school. But then everyone started talking about him. We were in the pub next door to the gym one time after boxing.

'Remember that weird kid from school?' Marco said.

I thought for a minute, chewing my crisps. 'Who, that girl who used to wet herself in class all the time?'

He cracked up.

'Nah, that kid called Sean Cuddell. You must remember him. Boy Cuddle! He was such a twat!'

'Oh, right. Quiet kid, yeah? The football teacher had it in for him.'

'Yeah, that's him.'

'His Dad used to beat him up or something, didn't he?' I said.

'Yeah. Anyway, I was talking to Louise Walker the other day, she reckons he's on the game!'

'He's had a sex change an' all then, has he?'

'No, you nob. You've heard of blokes being prostitutes before!'

'Oh yeah. So is he a bummer, then, or what?'

'Course he's a fucking bummer! The kid's a shirtlifter. He's an arse bandit.'

'I saw some of those in the arcade. One-armed arse bandits!'

'Nah, he's, you know, a rent boy.'

'Collects the rent, then?' I said.

Marco slapped me round the head. I don't think he's got a sense of humour.

It's strange. I looked Sean up. I wanted to see if the same thing was happening to him that was happening to me. I needed to talk to someone. I'd told Marco but he wasn't much use.

When I met Sean I felt like a little kid, totally out of it. I felt like I'd arrived just as he was finishing and he wouldn't wait. You know what I mean? He was the champion, I was the challenger.

And I found myself falling in love. And I hated myself for it cos I felt such a puff. I mean, I wasn't supposed to fancy blokes.

Christ!

So it wasn't a boy meets girl story. More likely boy meets boy; boy pays boy; boy shags boy. Up the tradesmen's entrance.

Sean let me near him. He let me sleep with him. He let me pay him. But I knew right off he didn't feel anything. I was just another desperate bender to him.

I didn't realise at the time that he *couldn't* feel anything. He was emotionally dead. I hoped he at least wanted me as a friend. Just another friend – me.

Christ, I wanted him for a soulmate, a lover, a confidant, a life assistant, my right-hand man, my closest friend.

I wanted to share my every feeling. I need someone to tell things to – to laugh at my jokes, to tear me down, to build me up, be violent with me, be tender with me.

To wonder what I was thinking, to smile when I say *I love you*, to respond when I love him, when I feel him and touch him. I wanted someone to think about me and daydream about me, like I did all those things about him. To worry about me, to miss me, to look forward to seeing me, to be reminded of me by silly little things like boats or colours or a song. And I'm sure I'll cry tonight. I feel like crying right now.

But he didn't feel any of those things. He didn't even think of me as a friend. Somebody once asked Sean about me.

'Is he your mate, then, that black kid?' they said.

It was down the pub or somewhere and I was so shocked and hurt when he said no.

After all we'd been through, I didn't expect him to say we were lovers, but at least mates, yeh. Until I realised he didn't have any idea of what the word *mates* meant - that implied a capacity for caring and for enjoying being cared for. Christ, even odd socks have mates. Somewhere.

Sean was the same way with everybody. He was good to everyone instinctively and he never demanded or expected anything in return, especially not love.

What hurt me most of all, though, was the tenderness I lavished on him – I wasted on him – that never touched him. That never got close. I didn't once make him smile or respond or be – I dunno – happy. It was like fucking a doll and it made me feel ill.

What the fuck am I doing? I thought. Jesus, use your fist, why not? Eh? Go on, fuck your own hand – at least it's got feelings! You got more chance of getting some response, anyway. . . But how could I help myself?

I tried to but, Christ, what a fucking temptation! So I fucked him, for free in the end, and he took it like the shit his mates fed him and I felt like a wanker and I cried.

So I used him, he annoyed me, I pissed off. And then when I missed him, when I missed all the friggin' shit farce of it all, I was back, sniffing his milk and making him tea else he'd have starved, the jerk!

I don't really know what Jenny thinks of me. I used to act the prick when I was with her and Sean. I never fancied her or anything and I don't feel like she stole him from me. Sean, I mean. I don't feel like she stole Sean from me cos, well, it's fucking stupid really, he was never mine, I mean he wasn't even gay!

It's very complicated. Christ! Remember that – Sean wasn't even gay! Marco was wrong about him.

So what did we have? No, she didn't steal him. Anyway, we've both lost him now, so. . .

I *do* feel guilty. And bitter and empty. You tell someone to fuck off enough times and they fuck off. I lost count, I suppose.

I once saw a little girl outside the Italian snack bar that sold home-made ice cream.

That stuff is irresistible on a hot day in July, when you can almost smell the warmth from the brown legs everywhere that disappear into arses in ra-ra skirts. This was a young girl, though.

I don't usually look at little girls. Not in *that* way, you know. But this one reminded me of Jenny who reminds me of little girls anyway. She was spinning on the pavement in the sweating summer, her white pleats lifting above smart pink pants. I felt myself watching selfconsciously each time her small arse turned, not wanting to but guiltily admiring the fresh smooth thighs and the curve of her crotch sloping away beneath her body. Really! What a pervert.

I got used to it. I got used to Sean, I mean, not being a pervert. He wasn't always so vacant. He was intelligent when he wanted to be. But he did persecute himself sometimes. It was so weird. He never told me about his past, his childhood.

But he told Jenny years later.

I used to do most of the talking. I just rabbited on, I suppose, with my stupid stories and opinions and my piss-taking. It was as if he wasn't there, which gave me a freedom that I needed sometimes.

So, yeah, I told him to fuck off a lot. So did Jenny, though. She went through exactly what I did with him. Except she didn't fuck his arse like I did and, as she told me this afternoon, like his father used to.

Christ! I almost choked up when she told me that. Everything bad I'd ever done to him just smashed me in the face when she told me that. When I was talking to Marco I thought his Dad just used to beat him up. I didn't know the guy used to. . .

Why didn't he tell me? It all makes sense now.

Like *Why do you never lock the door when you're having a shit, Sean?* If he's in the pub some pissed fart always falls on top of him when he's on the pan. And they say, 'Fucking lock the door, you cunt, what's the matter with yer?'

Does he enjoy that? I *did* wonder. But it was his old man, wasn't it? When the old man was on heat he didn't want no locked doors for little boys to hide behind, no sir! So it stayed with Sean, that habit.

I must have sounded just like the fat old git.

'Oh, Sean, I'm sorry. I *really* didn't mean to do that!'

'It's OK, Dad.'

There was an old joke I used to torture myself with when I was feeling really low.

> *What's the difference between the Boy Cuddle and a toilet?*
> *You don't feel bad after you've used a toilet.*

Anyway I used to go up north quite a bit with my Mum when she took me to visit our Gran.

I remember a pretty white Mum dragging her fuzzy little dark sooty boy by the hand through the wild eyes and strange accents of Morpeth.

And I remember Newcastle a time or two. Just rain and cold and big grey overcoats and everywhere I was impressed by the steel fingers knitted together in bridge spans across the Tyne.

My Gran lived in an insufferably gloomy pit house in a coal-soaked village in Northumberland. She had blackclocks – little cockroaches that used to crawl out of the walls and peg it across the kitchen floor scaring the crap out of my Mum.

The air was always thick and smoky and it must have been that dirty coal smell and the permanent dark patches of walls above the fireplace that finally turned Gran slowly and hilariously mad.

It was the coal dust in the mines that killed her old man. My last memories of Grandad are with his face strained and dark, blacker than mine, his bony hands clutching his bedside oxygen mask.

But Gran – she was always there.

Jesus, is that why I turned out so scatty myself? Those endless geriatric feeding-time afternoons having to listen to such absolute crap! The TV newscaster used to tremble when she started. . .

Van Gogh's Sunflowers *today fetched a record twenty-five million. . .*

'Bloody foreign muck!' in that mad Geordie accent.

What? Gran, this is a report on a Christie's auction! She was right, actually. It *was* French!

'Ah dunno! Bloody foreign this, foreign that! Is everythin' made in Hong bloody Kong these days?'

Your plastic incontinency pants certainly are, Gran.

It was funny at first and Mum used to glare at me as I giggled into my cocoa.

Gran was convinced she breathed through her ears for a long time. If she'd ever ridden the tube she'd have seen kids suffocating themselves with their squeaking Walkman headsets.

When she sneezed, she only used to sneeze once an' all. It's that second sneeze that proves you're sane, I reckon.

'Concentration camps! That's what these thugs want, like! That'd fettle 'em. That's what *he* could do with, bloody hell!'

Gran, that's Jim Callaghan. He's the Prime – Oh, never mind, pass us another sandwich. Then I found she'd put Colgate in them.

'Oh, away! Ah must be daft! Ah thought it was that cheese spread in a tube stuff. Ah always keep it under the sink, like.'

Jesus!

'They put muck in the food, though, y'know, Andrea. Ah'm *sure* of it!'

Poor Mum. I didn't realise at the time how much she was suffering.

'Oh, she's just old,' my Mum used to say as Gran droned on about her ongoing correspondence with Mike Baldwin and how she slags him off in her letters.

'Ah'm *sure* he's takin' some notice though, pet!'

And claimed to have spoken to him on the phone.

'She's just old,' while we sat and waited for a cuppa and Gran'd wonder why the tea took so long to brew with water poured on it straight from the tap.

'Ah ran it long enough – it was gettin' warm!'

Just old? Mum, she's completely friggin' mad!

An' I could say anything to her when Mum wasn't in the room – she didn't understand it anyway.

I said to her, 'Gran, my apple's got a stalk-on!' and I cracked up.

And neck of mutton! She lived off neck of mutton and expected me to eat the shit! Christ, it wasn't as if there was a shortage of sheep up north!

Y'know, I mean – who invented neck of mutton for Chrissake?

(*Right, what's the shittiest part of a sheep?*

Its cock?

Nah.

Its arsehole?

Nah.

Its neck!

Yeah, the neck – there's no meat there. Fuck me, no, just nerves and veins and bones and gristle. Perfect! Let's make it the regional fucking dish!)

Jesus, I'm not surprised Jenny fucked off to London where all the good bits of the sheep were being hauled.

(*Got some best lamb chump chops here, mate. Want 'em?*

Got any neck?

Neck? Nah, just this plump, juicy rump, y'know, and a bit of breast.

Oh, fuck that! Send it to London, them fuckers'll eat owt!)

Our Gran lives on our road now. In the old folks home across the road that used to be a loony bin. That's why our street's called Asylum Road.

Jenny lived with her Mum and elder sister, who was strong and dark-haired from what she told me. That's why I thought Jenny must have been adopted cos she's a tiny slim thing. Blue eyes and straight blonde hair.

Her Mum was grey and, I dunno, a little woman with resignation landscaped in the lines on her face. I imagine kindness and warm arms holding a little Jenny and hugging happiness into her.

And Jenny's sister had a kid. In fact I think she had two – a little boy and a girl, and they all lived in some pebble-dashed house in Sutton, St Helens.

I dunno, she never said much about home. Not to me, anyway. And I never asked if she was adopted. Perhaps it's just my fantasy.

You know, these days I can't look anyone in the eye without wondering if they've been either adopted or abused when they were a kid.

Or denied a dog as a teenager. I was. Couldn't have a dog, I mean.

It was my Mum – she hates dogs. Scared of 'em I reckon. But my Dad was OK about it.

That's something else my Gran used to go on about.

'Oh, them darkies!'

Er, Gran, I don't suppose you've noticed my dusky complexion, have you? I mean, you know, I could *be a child chimney sweep but—*

'They're all over. On the buses an' everything. Eh? Why don't they bugger off?'

My Mum never put her right and my huge Caribbean Dad never met the old looney, thank God. She'd have thrown a wobbler knowing my Mum was shagging some illiterate mud-black sambo. She'd have had him put in leg-irons.

I don't know how Gran accounted for me. *Oh, Andrea, doesn't that boy* ever *wash?*

D'you suppose Jenny used to wash before she left the northern counties of the Welfare State? Or was she constantly up to her elbows in niece/nephew baby shit and Giros that needed signing?

She went to college. She went to some little place in Lancashire, I remember that much. It was Geography she did, I think. And something about urban policy.

And then suddenly the three years were over. Her best ever three years of drunken, groggy, morning-after lectures struggling with closing eyes. And dressing up for dances and things. And sex.

Course it wasn't her first taste. She told Sean she'd grown up at thirteen. Christ, thirteen!

And at twenty-one she left college with a degree and the bank pressing her to cover her overdraft with a thousand pound loan she could never hope to pay off. No jobs, you see.

Oh, fine, Miss Graham. Of course *we'll increase your overdraft. Another couple of hundred? Why not, eh? And you don't need to worry about a thing for the moment, we'll just slap on three hundred per cent interest and repossess your house and disembowel your Mum when you graduate. Alright?*

Anyway.

Jenny's father had left. He didn't like seeing his gawky little daughters growing up so he grabbed the last of his bitter cans, his fags and his UB40 and shot off while Mother was still mangling the nappies.

(*Oh, fancy a bit of haddock for tea tonight, love?*
What? No neck of mutton? That's it. I'm off!)

No biodegradable nappies back then – the mould must have grown greedily around the drain outside the kitchen.

A backyard hung with steaming cotton and damp pegs. While the sky hung permanently dark and depressed over terraces of filthy brick and mortar crumbling like white Cheshire cheese. Or have I got the wrong impression of the north?

So how would her Mum feel if little Jenny left home now she's come of age? Who'd do the washing-up? Who'd fold the kids' clothes and hang them over the chair-back in the hall by the radiator? Their Mum? Yer joking!

And one day Jen said Oh, fuck it! My bag's packed (no more bags of shopping to carry now, Mum) and I can just about afford the fare to Lime Street and then on to Euston. My mates *did* invite me down, it's not as if I'll be homeless or nothin'. Oh, stop naggin', Mum, and don't worry – I'll write. OK? Bye!

Stuck the Walkman on an' she was off. In the pale early morning.

She slept on the train. You know how your head keeps falling off the headrest – well, mine does anyhow!

She probably felt even more tired and pissed-off when the tracks curved into Euston station and the Kennedy Hotel neon lights appeared on the skyline. They were off cos it was about eleven a.m.

So, let's see – no one there to meet her, but she knew that, anyhow. Look for the Underground signs – well, that's easy enough. And London Bridge is just along the black line, the Northern Line – about five stops but I expect she took the West End fork and didn't realise until she was at one of the Claphams or something and then had to turn round.

And I bet it was raining as she knocked high on a balcony in a crouching council flat depression factory. No one home, so she tramps around the splashing streets.

'Yeah, I can get to know London in an afternoon,' she tells herself. It don't look that big.

And later she's in at last and the old friends sit by the gas fire, laughing with wet hair.

Jenny's excited. 'It's great to be here. I'm so glad I came!'

They take her up Piccadilly Circus where the lights whirl around her head and buildings flash like Christmas trees. And in Soho and Chinatown, gorgeous smells of cooking waft along with the buzz of excitement. The girls giggle into the Top Shop windows and the wet streets shine. The streets lead them, wet, to the Dog and Trumpet. And beer.

I was with Sean that time, where was it? In some offices somewhere, I must've been delivering a package cos I did that for a while. So why was Sean with me? I must have took it round by hand, I expect. I'm telling you this cos, y'know, sometimes people really annoy me.

Anyway we were trying to find our way out of the building and it was all swinging doors and corridors. We walked through one door and this bloke and woman were behind me so I just held it open a bit till they caught up and they said *thanks*.

So I opened the next door and this young girl, quite nice, was there so I held it for *her* and she walked through, not a word, and off behind us.

'Oi, come here!' I shouted. 'Come here!'

She turned to look at me, surprised. Tried her best to look surprised.

'Look, I don't want to *fuck* you,' I said sarcastically. 'I'm only opening the door for you so at least say *thank you*!'

'Piss off!' she says. *Charming!*

And sometimes I go begging in the tube just for a laugh. ''Scuse me, sir, could you spare some change for a tub of fromage frais?'

I *did* see one bloke who really touched me, I really felt sorry for him. He wasn't asking for money – this was in Waterloo station – he just stood there saying *'Can I have something to eat please?'* Oh, that was so sad, as if he was asking his mother or something.

2 LITTLE BIG MAN

I bet Sean had a black and white TV in their house when he was a nipper. On all the time or set mid-channel and flickering black and white fuzz all over the furniture. Over the fluffy, crappy, falling-to-bits settee covers.

He lived out east. East London, Isle of Dogs an' that. And he'd sit and stare at the screen in the loud white-noise hiss like some pantomime audience heckling Captain Hook.

And I was still out on Canvey Island then before I moved into London and started at Sean's school. I remember making snow slides in the winter and playing Little Big Man on the move, skating on that ice and ducking down to pick up speed.

So there's little Sean staring at the telly, all crackling fuzz. A plastic plant sits on the TV set beside a cheap alarm clock. On a wobbly coffee table is a box of Kleenex and an empty scotch bottle, Sean's Dad's creased lip-prints on the moist bottle mouth. It could have been cognac – Hennessy – but I doubt he was that stylish.

But this quiet is shattered when a key cracks on the front door against the metal surround then rattles into the Yale lock and the child starts nervously.

Oh God, do you know what's coming? Do you know what I'm going to tell you? I don't know why I'm going through this again cos I've been through it in my mind a million times today and it still doesn't sink in. I still can't believe the ugliness of it. I don't know if it ever happened but Jenny said . . .

Jenny just told me today what Sean told her ages ago. Not much. Even after so long he still wasn't ready to talk completely and openly. So I just couldn't help the ideas occurring to me and I've been through them a million times already today, like I said.

Like this. Sean, the little boy, shooting a glance towards the door with terrified doe eyes. Then he jumps down from the settee and hurries to the hallway and *bang*! There's the fat old git at the door, beer down his stretched T-shirt over his belly and filthy stubble on his baggy cheeks.

Sean's off like a shot up the stairs. *He* knows what's coming. It's

so sick, why couldn't his Dad have been normal, just chasing the
kid for fun, y'know having a laugh?

'Oi, cunt!'

Oh, Jesus, Sean's heart tells him as it beats him madly up the
stairs.

'Come here!' And the baggy arse trousers disappear after Sean
into his bedroom.

The rustling noises sound like someone opening up Christmas
presents, tearing at the wrapping. Can you imagine the pain?

'Pack it in! Hold still! Shut up for fuck's sake!'

Cries and pleas under the old man's grunts. He's really going for
it now. He's really into it!

'Put them hands down! You behave or your Muvver'll be *well*
cross, now *be quiet!*'

And the boy stops but the old man's gruntings heighten. He's
whimpering, oh, he's loving it! Then they stop too. It's quiet.

Dad appears at the door, pulling up his flies, and disappears into
the bathroom. The splash of urine like the spray of a hosepipe and
a drum rolled into one, then a groan. Of misplaced self-pity.

'Bastard!' he shouts and his fist smashes into the bathroom
cabinet's glass front. He cries bitterly.

Sean cries, too, wondering what he's done to upset Daddy and
if Mummy will be too cross to cuddle him any more.

'Jesus, you *bastard*,' the sobs come from the bathroom. 'You
fucking bastard.'

That time on the tube with Sean. I didn't mention what I was
thinking. You know, when I was watching the albino.

Well, I remembered Sean (as a kid, what else?) at school and
somehow the memory was a dirty monochrome. A muddy football
field where the games teacher screamed into a young boy's face.

*'You're bloody spoilt! Spoilt and lazy! It's your bloody parents have
spoiled you!'*

A single tear melts from the corner of the boy's eye as the games
master walks away. The child stands on the lonely field in his dirty
games kit, the children laughing . . .

I don't smoke this stuff very often. I don't know why I *do* smoke it actually cos it's expensive and it only makes me shit.

Why *do* people make such a fuss over dope?

(*Hey, I had a fucking giant rizz last nite and spent a week lying face down on the carpet convinced I was Junction Thirteen on the M25!*)

What a load of crap! It doesn't do a thing for me.

(*Cor, crucial, man, I'm a piece of perspex – make an art deco coffee table out of me!*)

And it's such a bastard to skin up. I mean, it never crumbles properly and bits fall down the Zippo chimney (alright if you wanna get your lighter high) and it gets all over your fingers. And after trying to roll it for two hours you end up with a mouthful of Golden Virginia and the rizz nicely rolled round your dick!

Sean used to drink Hennessy. He used to drink it out of this grey mug he had.

No, this stuff just makes me want to go to sleep. And shit – I never know whether to lie down or dash for the bog.

I just want to forget today. And forget the past couple of years. Well, it's longer than that and I don't want to forget it really. Just get used to it.

It wasn't just Hennessy. Always brandy at home and sometimes a beer in the pub. But that's the one I remember. He used to sit and stare at the bottle. And it seemed to disappear faster once the first half was gone. He'd slowly sip the first bit then *whoof*! It was gone and he'd stare at the bottle. As if it would fill up again. Or perhaps he expected me to fetch him another.

I was kicked out of a place once. I was renting it and, anyway, I used to flick ash onto the carpet in my room. This was just roll-ups – not, you know, anything else. It started out beige when I moved in, this carpet, and it was like dark grey when I left. Black it was, nearly.

I've just been thinking about telling you about this letter Sean showed me once. From Jenny. Only it says the word *enjoying*. That's something I've got to stress that Sean just wasn't capable of. Enjoying anything. Himself or life or anything. That's the whole point. Well, it's one of the whole points. When it came to having a good time, Sean was a loser. I don't know why. Well, I do. It was his fucking Dad, wasn't it?

No, but I don't smoke on the tube. I never smoke there, it says no smoking *anywhere* on the tube. And one time I was going down into Oxford Circus tube when I saw this bloke coming up the stairs by the wall and he had a fag in his mouth and he held this cheap Bic thing up to it about to light it.

So I reached across and said *'No smoking anywhere on the tube!'* and pushed my palm against his head so that it cracked loudly against the paintpeeled concrete.

Then I shat myself and ran off.

That really winds me up, though, y'know. Some people just can't wait another second, they just have to light up even before they're out of the cinema or whatever.

And of course the other day that wanker got fined 25p for smoking on the tube and there was this smug picture in the *Standard* of him smoking. Twenty-five fucking pence! What a kick in the balls that was for the smoking ban. And for the poor bastards at King's Cross. I think it's fucking criminal!

That letter. She used to write to him quite a lot and I got mad one day and said did she *really* love him as much as *I* did? So I demanded he showed me one of her letters. He hadn't even opened this one. I couldn't believe it, opening this virgin letter like the Oscar nominations or something.

> Sean,
>
> Last night when I rang (Wednesday) and you were out
> I felt a thousand miles away and a stranger. I felt like
> I had no business bothering you like that – you were
> out and enjoying yourself with someone – a friend
> (boy, girl, it doesn't matter) and it was as if I had
> pushed open your bedroom door to surprise you and
> you were gone or asleep or something. Where once
> had been that reassuring familiarity (I felt we were
> Siamese twins for a time, joined at the heart and I still
> do) but last night for a mad moment you were a lost
> fantasy – untouchable, demure, sophisticated (which

you are) but so out of reach, so not me, not mine (but I could never own you). And I would never want to own you, but only to be comforted by your promises which would bind me to you as surely and gently and willingly as silk ropes. Or silk knicker elastic!

I think I felt guilty for wanting to talk to you constantly. I have so much to say but most of it must be said silently in love, in feelings.

You know I keep dreaming about you still, only now there's no frantic strangled feeling of helplessness when I see you (reaching out inside but afraid to move, yearning to say I'm sorry but knowing the words won't sound right, drowning in all the sentiments I'm *dying* to express and knowing I've destroyed my own future by stupidity, selfishness, a vain search for the impossible dream) no, these dreams are soft, feather touch, relaxing love dreams where you and me are together in understanding, in complete and fulfilled unashamed enjoyment of one another's mind, personality and, dare I say it, body. You make life full, you add a whole new depth of meaning to everything I do. I can consider all things in relation to you and how much we love each other – it's fascinating and lovely. (Like you.) If you're at home when I phone I chat and love it. If you're out I feel afraid and alone but happy and inspired – grateful – that I have someone to be afraid of and alone without and to tear out my heart yearning after. This is it. The real thing. Let's make it good and make it last. Yeh?

Sean, you know, he just didn't care. How he looked, I mean. He'd walk about with his skirt on and stuff. And sometimes he'd go out, like to the Piano Bar, in his women's gear.

It was always tight skirts and a top he didn't have to stuff anything down. Some crossover thing. I mean it was OK in the club, y'know, but he used to be on the streets the next morning. Coming home after . . . Well, you know what he did. For money, I mean. You *did* know? Well, he didn't care.

Did he give a shit about what people thought of him? Did he give a shit about himself? I don't fucking think so!

And did he care if, walking along Southwark Street, some darkie billboard paster sees him from up his ladder. And Sean's swinging his wig from his hands.

They have these big brushes on long handles and the darkie splats some glue over his shoulder and onto Sean.

'Fucking faggot!'

But of course Sean *wasn't* gay. That's the crazy thing.

I shared a house once with this bird. I fucking hated her.

One morning I didn't have anything in the house for breakfast just these frozen peas.

She says, 'Peas! For breakfast!'

I said, 'Shit! For brains!'

I couldn't stand her, I tell you.

3 PRETTY BACKSIDE

Jenny's mates left school together at fifteen.

And if you weren't already pregnant there weren't too many careers open to you in St Helens.

The blokes went to work for Pilkington Glass. The lasses either ended up packing bananas at Geest or down the checkouts. Or they *got* pregnant.

Then watch your fella piss off in a cloud of baby powder!

That was it. No accountancy. No estate agency. No trendy Covent Garden stalls selling cloisonné pigs or psychedelic hand-knitted sweaters. It was in the club or down the super', you took your choice.

But of course Jenny broke the mould. Wonderful Jen. She must've been the only kid in Merseyside to stay on for 'A' levels.

And then she went to college. I mean, is there no end to this girl's talents? The girl's a genius, a poet, she's a modern thinker. Leonardo da Vinci and his helicopters? Forget it! This girl did sand dunes in Geography!

She was also . . . well, a bit romantic, you know. No, I mean she fucked a lot. She was a nympho. When it came to fucking around she didn't fuck around!

But she grew up, she really grew up a lot at college. She got a degree, she dreamed of owning a lovely big car and a lovely big house and an endless succession of lovely big-nobbed concubines.

But she ended up on the checkouts just like the other desperados. Only she was five years late and a grand in debt. And her mates were long gone. They'd moved south to find warmer weather and new, unexplored banana warehouses.

So Jen didn't last long. She handed in her notice. It said *No Fishing* or something!

'Jenny, what *do* you think you're doing?' said her mother. 'Come on, now, you've got that overdraft to pay off yet, I'm not having you finishing work now.'

She probably replied with something straight out of *Brookside* like '*Oh, ey, Mum. Behave, will yer!*'

The lure of London was spelled out to Jenny by her mates. Oh, it's *sound*, y'know. There aren't fires in the tube *all* the time. Every day, yeah, but – well, it's still safer than, I dunno, sticking a pound of Semtex up your arse and blasting your way to work. OK, so it's not.

And the muggings – I reckon they're made up! I've never seen anyone being stabbed. To death, anyway. And the air and water are fine. Pollution? Bollocks! I've *always* had cancer of the liver and lead in my blood? Well, it runs in the family!

So the rents are high, they said. Well, not for us – we got a council flat. *What?* Yeah, we were lucky. And with Monica moving out (cos of her new job – she can afford a decent place now) we've got a room spare. What do you think, Jen?

Well, she thought *brilliant*! She thought *yes*!

So, there's no nappies down there, yeah? No kids in the flat being sick in your bed? Great, I'm coming!

When I met Jenny I thought she was so sweet. Her blue eyes were always wide open and attentive and she had pretty little thin pale lips that look better than they sound.

Her blonde hair was tied back in a pony tail at the time and a straight fringe was brushed down onto her forehead. And every time she spoke her voice sounded like bright, refreshing laughter and when she laughed it was too much for me. I could've cried.

She was like a January blonde – the first girl in the calendar.

And this girl had come to see Sean! Why the hell was such a fine portion wanting to see that bleeding retard? I thought *I* was the only dozy bastard who couldn't keep my sordid hands off him.

Well, she wasn't incredibly pretty or anything. But she looked so young and innocent, like a little girl. But, you know, it wasn't as if I fancied her or anything. Not especially. I just could see there was something really nice about her.

It wasn't till later that I realised she was a completely mixed-up bitch. For a start she was a frigging nymphomaniac. She just couldn't relate to anyone in any other way but sexually. Affection and friendship for her were attainable only in the bedroom. Love could not survive outside of the sexual act.

She was insecure. That's what they say. Anyone who sleeps around so much they get bed sores is called insecure. They feed on affection, love, attention, and if sex is the only way to get their fix, hey, they'll take it lying down. Guilt just doesn't come into it. That's blocked out through sheer desperation.

So whereas Sean was incapable of loving anyone, even himself, Jenny was incapable of doing anything else.

Oh, and she was scatty for other reasons. Apart from acting like a nipper in McDonald's – '*Oh, I want a Happy Hat! I want a Happy Hat!*' God, I could've puked (or was that the cows' knackers in the burger?) – apart from that she was just *so* useless when it came to responsibility, but that's later.

I'd like to portray Sue as a porky git. But I'm not sure how to do it best – how to make you see her gross features and the way her greed hung in rolls over her skirt band. Perhaps I'll just say she was a porky git.

It's a shame cos her face was alright under all that puffiness. But still I can't imagine – I can't understand how anyone would want to give her money to shag her. But that's how it was. Sue was a slag. And she made a living out of it.

She was one of Jenny's mates. She shared the council flat near London Bridge with Karen and Lesley (also Jenny's schoolmates) and Monica who was a Londoner and vaguely related to Sue.

Sophisticated Monica who wore a dyed scarf tied around her ankle, flat court shoes and those flimsy, baggy, calf-length trousers that really show off a bird's arse and knickers when she bends down and flap around their legs the rest of the time like ridiculous sawn-off Lionels.

Anyway, Monica started it. Shagging for money, I mean. She probably got it off her Mum, they all do it in Stockwell. When they're not being strangled, that is. So her mates copied her.

And got strangled – no, became tarts, I mean!

No, it wasn't as if they were professional call girls or anything. They were either on the dole or temping most of the time but they were on the take for the odd shag if it suited 'em.

And I bet the Labour councillors at Southwark didn't know where their rent money was coming from! Or if they did, they couldn't give a toss.

No, but they worked hard. Yeah, they worked like dogs. Well, they *were* dogs!

Anyway, Monica moved out and Jenny moved in. Now, here's a funny story. Y'see, Jenny used to knock about with her mates and they'd go out quite a bit, looking for talent and stuff. Yeah, looking for a good stuffing. Jenny knew what her mates did but wasn't interested herself – she fucked for free.

Anyway, Jenny gets off with this bloke in the pub and her mates are taking the piss.

'You old tart! You can't keep your hands off these blokes!'

'Oh, piss off!' Jen says. 'Look, we're off in a minute so I'll see you tomorrow, OK?'

'What, you going *home* with him?'

'Yeah, *ssh!*'

He comes back from the bog and she says, 'Oh, I'll just nip to the loo 'fore we go.'

Sue waits till she's out of sight, then looks up at the pissed fart, swaying as he stands.

'Here, you'd better pay us now,' she says.

'Eh?' He's a little slow on the uptake but it dawns on him. 'Oh, I was gonna give it to her later on.'

Sue giggles. 'Yeah, I'm sure you were. Nah, she's embarrassed about taking money. Come on, give us twenty quid – she asked me to look after it.'

'Hang about, I've only got a tenner.'

'That'll do!'

It was a close one. They'd just prised the poor bloke's cash from his hesitant fingers when Jenny minces up.

'Come on then, love,' she says, taking his hand, and off they go.

So later on the scene goes like this:

His panting slows down. Jenny's brow creases in the half-light, her breasts flattened beneath his body.

The curtains are open and moonlight makes the bed glow silver. A dog-eared poster hangs down off the wall beside her face and she can see the mildew on the bare plasterboard.

'Why've you stopped?' Jenny asks. She looks up at him and an inane grin spreads across his face. He belches.

There is a long pause. The grin comes and goes. He looks like he's about to be sick.

At last 'I want my money's worth,' he explains.

Well, Jenny doesn't know what the fuck he's talking about but he *is* pissed and she's tired and who cares. But then, Christ, did he—!

'What?' she almost spits in his face. He looks confused and concerned.

'What money? You'd better tell me!'

And back in the flat the girls slip Jenny's wages into her dressing-table mirror frame and absolutely piss themselves.

I was walking along Southwark Street one time, just where it meets Borough High Street. And . . .

Actually I'd better go back to the start. But I wasn't going to mention this. Oh, fuck it, I might as well. I don't give a toss anyway.

Sean wasn't in that time when I knocked. This was only a few months ago. He was in hospital having tests on his kidneys. Oh yeah, wait till I tell you about that. Jesus, he looked bad when he got back and I saw him. All pale and that.

So anyway the door was open, it was ajar, and I pushed it and went in saying *Sean, are you there?* and all this. And just as I went in this fucking big bastard jumps me, and Christ I shat myself!

I didn't dare try to hit him or anything, I just froze and he ripped off my pants and I thought he was gonna rape me. I was really shitting it now.

Well, the cunt fucked about with me for a bit – he was pissed. I could smell his stinking breath, hot and damp and like tobacco. And he tried to put his half-limp cock in my mouth but I wouldn't do anything to it so he ended up tossing off into my face. It was fucking disgusting and I felt really sick and scared. I remember hearing a phone ringing far off and I couldn't do anything but listen and count the rings.

I could almost hear him saying *Come on, do something you little twat! Try and stop me why don't you? You* want *it really, don't ya?*

But I couldn't do anything. I felt so weak and useless. Why was he doing this to me?

Well, he fucked off eventually. But before he went he bent down and kissed my mouth. He actually kissed my face with all his come all over it. God, it stank.

I shut the door, the lock was bust, and had a shower in Sean's bathroom. And while I was washing I was crying. I had red eyes when I looked at myself in the smeared mirror.

So it was just a few minutes later, like I said, when I was going along Southwark Street to the station. And I just wanted to get home as soon as I could.

Anyway there was this couple in a big doorway and the bloke was pretending to hit the girl. He was doing it really openly, showing off, as if he wanted someone to have a go.

Well, I just walked past, hardly noticing them – I didn't want to know.

Then this bird breaks away from him and runs up to me. She kept saying *oh, can I come with you? He keeps beating me up. He'll kill me*. And she was getting bloody hysterical and I knew she was only pissing about so I kept pushing her out the way.

So the bloke catches up now and he's giving it, you know, *leave off my bird, will ya! It's none of your business, just fuck off, OK*?

And I said I am fucking off. But he comes in front of me and pushes me and says *what are you trying to do? You got a problem?*

So I smashed him one in the gob. I was getting so pissed off with all this fucking hassle, I tell you, I could do without it so I belted him one.

He was sitting on the paving stones, feeling his teeth, almost crying, and she starts thumping me so I slapped her as well.

And I ran off. Not cos I was scared but just to fuck off before they started again.

On the train my hand was bleeding. I'd taken a bit of skin off the knuckle. And it hurt, too. It was tender for about a week after that. But I saw those two in the pub later on. They didn't say anything. It was when I was with Sean, he looked really ill.

I put as many brandies down him as he could take, then he looked better. I'm sure it did him good. Well, even though the doctor said he should only drink pure water like the mineral water from the super', only a special kind – I don't know, I can't remember. I think Evian or something.

When I got off the train at the Queen's Road it was raining. The water splashed off the rounded carriage roof and fell in a fine spray between the train and the shelter overhead.

It felt like the soft kiss of a young girl. A strange . . . A stranger. A girl who would come and kiss you in a station like this and then go and you'd never care who she was or what you meant to her or what you could have had. And her cheek would be warm and with peach flesh skin, alive, tingling with a soft bloom like the fruit's delicate fur.

But why the fuck should it happen in Peckham!

Jenny felt sick with herself. She'd done nothing illegal. She hadn't solicited anyone. Her mates had done that for her. But she still felt guilty. She had committed what was for her the only sin – fucking for money; and that made her a common prostitute. But no, fuck that – she'd been tricked and she was mad! She gave them shit when she got home.

But they just said, 'Oh, grow up. You know you're a slag so why not get something out of it?'

Jenny felt betrayed. She didn't speak to them for weeks. She began looking for another flat but they pleaded with her. *Oh, we're really sorry. Honest we are. Don't go, we'll make it up to you! We didn't mean to hassle you!*

So she stayed.

And then one night she came home with a big grin and proudly slapped thirty quid on the table in front of the girls. She'd fucked one bloke and blown another off down the Bermondsey docks!

Sean had probably seen Jenny long before they met. He used to go up around Oxford Circus, Carnaby Street and just sit outside the pubs. I don't think *he* knew what he was doing.

He used to go up there in the winter when the air was almost solid. Really crisp and sharp – it made you feel clean right through to the bone.

Not like the sticky heat when everything is slow and like a dream.

And he used to wear a T-shirt under his stripy black and white cotton blouse and then this crappy old khaki Pierre Cardin raincoat over the top.

It was bleeding awful, this coat. Everyone took the piss out of it. It just make him look like some old flasher or a tramp.

And faded jeans with holes in the knees. He had holes in his knees long before they became trendy. And he often didn't wear socks, even in the winter. So he'd sit there in his white boating shoes with his toes freezing to the canvas.

So I reckon he must have seen Jenny. He must have sat outside the Dog and Trumpet against the railings and seen a bunch of drunk tarts limp out of the door in high heels and then some arsehole blokes squeeze out behind them.

'*She*'ll do it. She'll do anything!'

'You frig off!'

'What do *you* do then, love?'

'You'll get a kick in the balls in a minute!'

And I wonder if she staggered back into him – Sean on the railings – her heel stabbing at his poor dumb frozen toes. But he wouldn't even have flinched. He's that stupid.

No, that's not fair, now I know the reason for it. For him. He wasn't stupid, just numb. Anesthetised to any kind of feeling.

'I'm pissed,' one bloke slurred.

'Fuck off home, then!'

'Are *you* coming?'

'Where?'

'Not with him!'

'What do *you* think, Les?'

Oh, for God's sake, let's see some money flash and then you can all bugger off to your sordid business. Bloody arseholes the lot of 'em. Giggling like schoolgirls and leading the puppy-eyed boys on. Go on, piss off!

But what did Sean think? Oh, he was in a different universe.

After dark Tottenham Court Road closes up its hi-fi and video stores and the all-night neon lights come to life in the windows.

This is when business starts in the pink trading areas. The gay areas. The tarts an' all.

Areas scattered between Soho and Centre Point at Tottenham Court Road and reaching right up to King's Cross.

Them pale, nervous faces looking like they should be somewhere else somehow. An' just making a nod, a word, you know, it works. And in ten minutes – two men grunting on soiled sheets, casting stark shadows from the bare overhead bulb – but it's the way some people make a living.

So what's wrong with choosing not to make your way to an office or a building site each morning?

Lights flood the concourse at King's Cross and wash out onto the pavements, and down in the Underground tunnels, and out on the streets not far away, each desperate face is lit by the same artificial filthy light.

From the benign smiling trilbys in St Pancras to stained-glass winos hanging out by the YWCA to eye up the girls. And kids sniffing round Centre Point looking for a home but first for some slack-arsed suit-and-tie who'll pay hard cash for a sloppy blow job among the car park columns.

These are the places Sean took me to a few times. I wanted him to show me where he met the people who did all those amazing and disgusting things to him that he'd told me about. I wanted to feel the thrill of just being there – if there was any thrill to be had.

And we stood beside a phone booth outside the concourse and I tugged excitedly on his arm. What's he? What about him, is he gay? Is that one buying or selling?

Before I could react there was a big cunt in front of us and he knew Sean.

'What's your mate do, Sean?'

Sean turned to me for an answer. Christ, don't put me in the shit, I thought – he's *your* freak!

'Oh, I'm just watching,' I said.

I felt a right nob. He laughed and I felt sick.

There were boys of fourteen or fifteen, fear showing through the wisecracks in their confidence, drawing on King Size B&H that flared in the gloom like beacons for snipers. And through pouting lips the smoke would emerge and tunnel the crisp air then dance away and vanish.

And the buyers weren't all City brokers or estate agents or even MPs – y'know, the usual bent crew. Straight from work one bricklayer, clutching his dusty level and holdall, mouthed a tight-lipped come-on through Desperate Dan stubble.

And off they went. Why didn't they skip away, gaily, hand in hand? Could it have been more obvious?

And some fingers wore wedding rings. Some blokes had wives at home, kids. Wives who had too little to offer because they were clean, loving little women with tidy tits and cute arses. Too little to offer cos they weren't under-age runny-nosed kids with stiffies in their creased cords who'd wank you off for a fiver.

The whole thing was fascinating. I mean, I'd just found out I might be gay, then I'd met Sean and fallen in love and now he was showing me all this. How had he got into it?

It can happen to anyone, you know. You're hanging around outside the gay bars up King's Cross, like you do, and all it takes is some insistent old queen to whisk you off to his pad in north sixteen and roger your bottom and you're hooked. You're a hooker!

Course, most people would have thrown in the towel and vaseline right from round one. But not Sean. He hasn't got the sense.

Then he found the drag scene – the nylon bustle of Soho and the Piano Bar. And the middle-aged mascara'd banker nancies took to him. They bought him his first clingy dresses and minis providing he model them for us, next time, ducky!

And, as they say, one up the bum no harm done provided the cash flows as freely as the – well, you know.

And did I mind? I had mixed feelings. I knew he didn't enjoy it cos he wasn't gay. But then, I knew he didn't enjoy anything. It wasn't my place to be jealous, anyhow.

Now, well, I suppose it reminded him of his roots. His childhood roots. If you know what I mean.

How far it is from London Bridge to Elephant and Castle? I'll have to check it in the *A–Z*. Anyway, that's where the squat was. That's where the girls used to go. They knew some scruffy bastards down there.

Fucking—! Jesus, it's miles! They went all that way just to get porked by some purple-haired acid heads!

Karen found something interesting in an old banging mag Monica had left behind. As well as the price.

'Bleeding five quid,' she squealed. 'That slag must be rolling in it!'

'Well, she is French,' said Sue.

'My arse!'

'They like a bit of French.'

'She ain't pissin' French! She did it at college, yeah. That's all.'

Sue pouts and narrows her eyes sexily, at the same time stirring seven sugars into her coffee. Sue's the fat one.

Anyway, Jenny and Lesley still hadn't come home after last night. Still, it was only eleven in the morning.

What Karen found interesting was an advert with a box number.

'Listen to this,' she said. 'It sounds good. *Attractive live-in girl wanted. Accommodation and excellent wage in return for company and favours.*'

Sue wasn't listening. Karen read it again.

'What was that?' the fat girl asked.

'Oh, Jesus – you deaf?'

'No, I heard,' she laughed. 'You fancy that then, do you?'

'Yeah. Sounds cushy.'

'Nah, it'd be like being married. Living with someone. You'd lose your freedom.'

'A wage, lovely house, no bills? Just the odd shag. He's probably ancient. I bet he'd leave you alone most of the time.'

'How do you know it's such a smart house? It might be crap.'

Karen tears out the ad carefully. 'It's a big advert. Reply through the mag. I don't think it'll be crap. He must be rolling in it.'

'What you talking about? They're all box numbers.'

She grins humourlessly and makes a show of slipping the ad into the breast pocket of her leather.

'He's mine.'

'You can have him,' Sue mumbles.

At about twelve the two girls made their way down Borough High Street and then past the gaudy green plastic shopping centre on Walworth Road. I've never seen such a disgusting looking thing, I tell you.

They walked all the way down there, it must have taken them over a half hour to reach that circus of boarded up, broken down squatsville tenements. No offence but Elephant and Castle ain't well known for its opulence. More like for being one of the dingiest camps in town. Tower blocks of council apartments stacked up to the sky like great square monsters with thousands of broken eyes.

In these Labour councils, if a place gets run down then it's boarded up and forgotten. And if squatters move in they're warned out but rarely actually evicted cos the Council just can't afford it. It's cos the Führer's a bit tight with the housekeeping.

So, anyway, the girls turn down Browning Street and here they are, at the knackered old terraced squat.

Sue knocks a couple of times. There's music coming from an upstairs window. Is this really worth waiting for? I mean, how much money can these scruffs have? And how many diseases?

As Sue knocks again the lock is turned and a thin pale face with untidy black hair looks around the door.

He disappears into the messy hallway and then upstairs. The girls follow him and at the top they find a smoky kitchen. A sink unit stands selfconsciously alone in the room – the only piece of furniture.

I kind of imagine a perpetual party going on in these places but I bet it was quiet really.

Karen takes off her leather and drops it in the corner. The thin boy says 'Topper's in' to Karen.

'Thanks,' she says and goes off to find Topper who's probably lying on a nest of old mattresses and sleeping bags in some darkened room where a thick blanket hangs over the broken window.

'Come an' sit down, girl,' he calls.

Sue sits in the kitchen against a wall and smokes with Roger and Aero. Roger is the thin guy who answered the door. He wears a ridiculous Starsky and Hutch chunky knitted cardigan. Aero is Catalan. He's funny and friendly and his dark hair is bleached to an almost orange colour and his DMs are polished one green and one red.

Topper draws cartoons and they're good. He's got books full of them and they show the characters of him and his mates and what they do. But he's a bit behind with them. Things happen faster than he can draw them. One day he'll finish off the backlog and maybe publish.

The boys like Sue but today there's no one who'll pay to stuff her so she sits wondering if she should fuck off somewhere else. She supposes Karen's getting nobbed. Well, she's OK, she's slim.

If Sue was going to leave she decides not to when Jenny turns up.

'I *knew* you'd be here,' Jen giggles. 'Hi, Aero. Hi, Rog.'

And of course Sue wants to know all about last night even though it's the same old shit. Ooh, d'you know, I got laid last night and got *paid* for it too! Would you believe it? That'll help with the rent.

Aero passes the roll-up to Jen but she doesn't want any. She can't stand smoking and dope is out of the question.

'Did you know I've moved?' asks Aero. He makes it sound like Hammersmith to Chelsea instead of just another boarded-up door he's booted in.

'Have you?' says Jen. 'Oh, you'll have to show it us. Where is it this time?'

Jenny digs a pen out of her handbag.

'Swanbourne,' Aero says.

'Sue, you got a bit of paper, love?'

Sue shakes her head. 'Oh, hang about.' She squeezes her fat fingers into Karen's leather and draws out the crumpled ad.

'Here, use this.'

Jenny opens it up. 'Don't you want this? It's an advert from a contact mag.'

'No,' says Sue, 'I've changed my mind about it.'

'Swanbourne,' Jenny says. 'What number, Aero?'

4 HE'S NO TRAMP. HE'S GOT TODAY'S APPLES INSIDE HIM

 I always say to Socialists 'Don't worry, everyone's the same height sitting on the pan!' That's the sort of thing that occurs to me when I'm alone and half-asleep.

I remember waking up cold. When I'm cold in bed I lie on my side and curl my knees up as high as they'll go and bury my arms between my legs. But my nose is always still cold.

It was one of those bleak wintry midnights. The digital clock said 00:55 in red numbers and I woke up cos Sean came in from one of his mindless wanderings up town. He'd probably walked from Carnaby Street and that was a long way. Longer in the winter. He came quietly into the bedroom and turned on the little lamp clipped to the bedhead that just made a warm pool of light on the carpet. I wasn't too bothered, I knew he hadn't meant to wake me.

Anyway his mug of brandy was waiting for him so he had a bit. I watched him for a while. I could hear his gentle breathing and the soft rustling of his clothes, almost feel the heat of his presence. It's funny how different a room feels with someone else in it.

Someone undressing. The jeans and shirt came off first and I thought *what's he doing? Is he ready for bed?* No. He pulled out a pair of leggings – black cotton ones, the sort birds wear – and put them on. And there, squinting into the gloomy mirror, he began putting on make-up. He was still drinking so now the mug had a lipstick stain on it, the impression of tiny creases and folds in the lip.

Then it cracked back against the bottle.

Finally Sean took off his trousers and snapped off the light clipped to the bedhead. And he went to sleep on the floor.

Monica and Jenny walk past the moored boats in St Katharine's Yacht Haven and into the Dickens Inn.

They join the crowd at the bar.

'How's it going in the flat?' asks Monica. 'You all still getting on OK?'

'Yeah, alright. Well, sometimes Sue's a bit . . .'

'Fat?' suggests Monica. They both laugh.

'She's a bit hard to get on with sometimes.'

'Yeah, I know. You should move out.'

'I threatened to,' Jenny shrugs. She pulls at a thread on her coat. 'But I couldn't afford it yet. Oh, I've got something to show you!'

She searches through her handbag and pulls out a crumpled magazine advert. There is an address scribbled in the margin in red ink.

'Here y'are, look at this.'

'What's this?' Monica takes the paper, looks at the address and begins to read.

Jenny waits a moment then says, 'I've applied for it.'

Monica looks up with her eyebrows raised. 'Company and *favours!*' she giggles. 'Where'd you get it? It sounds like the sort of thing *I* read.'

'Oh, I just wanted to jot down the address; I'm sure Sue nicked it out of Karen's jacket.'

'What? The magazine?'

'No, just the advert.'

Monica's mouth drops dramatically then she laughs loudly. 'She *is* gonna be pissed off!'

'You don't think she wanted it?' Jenny smiles.

Monica thinks she probably did.

'What do you reckon, then?' Jenny asks, nodding towards the ad.

'Best of luck to you, love.' The bare floorboards creak. 'When I was in France a girl at the college got herself a sugar daddy. He was quite sweet but not very rich. She was trying to dump him for ages and finally chucked him when he took us to the Carnival in Venice. I had to listen to him crying all the way back!'

Jenny looks towards the bar, absently.

'I just wanted something solid.'

'Don't blame you,' says Monica.

Jenny's eyes plead as she fixes on Monica. 'Doesn't it seem crazy?'

'What? Applying for this? God no! But I bet your old mates from home would think our line of work's a bit strange.'

'I bet they fucking would!' snaps Jenny angrily.

'Look, Jenny —'

'I'm getting so pissed off with all this!'

'Listen,' Monica takes Jenny's hand. 'I hope you get the job, I really do. If it's what you want. It'll be a big break. And look, I managed to get proper work so anyone can!' she laughs and Jenny's frown fades.

They are at the bar and Monica orders the drinks.

The two girls sit in the Pickwick room by the window and they look out across the dock at the lights on the boat masts and, under the water, the strange glows. Samantha Fox's boat is out there somewhere.

Monica lights up a Gitane as a pair of wideboys approach and begin chatting.

I went up to Sean's today after I met Jenny in the pub. I didn't have the key. Haven't had it for ages. I would have liked to look around for a bit but of course it was all locked up.

And it was getting dark when I walked back from the station. People's lights were on in their front rooms with the curtains still open.

It's a funny time, that. Those rooms were on show and you could look in and see just nothing – an old boy watching telly waiting for his tea or just some family sitting about, nothing exciting. But it's part of their lives and it's exposed for a few minutes.

Sometimes a pretty girl, and she might look out at you and you wonder *what would happen if I knocked? Would she be interested? What if she was wishing I would?*

And what if anyone had looked in on me and Sean? I wouldn't have cared and I know he wouldn't.

He'd be in a trance or something. Thinking about his Mum on a picnic somewhere years and years ago.

'Eat your sandwiches, dear.' As they sit on a thick woollen blanket in the picnic park out in the sticks.

And Dad's nearby, reaching into the car for something. Another four-pack.

Hey Sean! Is something wrong, boy? Why you looking like that at your Mum? So desperate, begging to be noticed, bursting to tell her something you daren't even think about?

'What's the matter?' she asks impatiently.

'Mum,' little Sean manages to say but his voice is weak.

Hang on, where's Dad? Oh, there's his arse sticking out of the car.

'Mum,' he swallows with a dry throat. 'When me and Dad went for a walk . . .'

Mother frowns nervously.

'When we stopped. My Dad. He . . .' There are tears in the young boy's eyes.

'Sean, stop it!' she snaps.

There go those eyes again. They plead with her to listen and help but she turns away. She looks away! Little Sean moves to his Mum and put his arms around her neck tenderly.

But she firmly removes them and sits him down. She gets up and walks to the car.

'Mum,' but she can't hear. His eyes follow her blankly. Little boy.

You've always got to check. Look at their left hand. Check for a groin. A diamond ring, I mean.

It's so sick. I hate seeing birds with engagement rings on. I reckon that finger should be cut off from birth. Nah, they'd only find another one to put 'em on. Birds who get engaged. It really makes me puke.

Monica was the sort of girl who'd get engaged for any fucking reason. You know, just cos she thought it made her seem important or mature or wanted.

Look, girls, I've found someone who's stupid enough to buy me a cheap cubic zirc ring. Yeah, it'll last a few months just to get me to agree to unnatural sexual acts then he'll fuck off with the print room key operator from the office!

And as soon as she met Jenny, well, they were best mates right off! Jesus, she just fell in *love* with the girl, y'know!

Oh, she just needed someone to act to, to mouth off to. She needed an audience and Jenny was easy-going and a good listener. Good to be with, so Monica took to her.

But I couldn't stand her. Monica, that is. When Jenny was there Monica wouldn't think twice about getting on the pan with the bog door open which faced right back into her room and she'd carry on a conversation with her knickers stretched tight across her knees, streaming piss into the rumbling bowl.

Oh thanks, Monica, y'know. Could I just see that again? The bit with the wad of bog roll. Oh, and then look at it afterwards. Yeah.

And she'd sit on the bed doing her nails while Jenny examined her complexion in the dressing-table mirror.

'Bastard zits! I really must stop having sex.'

'Is that what causes them?' says Monica.

'Yeh.'

'Or is it just the way *you* do it?'

Jenny smiles cattily.

'You know what it is, don't you?' says Monica. 'Just looking in the mirror gives you spots.'

Jenny turns and pulls a face at Monica.

'So, what did it say in the letter?' Monica asks excitedly.

Jen smiles, smoothing on some foundation. 'Well, it was an invitation to a club near Oxford Circus—'

'*Where* near Oxford Circus?' Monica is suspicious. 'Soho?'

'Well, near. No, not really. Anyway you have to take the letter to get in and it's like interviews. It's like applying for any job, I suppose.'

'You've missed a bit under your chin. No. there, that's it. Just smooth it in. So, er, how many others are going?' Jenny shrugs. 'You won't know, I s'pose.'

'I bet he'll line us up,' Jenny grins. 'And pick out the one he fancies.'

'Yeah, lovely. Not like a cattle market at all!'

'No, I dunno. He'll chuck out all the old dogs first. We had to send a photo, like. But, I mean, you could've sent anyone's.'

'You sent mine, I suppose,' teases Monica.

'Sure. They recommended you a good plastic surgeon.'

Jenny holds up a lipstick. 'Can I use this one, Babes?'

Monica nods. 'What is it? Damson? There should be a pencil that matches somewhere.'

'Oh, here's a black one, that'll do.'

Monica looks horrified. 'Black! Christ, you're a fashion victim, Jen!'

'I wonder where he lives. I hope it's somewhere nice.'

'How do you think you'll do?' asks Monica.

Jenny shrugs. 'Dunno. About as well as I usually do at things.'

'Oh, God, cheer up, will you? It's confidence you need. You're not shit, you're lovely. And you'll get the job if you want it.'

'Lovely. That's just around the corner,' said the cabbie.

Jenny had waved him down outside Oxford Circus tube. She thought it'd be cool to arrive in a taxi.

'Poland Street, please,' she'd said.

They love short trips do cabbies. Two seconds' drive and then they can charge the sort of fare you'd object to after being carried barefoot to Basingstoke.

Anyway it was midday and the roads were choked. I don't know what they were so upset about! (Just a little joke there.)

The taxi crawled painfully slowly over wet roads, a dull black greatcoat pensioner shuffling in the traffic queues like at the Post Office.

A patch of sky breaks the clouds. It's rare today. Like a bank teller's smile. And the blue sky, exposed like soft thigh flesh, is as smooth as the lace cloud edge drawing back.

The light glistens in rippling puddles where tyres trample, reflecting the tarnished aluminium hubcaps of the staggering black oldman taxi.

Jenny in the cab looks out, her arse flattering the filthy leather seat and stuck out towards the middle with her shoulder resting against the glass, her lips just a sharp jolt away from the cold September window.

And it stops, like the end of a fairground ride. Only this time you have to pay before they let you off.

She paid and savoured the moment of uncommon extravagance.

Here it is. The New Edwardian. There's a narrow doorway leading upstairs and girls spill out onto the pavement like overflow from a blocked drain.

Christ! They're early. Mind you, they're rough most of 'em.

There's a huge black-tux bouncer outside who sees Jenny stepping out of the taxi and smiles.

'Got your letter, luv?' he rumbles.

Jenny holds up the paper she's clutching. 'Yes.'

'Thank Gawd for that! Another boner fido one. Listen, ignore that rubbish, they're all gatecrashers.' He nods towards the overspill of girls on the street and lining the narrow stairs. 'Right, go on up. See the man at the desk.'

Jenny pushes her way past the crowd of girls who eye her jealously. One clutches her arm.

'Here, get us in, love, will yer?'

What could she do but look helpless?

'I can't,' Jenny says. 'Won't they let you in?'

The girls laugh and Jenny pulls away and climbs the stairs.

At the landing there's a desk and a Spaniard. A Spanish waiter-type. But he seems to be in charge.

The Spaniard, he say 'Hey!' He shout 'Can't you get reed of all thees lot?'

The bouncer shrugs.

'Come on!' he shout. 'Go home! You not eenvited!'

The gatecrashers frown, slouched against the wall, as if waiting for their lives to begin.

The Spaniard stares for a moment. At an attractive wide-nosed Italian-looking girl with rare eyes, intense, expressive.

'Hello,' says Jenny.

What? Oh! The Spaniard he smile. 'Hello.' He holds out his hand for the letter and disappears behind the desk.

She's gonna get a little badge with her name on. All the girls get one. Pathetic, isn't it? Like some school trip. *I'm Jennifer and if I get lost, smack my arse and send me home to . . .*

'We have to check out, you know, the photos,' the Spaniard he explain, searching for Jenny's face on the board of passport photos. 'Some girls send pictures from ten years ago . . . We have to say *sorry*, you understand?'

Christ, I was right, thinks Jenny.

So the little guy finds her photo and it looks like her so she gets her badge.

Ruth is called over in her tights and a leotard that seems to disappear up her arse. She's what they call the waitress, capable and quite pleasant.

'Why don't you get a drink,' says the Spaniard, handing Jenny over to Ruth.

So Jenny finds out about the place. Mr Fitzsimons will see all the girls here today. He'll take a selection home and talk to them there, then make a choice.

He was pleasantly surprised by the response to the advert but, Christ, it's busy! All those slags out there turned up on spec like vultures when they got a sniff of what was going on.

'Is this a nightclub?' asks Jenny.

'Yeah,' says Ruth. 'Nightclub, hostess club, whatever.'

Christ! A hostess club! A classy dim-lit ballroom of smoky shadows where girls sit and entertain and wait to be hired out.

Yeah, Ruth confirms. Mostly they just sit and talk, it seems. But occasionally a girl will go home with a bloke. Well, to a hotel.

'Does Mr Fitzsimons own the club?' Jenny asks.

'Who? Oh, no – no, he doesn't. Sorry, I didn't know who you meant for a minute,' she laughs. 'I haven't met him, actually. No, it's Mr Grant, my boss, who manages the club. I don't know if he owns it. He's just a friend is Mr Fitzsimons. Mr Grant is just letting him use the club today.'

Jenny nods. 'I'm a bit nervous,' she whispers with a coy smile.

'Don't be! Just be yourself. I haven't actually met the bloke but I hear he's quite nice. Malcolm is always going on about him. They're like that!' Ruth holds up crossed fingers.

Through the bead curtains is the dance floor – a small area surrounded by wallseats, tables and stools. It's usually dark in there so you can't see what dogs the tarts are but today it's quite well lit. Fitzsimons wants to see what he's buying.

Jenny goes through to join the other girls who are mostly standing around, looking nervous. A few sit at the tables and smoke.

Which ones won't get through the vet, Jenny wonders. Some are obviously too skinny, too fat, too lumpy. Jesus, I wouldn't pick any of them, she thinks. I'd pick me.

There's a window through to the bar. Ruth is perched on a stool, sipping something fizzy. And tight-lipped bouncers prop themselves on the sticky bar where the beermats huddle in damp pools.

Jenny sits by one of the tables between two groups of girls and crosses her legs. Girls look so sexy with legs crossed and you have to sit down to cross your legs. So she sits down. Unless you're dying for the loo. But she wasn't.

And eventually the randy old git himself turned up. Fitzsimons and

Grant splashed through the bead curtains, the club manager fat and bearded with a permanent grin on his face.

Fitzsimons probably said something like 'Ladies! Thank you for coming, I do hope I'm not too late,' with a *Horse & Hound* smile.

He's middle-aged and silver haired. Hardly a paunch next to Grant, and his eyes are alive and sincere. Not wet and sloppy like some smarmy little bastard's, but not dry and cold either. Yeah, he seems OK and he looks smart with his funny little chain fastening his tie to his shirt.

And gold and silver flashes appear from beneath his cuff from time to time. A Rolex? Could be a Chinese fake.

Anyway he looks like he's got some money and he smells *gorgeous*! And it's not from Boots, neither – you can find Kouros on any skinny little short-trouser and vest kid's shelf!

This was something else, something special, all him. He'd created it himself, Jenny was sure: created it with orchids, pine blossom, lemon, and with infinite skill and delicacy, the fragrance that was having such a strange warming and spreading effect on Jenny's crotch.

Yeh, she fancied him like hell. But that didn't make him exactly unique among men.

More than that – he was a hero. Jenny was in a daze. In a dream. She was already beside him in his sex-red Carrera, pulling away from their Oxfordshire mansion. Fitzsimons's sexy hands were everywhere – one on the wheel, one on the gearstick, one on Jenny's milky inner thigh, slipping his fingers into her stocking top, then tracing the line of her suspender upwards and finally sliding those thick, smooth fingertips behind her black silk French knickers and into the warmth of—

Christ! I was miles away. Oh, God, I think I'm going to blush. But she stops herself. Fitzsimons is talking to her.

'Where do *you* live, Jenny?'

Fuck! How's he know my name? Oh, the badge! Stupid bitch! Jenny's almost breaking out, her forehead is burning but she composes herself.

'Oh, London Bridge, actually,' in her poshest scouser accent.

'Which platform?' puts in one of the girls and they giggle. Jenny could've punched her fucking face.

She couldn't think of anything to say except *fuck off* so she didn't bother. Fitzsimons wasn't here to enjoy a girly slagging match.

'No, we live just off Borough High Street. I share a flat with some mates from school.'

Jenny eyes the witty tart, waiting for some smart tit comment as she realises she's left herself wide open again.

'Do I detect a provincial accent?' Fitzsimons tries. 'Or is this the fashionable way to speak these days in West One?'

'Does it show?' Jenny laughs.

'Indeed. I'd guess somewhere in Lancashire. Or the Wirral.'

'Close. St Helens, actually. Not a proper scouser I'm afraid.'

Fitzsimons grins. 'Good heavens, St Helens! Where I knew my first love.'

'Really?'

'Oh yes. Your rugby team. I was fanatical.'

'Oh, *my* team,' she smiles. 'Yeah, I wondered why it was always so crowded in our house!'

He smiled! I made him smile! Fucking hell he loves me! I'm in!

For the first time Jenny notices the plastic badge pinned to Fitzsimons's lapel that completely ruins the look of his Yves St Laurent suit. It says *Laurie*. So it's Laurie Fitzsimons.

Jenny realises she and the other girls stood up to meet Fitzsimons. Now he invites them to sit down and they pull up stools and surround the guy.

Everyone wants to know about his job, his house, his money. Some are less subtle than others but anyway Fitzsimons isn't giving much away.

He wants to know about the girls. Their backgrounds, any jobs they've had. He'd like to ask each one about their sexual medical history but that'll have to wait.

They sit and talk and Ruth whisks in and out, bringing drinks.

Fitzsimons is satisfied with the atmosphere, it's relaxed and the girls are having a laugh – mostly at one another's expense.

So finally he's learned all he wants to know and he excuses himself.

Ruth pops back again a minute later. 'If I read your name out could you come through to the bar, please.'

Oh God, thinks Jenny. *This is it*. The ones he's chosen. And she waits while one by one the girls get up and leave. Waits for her name.

But they're the losers, the ones who went. It's OK, those are the ones he's got to palm off out there with fifty quid apiece. That ought to sweeten 'em. And 'Thanks for coming' – 'Thanks for your time' – 'Bye.'

But Jenny's still bricking it cos she thinks her and the five quite good-looking girls left in the lounge are for the heap and Fitzsimons is out there screwing the others, trying 'em for size. But she *is* an insecure silly cow, after all.

So there's six girls left. Jenny and five others when Fitzsimons returns.

She longs to run to him and sink into his arms. *Oh Laurie! Make love to me here! I'm good! I'm drowning in my own juices.*

'There are taxis waiting outside,' says Fitzsimons. 'Will you come with me to Wimbledon?'

'Yeah.'

'OK.'

'Is that where you live?'

The girls jump to their feet excitedly.

It's like a game show. *You six lucky ladies are through to this week's semi-final! Yes, going for our star prize today of twenty glorious years of live-in shag slavery at the hands of 'Mad Jackboots' Fitzsimons, the demon semi-retired City broker of old Liberty town!*

And when they're outside Jenny's like a girl on the school trip – she's *got* to get in the same cab as Fitzsimons. She's practically *kicking* the others out of the way as they scrum down trying to push the first three or four girls into the first cab. Right, Fitzsimons has got to be going in the second cab so in they dash.

Fitzsimons closes the door for them. Fuck! He's still outside. Jenny pushes her face at the window craning to see him like a trapped dog.

'I'll see you later,' he calls and disappears into his Scorpio.

It wasn't Liberty anyway. Liberty used to be down Wimbledon Broadway towards Merton High Street before they changed the phone districts. Fitzsimons lived up by the village. On the Hill.

If you dial LIB on an old phone you get 542. That's the exchange for Wimbledon. Uncanny, isn't it?

Anyway, he was a rich bastard. Only rich bastards lived up there. Anyway at least he didn't have a sex-red Carrera.

What he *did* have several days later, though, was a new housemaid. She learnt new techniques of French polishing, meat tenderising, enjoyed making bacon and stuffing in the kitchen and sometimes she'd sit on his face and wiggle!

And of course Fitzsimons took her to the ballet and opera (which she didn't understand), or to a movie (which she did), or for a slap-up/chuck-up meal (where she stuffed her face), or to a nightclub (where she'd get *out* of her face).

But Jenny's mates weren't jealous. They didn't hold it against her. And do you know why not? Cos the bastard hadn't chosen *her*, had he?

No, she was sitting on her arse at home while all this was going on!

Yeah, she fucking hated him now. She hoped he got the frigging clap off that tart he was shacked up with. She hoped the old slag would have an eppy when she was blowing him and bite his fucking dick off! Or she'd dog-knot on him and they'd end up in St Thomas's casualty, stuck together like Siamese twins, waiting for the fire crew and the cutting equipment to arrive.

And she was unbearable to live with, was Jenny. She was miserable and snappy and she refused to go out.

'How do you expect to make money?' they asked her. She didn't answer. But she thought *Fuck off!*

'Well, if you can't pay your rent we'll have to find—'

'OK, OK! I know!'

But she wouldn't talk any more than that. So, like good mates should, they ignored the stupid bitch.

This is actually making me feel better. A bit better. You know, getting it off my chest. Talking about it. Even if I am talking to myself in my own front room.

Do you know what I'm drinking now? Hennessy. Out of a glass, though. Whatever happened to Sean's mug, I wonder. He probably chucked it.

It seems ages ago since I spoke to Jenny in the pub. It was about twelve but I haven't done much since. Went to Sean's. Bought this bottle from the offy. Cried a lot.

My Mum's still out. Dunno where. Probably at Skelly's. And the curtains are still open but it's dark out. Now everyone else in the street is walking about looking in on *me*. But I don't care if they see me. Crying.

When I lived out on Canvey Island my mates used to take the piss out of me saying I was a northerner. Cos I used to go up there quite a bit and cos of my Mum's Geordie accent.

They used to ask me if it really was black and white up there like in the old photos in books and stuff and if everyone wore flat caps and clogs and raced whippets and kept pigeons. So I used to say *yeah*. Cos it's true!

This kid I knew, Kev, went up to Nuneaton once. His first time in the wilds of Warwickshire. And he had to go to the shop for some bread.

'Hello, loov,' said the fat woman behind the counter. 'Can I help yer?'

Kev saw a Champion loaf. *Fucking champion!* He always associated those two words when he was taking the piss out of northerners so without thinking he said:

'Can I have a loaf of fucking Champion bread, please?'

The look she must've given him!

I cracked up when he told me that. What a thick twat! Sorry, Kev!

But then, when *I* was a kid I used to think we lived on a real island. I thought Canvey Island was about three thousand miles out to sea! That was pre-school age of course.

Jenny was still sick about not getting the job. She made things up to herself about the tart Fitzsimons had chosen. A hundred quid! That was her consolation prize. It sat on her dressing table and drew scornful glances every time she noticed it.

It was while she was emptying the pockets of her jeans cos she wanted to wash them that she pulled out this card, like a business card. It had a picture of a horsedrawn carriage on it and it said The New Edwardian.

Then she remembered Grant had handed one to the last six girls on their way out.

Pop round for a chat sometime, he'd said. *Or give us a ring.*

But of course all the girls thought *fuck that! We're off to sell our fannies into slavery!*

But now the whole thing started to look a bit cushy.

At about nine that evening Jenny slipped off and found a phone box on Borough High Street.

'Hello, can I speak to Mr Grant?'

'Speaking.'

'Er, it's Jenny Graham. I was at the club on Sunday for Mr Fitzsimons's interviews – do you remember?'

'Oh yeah, yeah, I remember, Jenny. Yeah, listen I'm glad you rung actually. I said you ought to, didn't I? What did you think of the club, then, luv?'

'Oh, I thought it was nice, I—'

'Yeah, but you didn't meet any of the girls. You know you ought to – you'd *love* 'em. Oh, they adore this place. Second home to 'em. *First* home to some of 'em!' He bubbles with laughter. 'They could tell you some stories about this place, but they all love it here – it's like a playground, it is, Jenny.'

'Yes, I *would* like to find out a bit more about it. That's why I rang really.'

'Yeah, Yeah, course you did, luv. Listen, why don't you pop round, Jenny? Can you come and see us tonight? Honestly the girls'd look after you like muvvers, they would, an' everything. You could just sit and talk to 'em and perhaps to some customers, who knows, and see how you liked it. What do y'think?'

Jenny's heart was racing. She loved the idea. She could start right away. Christ, she was working it out, how many could she fuck tonight? She stood to make hundreds in a place like that.

But don't sound too keen. Keep reserved and he'll stay on his toes.

'Yes, alright, Mr Grant. I'll be there in about an hour, is that OK?'

'Yeah, love. Listen, call me Malcolm, everyone does.'

'OK. What shall I wear?'

'Oh, anything you feel comfy in, love. Quite smart though, eh? I'll see you later on then, Jenny, alright love?'

'Yeah, bye.'

She practically skipped home. But, shit, what was she gonna tell the girls? She hadn't been out for days and now this!

5 DO YOU MIND IF I FALL IN LOVE WITH YOU?

It takes all sorts, they say. Well, there's worse things in the world than wanting to watch someone fuck somebody else. A mate of mine watched me fuck a bird once but that wasn't the same. He didn't want to, as such. He didn't *pay* for the privilege, he just happened to be there cos we were pissing about.

Anyway, what I'm getting at is that some guy offered Sean to make it worth his while if he'd shag a bird and let this geezer watch. Appalling, isn't it?

Course, Sean didn't mind. The only thing was, convincing a third party of how much fun it'd be.

This geezer was Simon McGurk, an Irish bloke who weren't really a *mate* of Sean's. He just muscled in through contacts in the gay scene.

Anyway, he took Sean up town and they found a club. A knocking shop. And guess who just happened to be working there?

Course they didn't know each other yet, Sean and Jenny. In fact, they met in the club for the first time. If you can call it a meeting. He was in his usual autistic daze, she was trying to turn on every bloke that came through the doors. Such an unlikely couple of buggers coming together under one roof! Amazing. That she actually saw anything in him.

But she did. She felt that excitement and taste of desire. The kind of sweet, bursting taste under your tongue when, at the sight of a smooth leg or the touch of a tender hand in the pale light strained by drawn curtains, the blood melts slowly into your groin, pressing into that sadly-imagined lover before you but going nowhere – just outwards, erect, padded, flushed. And the brow prickles and perspires in a frantic dance of suppressed sexual buzz.

Then she looks away, embarrassed, and hides her hands as if the tingle of dope resin under fingernails has betrayed itself, guilty, silent, staring.

Sean's face would stay serene through all this. Even if he noticed her he'd stay the same. Not like when you're deliberately acting detached with someone – playing cool on the outside when really you're fired up and dying to jump on them if they'd just make that sign, Christ, or flared nostrils or something. Dilated pupils, irregular breathing, that scent, that sex smell that cuts through all perfumes. And blood rushing to the lips. Shame you can't see that through the lipstick that's trying to simulate it. Sometimes women ruin their own chances!

He looked quiet and experienced, somehow. Which he was. He *was* experienced, he didn't need to call someone naive in a sixth form common room to gain that powerful impression of experience that can only survive off someone else feeling small.

The poor bastard had never made anyone feel small or feel like shit in his life. And I used to slag him off for being brain-dead. It used to be something that annoyed me, why couldn't he just turn round and fuck somebody off one time? Just once? He never hurt anyone. He didn't have the bastard brain to, cos it had been bullied out of him.

His Dad made him leave the bathroom door unlocked. Can you believe it! I've mentioned that already. What does that sort of thing *do* to you?

Christ, I used to *love* my privacy. Still do. Sitting on the pan dumping your load. I loved the feeling that I was completely secret, everyone else locked out – I could pick my nose, fart, pull faces, I dunno – wave my arms about, anything. There's nothing like it. Being on your own just for a few minutes a day. Without that how could anyone develop normally?

How could he relax on the pan knowing his Dad could come along any minute? And would Dad resist the temptation to push open the door to his little perverted sexual larder? What's it like trying to dump when your prick's being pummelled by the huge fat rough hands of a beer-breathing git?

McGurk and Sean didn't even know about the club. They were just wandering about outside the Piano Bar. If it was gay clubs you were after, yeah – Sean could find every one in London blindfold. But tarts? Where were they to be found? McGurk was still finding his feet – he'd only been over from Downpatrick for a few months.

A bloke came up to them outside the Piano Bar. Short bloke.

'Don't bother with the topless bars,' he said. 'They just rip you off. You looking for girls?'

McGurk nods, not really interested.

'Listen,' the bloke goes on. 'I can get a car for you, take you to a smashing club – it's not far, about ten minutes – lovely girls and a cabaret and everything.'

It was a cold starry evening. McGurk had met Sean in a Covent Garden bar and together they'd walked to Soho, Sean wearing the suit bought for him for tonight so he'd match McGurk for smartness.

And they'd had a few so the street lights were blurred and washed out into the night. The little man swayed in his enthusiasm and the drowsy evening.

'Where is it?' asks McGurk.

'About ten minutes away, mate. Here's the car, just here.' He points to a Granada squatting at the curb.

McGurk looks at Sean.

'Come on, then,' he decides.

A dull man drives them, talking about the cold.

'What's the name of this place?' asks McGurk.

'New Edwardian, Guv.'

I don't believe it! Did he really say *Guv*? Perhaps it was *luv*. Perhaps he's gay.

'It's just five pound in,' he tells them. 'Then buy the girls a glass of champagne and they'll talk to you an' everything.'

'Yes, thank you,' says McGurk, cattily. 'I'll *do* that.'

It's all very professional and polite. A doorman at the Poland Street entrance meets them and takes them upstairs.

'Sign names here, please,' says the Spaniard behind the desk.

McGurk sniggers to himself, laughing at the Spaniard, and pauses for a second before signing his name. He decides to use his real name. Sean signs and McGurk hands over a tenner.

It's five quid for half a lager. Five quid! Well, I suppose it's nightclub prices. And the champagne list starts at fifty quid going up to Mumm at seventy.

That's all they serve. Lager and bleeding extortionate champagne! And you have to buy champagne to keep a bird talking at your table for more than five minutes. Not just a glass – a bottle.

As soon as the plain little Munich girl realised she wasn't getting a whiff of it she sodded off. Well actually, McGurk waved her away like an old woman might wave a dog from her grandchildren.

'Are you going to buy me champagne?' She looked desperate. Are we *fuck!*

McGurk is trying to talk to as many birds as he can before he has to buy any champagne. A sensible idea but it obviously isn't popular with the girls. They mention it every other word. And McGurk's firing the questions like it's *Whicker's World*. He's asking 'em all sorts.

Sean sits staring at his thumbs pressed together in his lap. McGurk must have asked himself why the fuck he chose this lame bastard as his leading man. Watching most other people take a shit would have been more interesting than watching Sean perform!

But the two sit together in their suits, suspiciously innocent.

They talk to a Liverpudlian called Natassia. Her fingers circle the glass stem beside red glowing lampshades. She's messing about with the empty glass so much McGurk gives in and buys a couple of bottles of Mumm.

Natassia smokes her cigarettes through plastic filters and stirs her champagne.

'Oh God – these bubbles! I've tried to stir them away with me little stirrer but they don' 'arf go to yer head quick, like, don' they?'

McGurk says, 'So, tell us about this, then, why the champagne?'

'Oh, it's house rules, luv. It's just, you know, you buy the champagne for us, it's like a present, and we talk to you.' Her smile is sickly sweet.

'And what about, er, do girls often leave with customers?'

'Oh, yeah! Quite often! Not always, though. I mean I like to sit and talk but I'll leave with someone if I like the look of 'em. It's—'

'So you have to *want* to go with them?'

'Oh God, yeah! If we had to go off with any old weirdo, God 'elp us!'

'How are the girls paid? Does the customer—'

'No, you pay for the girl here,' she draws meaningless lines on the tablecloth with her red bullet fingernails. 'You pay the club a hostess fee and then she gets paid by the club, y'see.'

'She gets all of it?'

'Well, no. Not all of it.'

McGurk waits, looking.

'Half?' he tries.

'A third, actually.'

He nods. Natassia looks into Sean but his eyes are walls.

'*You're* not asking questions, are you, luv?' she says. 'Not like your mate. Never *heard* so much questions.'

McGurk smiles but it doesn't quite reach the eyes.

Natassia's eyes pierce out from fine lines smoothed over with cornsilk. Her breasts are sharp and underdressed, pressing out through her frock which hugs her arse and thighs and ends high, turning into stockings, knees, calves and feet strapped into red shoes.

'I think you quite like Sean, don't you?' asks McGurk.

'Ooh, I do, yes.'

'What about you, Sean?' he says.

Sean just looks at McGurk and shrugs. 'Yeah, she's nice. I don't mind.'

Actually Sean thought she had a face like a tin of biscuits. But it would have been less than professional to mention it.

'What don't you mind, luv?' she laughs.

'Oh, this is my little birthday treat for him.'

Natassia chuckles. 'And he's choosing his own present? Hear that, Jenny? Ever been anybody's birthday present?'

Jenny smiles and looks again at Sean with her mouth exploding. Natassia had called her over to join them.

'Jenny's from Merseyside, y'know, like me. Here, come and sit here, luv.' She pulls out a chair beside her. 'You don't mind, do you?'

McGurk shakes his head. 'Not at all. Come and join us, my dear.'

'Only, y'know, it makes up the numbers better. I always like a foursome. Three's a crowd an' all that. Four makes it better, like, you know! Have some champagne, Jen.'

Natassia begins to fill Jenny's glass but stops mid-pour. 'That's alright, isn't it?'

'Please, go ahead.'

'Hey, wait'll you see the stripper! She's brilliant, isn't she, Jen? You know what? No, I'll tell you in a minute.'

Two black girls arrive and splash through the bead curtains.

'Oh, Anne!' calls Natassia. 'Y'all right, luv?'

Anne is shy and she slowly approaches the table. 'Hi.' She draws out the word.

'Will you join us?' invites McGurk. 'There's plenty of champagne. Anne and . . .' he raises his eyebrows towards the second black girl.

She smiles broadly and attractively; she looks like Whitney Houston, only slightly darker, and her accent is Parisian.

'Thank you, I'm Veronique.' She holds out her hand and McGurk takes it.

'Very pleased to meet you.' He shakes the hand delicately as if it was Swiss made. 'Simon McGurk.' No one really notices Sean.

Veronique is gorgeous. A young, beautiful black girl, glowing deep and rich like a dark wood ember in her blazing fiery youth. But hold on to your heat, babe – it'll swell like the cool tide then burn out quickly, much more quickly than a thin willow white bird.

She's at college in Paris – lives in the Latin Quarter in digs, where the street walls are plastered and washed a dirty pale yellow, almost cream. She's over here on her year abroad from the English degree course.

'The idea is to get a flavour of English customs and experience the language in its natural home. I certainly have had much experience in London!' She laughs happily and looks from face to face.

'Do you do this sort of work in Paris?' asks McGurk.

'Oh, yes! It's nice to have a little extra money. You know how poor students are!'

McGurk has a slight grin on his face as Sean looks at him watching the girls talk about knitting patterns and the best shops for wool. This is what they talk about in hostess bars, believe it or not. And about their boss, the fat greasebeard wideman.

High heels click across the dance floor.

'Is this the cabaret?' asks McGurk.

Natassia twists her head round to see.

'Yeah. That's Lucy. She's really good. Just watch.'

The disco lights come on beneath the floor and spotlights on the ceiling, and recycled Glenn Miller farts from the p.a.

The stripper has a silky dressing-gown on and a fake fur stole and she mimes into a microphone, passing it from hand to hand.

The stole goes first. Then she peels down her long mauve gloves. Under the dressing gown she wears a tacky gold bra and panties.

Natassia leans to McGurk. 'I've got something to tell you,' she winks. 'That's a man, is Lucy. She's a bloke.' And she smiles at Sean.

'Really?' says McGurk. 'In drag?'

'No, not that! I mean she *used* to be a man. You can tell she's a woman *now*! You know. She's really lovely, though, really nice.'

McGurk looks again, surprised. The girl unhooks the bra and holds the cups to her breasts, leaning far over on her toes. Then soft breasts leap in the gloom. The panties are untied at the hips and fall from her muff, dark against a pale belly.

And the fleshy arse, almost firm as she turns. Narrow hips and the thighs smooth but not quite feminine.

The music stops and the girl disappears with a smile, clutching her clothes.

'That Lucy – she's great!'

Well, McGurk's had enough. He leans across to Sean.

'You take your pick now, Sean,' he whispers. 'Don't be too long, I'm off now. Sure you know where to go, don't you?'

'I've got the room keys,' says Sean, patting his pocket.

'Couldn't you try to get the French girl, Sean? The pretty black one, eh?'

Sean watches McGurk as he stands to leave.

'Oh, you're not *going*!' insists Natassia. 'Come on, sit down, have one more drink at least. What about your mate, it's his birthday!'

'I'm afraid I really must go now, ladies. It's been lovely to meet you. All the best, now!'

The girls still protest but he drags himself away.

Sean sees the Irishman out at the desk beyond the bar and he's flicking through his wallet for his credit cards.

Natassia leans back on her chair and peers through the bead curtains. 'Your mate's paying for one of us, isn't he? For you.'

'Yeah, that's the idea.'

'So it *is* a birthday present. I thought he was kiddin'.'

Now Sean's alone with the girls. He's got a job to do and he knows he has to be professional about it.

'Do people use the dance floor much?' he asks.

'No, luv, not really,' says Natassia. 'They're too old and boring, most of 'em. *I* fancy a dance though, do you?'

She looks around with enthusiastic eyes.

'What – to this crappy music?' says Jenny.

Sean asks, 'Can you get some Madonna on?'

Natassia asks Ruth to change the music and she nods.

Anne talks about *Cruising* that she got out on video the other night. Al Pacino. They get on to talking about *American Gigolo* and wonder if blokes really do that, you know, go and sell their favours in the rich old women's graveyard of the Riviera.

The synthesised toms of *Dress You Up* pop from the p.a. and to the beat of the driving bass Sean moves down onto the flashing dance floor, taking Veronique's hands and leading her with him. The other girls join them.

Sean has no fears, no inhibitions. He doesn't care how he looks, no reservations. So he just goes for it, performing as if he was enjoying himself, and ends up looking good. Which is the way it goes.

Jenny's gutted and she tries to get near him.

Sean moves closer to Veronique. 'Can I take you to a hotel?'

She grins and, with a slight shake of the head, looks away modestly.

'What's the matter? Don't you wanna come?'

'It's nothing against you. I'm just talking tonight. I wasn't going to leave with anyone.'

What a blow-out! Only Sean could be anything but seriously insulted by a snub from a tart. He just shrugged.

'Why don't you take me?' Jenny is at his side, looking her sexiest.

Sean stands for a moment, fixing her eye. Jenny's knees wobble.

'Why not? That'll be fine.'

She almost faints. Wow, it's heaven. She's gonna fuck him!

Grant fusses around her, telling her it's OK, she's been paid for. And Sean gets his jacket and waits patiently while they're pissing about.

Jenny doesn't give a toss if she's been paid for or not. She'd pay for herself if it'd get her out of the door any quicker.

They walk down the steps and Sean slips his hand into Jenny's. Hers is warm and incredibly soft and trembling like a frightened baby bird.

A cab pulls up for them. It shines like a black puddle of oil beneath the streetlights, its body almost rippling.

There's a toothless old guy behind the wheel with grey stubble covering his chin. On a rushed Saturday afternoon he'd be lucky to get as much as a despising glance from a fare but tonight he was part of the dream to Jenny. He was her pumpkin coach driver, handsome in frills and dark tails, and she could've kissed him for joy!

That's the way silly little girls like Jenny get when they've got a crush. Take Sean away and she'd have probably settled for the cabbie.

He would've been chuffed, too! Better than the roller-haired old bag he had at home. With her teeth falling down every other word. *'Where've you been all night, you old git?'*

'Yeah, I know it, Guv.' Christ, there's another one! Do *all* cabbies say *Guv*? Why do they do it? People take the piss out of cockneys for that sort of thing.

'Yeah, I know where that is,' he said when Sean told him the hotel. *Cor, have a word, mate! Sort your life out!*

I bet he wasn't a proper cockney. No, he probably couldn't hear the Bow Bells from where he lived. Too much noise from the Blackwall Tunnel northern approach. Agh! *Northern!* That bleedin' word again!

Anyway, the old guy knew where the hotel was. He should do, he spent most evenings tramming tarts and jockeys from the club to hotels so he knew where most of them were.

This one was quite unusual, though. A bit classy. But he had the tact not to say so. I think Jenny would have liked him to.

At the hotel Sean buys drinks at the bar and asks Jenny to wait for him.

'I'll go and check in,' he says. And Jenny sits by the fire with her Tia Maria.

Sean walks past the desk and slips upstairs where McGurk's waiting by the room door.

'Ah, you're here, Sean, good. I've been getting some funny looks from the staff,' he grins.

Sean unlocks the door and McGurk slips in.

'You know,' he says to Sean. 'It just struck me. I hope we didn't have the same taxi driver. Bit risky.'

'An old guy with no teeth?' asks Sean.

McGurk laughs. 'No, it's alright then. See you later now, Sean.'

Yes, see me later. But Sean presumably wouldn't see McGurk.

Jenny doesn't mind Sean wanting to leave the lights on. But she draws the curtains.

'Look, people on the other side can see in,' she smiles.

'You shy, then?' Sean says.

They undress one another sensually and slowly. Sean kisses. And when he kisses he caresses her neck beneath her soft hair and up around her ear. And he gently rubs high on her back with his long, strong hands.

He flicks his eyelashes on her cheek and brushes his nose against hers, then presses and rubs it until her eyes close and their lips melt together again.

His tongue searches for hers and they slip together. He holds his mouth tight and she penetrates with her tongue and he licks its tip. The tongue searches behind her lips and he feels the teeth, hard and smooth with tiny ridges, and their mouths open so wide and their heads roll and then slowly their teeth touch like the soft ringing of a bell, then lock together and bite down hard.

Jenny gasps and her knees tighten around Sean's thigh pressed close into her. Teeth clamped like animals, their whole bodies seeming to connect at the head, fused in tooth sex.

A kiss *can* have a climax with teeth grinding and hearts beating and hips thrusting together, mouths wet and uncontrollable, yearning to get even closer and there is no closer kiss than with teeth.

Sean cups a breast through the bra, soft flesh pressing a lace pattern into his hand, and he moistens her ear with his tongue then blows gently into the wet. She shivers. Her spine tingles but it's lovely.

Sean unhooks the bra at the front and lifts Jenny's long slim milky back, slipping the straps over her arms. He holds her backside, pressing her tighter against his thigh, and traces a wet trail across the breast, dampening the soft nipple then blowing, and it stiffens into a blood-red pulsing peak.

He takes it between his teeth and softly bites it, sucking in flesh and then letting it go and madly licking and kissing.

Sean reaches down and his fingers begin to push down Jenny's knickers. He pulls the thin bands over her hip bones and she lifts her arse as he slides them right across her thighs and down to her knees. She raises one leg then the other, and the damp material slips through Sean's fingers as he drops them to the floor.

Sean follows his tongue, leaving a shiny pathway across her soft belly and pausing for a second in that bush of dark brown curls sweetly scented with talc.

His arms circle her thighs and he pulls her to the edge of the bed, dropping to his knees on the floor as if saying his prayers. And he lifts and parts her tender thighs, kissing into the soft flesh inside her legs and closer, then backing away. She moans in torment.

Then his tongue touches her lips and that sweet acid taste fills his mouth and the glistening opening begins to come alive and flow.

Sean's tongue squeezes inside and strains to press and curve upwards and Jenny's thighs bear on his head like deep sea pressure. His tongue is burning with the effort but he pushes harder and each time Jenny gasps.

He allows the tongue to slip out and begins searching among the outer folds where the taste changes with each new discovery.

And the soft curls brush his cheeks, the sandalwood talc fills his nose and his tongue finds the place where Jenny catches her breath and her legs tense.

His mouth cups the area and the tongue presses and rubs insistently. Jenny's hands reach down to Sean's head and her fingers disappear into his hair, pulling at the roots.

She's calling out, now. To God, for some reason, and her hips are rising and falling, her thighs clenching and releasing. She's panting and her face and lips are flushing and her eyes are tightly closed.

Sean's hands hold tighter as the hips almost shake him off then they rise quickly and freeze, quivering as Jenny moans, the tension becoming unbearable and Sean's chin is dripping and his face wet. Jenny screams and almost cries and for another second she holds her position, her face screwed in agony, then she gasps for air and the hips drop.

Sean wipes his face on the sheet and moves up onto the bed to hold her. Jenny clings to him, her head on his chest, her face angelic and happy. She strokes his forearm and takes the hand, holding the fingers to her lips and kissing each one.

She looks up into his eyes and hers are wet. A tear runs from the corner and onto her nose.

'Kiss me,' she says. Her voice is young and childlike.

Sean draws her to him and gently kisses her. Then again and their mouths open and moisten, lips pressing hard now and their limbs begin to link.

Jenny feels Sean swelling hard against her belly and she peels down his boxer shorts, her palms sliding over his buttocks. Sean pulls them down and over his feet. He can feel Jenny's pubic hair around his prick and he reaches down around her arse and underneath where his fingers slip into that wet cleavage and he finds the hole.

'Just a minute,' Sean says and reaches for the Durex he's already opened beside the Bible.

'I wasn't going to say anything,' Jenny admits.

Sean says nothing but realises if she's *that* stupid, he's glad of the protection.

In a second he's rolled it on, black and sleek, and it makes him feel even harder and bigger – the blood pumping tight against the ring at the base of his prick. He presses her against the bed with his chest and lifts his hips away, letting the erection stand out between them like a jib-crane.

Jenny's breasts flatten and her legs spread wide, rising up with her soft thigh flesh pressing into Sean's side.

He explores the opening with his fingers and guides his erection close, then holds Jenny's hips as he slides easily inside and she gasps.

Her lips search for his and lock on tightly as their rhythm matches and she pushes, her heels digging into the bed, spread wide.

She's holding his arse, pulling him tighter and then stroking his back and gripping his neck.

'Oh, God,' she groans.

Half the time he's thrusting hard and panting hot air onto her neck and shoulders and gently biting her flesh, then he'll slow down and savour the easy penetration, and how his length is sucked warmly into that yielding slippery vagina and it's held tight if he stops and Jenny massages him with her versatile internal muscles and her eyes smile to him.

He can hold still, pushed up to the buffers inside her and the hard bones under her muff are tight against the base of his stiffy.

Jenny's frantic heartbeats flutter against his chest and she can feel every tiny move he makes inside her.

Then motion again – strong and deliberate strokes, Jenny's voice begins to rise and she's whimpering. Then Sean grunts and his eyes close in luxury and his fingers tighten like a dead man on her spine as he comes, his whole body stiff and his whole consciousness shooting out of his prick and a relief fills him as he releases and softens his weight onto the girl, remaining inside her.

Jenny's mouth is smeared with damson lipstick. And mascara washes down her cheek in tears of happiness. She clings to Sean's neck as he withdraws and lies on his back, peeling off the condom and tying it.

Sean takes her and she lies in his arms, her breathing slowing to normal. She buries her face beside his neck and stares into the bright corners of the room, still smiling, content.

Night noises press against the window outside. Footsteps echo around the hotel courtyard and a faint faraway cough is caught up in a short burst of song. Car noises swell and fade on the road and tyres crackle by on hard stones.

It's the darkest part of the night, the time when the winking lights of planes look most like UFOs – their lamps digging glowing tunnels in the high clouds.

And warm inside, the two lovers lie in the artificial full light of the room.

'We ought to go now,' says Sean.

'Already!' sulks Jenny. She frowns and stares at the ceiling. 'I want a shower first. Can I have a shower?'

'Couldn't you wait?'

Jenny leaps up.

'They'll have towels, won't they? Come on, do you want one? We can have one together.' She's halfway to the bathroom.

Sean raises himself onto his elbow.

'Don't go in there,' he says.

Jenny stops.

'Why not?'

Sean sighs. 'There's someone in there,' he says flatly.

Jenny's jaw drops. She's quiet for a second then—

'What!'

'There's someone in there.'

'In the bathroom?' Jenny shouts. 'You're telling me there's someone in the bathroom?'

She almost jumps off the floor when a voice comes from the tiled darkness beside her.

'Shut up, Sean. No, there's no one in here.'

'Jesus Christ!'

Jenny dives under the covers piled at the foot of the bed. 'Who the fuck's that?'

McGurk strides from the bathroom and across to the door.

'Well, I'd better be going,' he says. 'So long now, Sean. The doggy position would have been nice but there it goes.' And the door slams behind him.

For a second Jenny stares at Sean in disbelief from her nest of sheets.

'You fucking slag!' she shouts, digging her clothes out, searching for her knickers. 'Jesus, you bastard!'

She hops around, her heel caught in the arse of her pants.

'You *like* being watched, do you? All that was just showing off or something, you pervert?'

Sean just watches.

She stops and looks at him. 'You're a weird bastard. Well – fucking explain, then!' Her shouts are alarming.

'I'm sorry you're so upset. He wanted to watch – *I* didn't mind.'

Jenny stares. Then shakes her head and begins to pull on her skirt. 'How did you think I'd feel? Oh, fuck off! You've made me look a right wanker!'

She's still wriggling into her high heels as she opens the door and storms out, leaving him with a last scornful sneer. 'You fucking dickhead!'

Jenny stands with her back to the wall outside the closed door and sighs heavily.

She expects McGurk to turn the corner any second and offer her a drink. And all the time she waits is more time for the staff to see her and ask her if she's OK and then Sean will hear and he'll know she's still out there. And silly things like that worry her. If she's so worried about him knowing she's out here why doesn't she sod off?

She looks at the rich carpet between her shoes. Black court shoes. How the thick pile stands proud around the rim of the leather soles that press the fibres flat.

Ted Hughes comes back to her, talking to her of the rolling Pennines. But then another line of verse she read somewhere.

> Deep down I must not realise
> How far I am from you
> For the miles must surely add up
> into insurmountable pain
> That you are so far away.

Little things like that spark off such deep feelings in her. She's at a railway station waving goodbye to Sean who's off to Africa and she's crying cos she's already missing him a hundred years.

There she stands for twenty minutes, outside the room. A couple of times she almost gives in and rushes away but she has that strange feeling where your spirit strides away then is pulled back sharply as it realises your body hasn't moved. Like it's on elastic or something.

And she feels like she's plucking up courage to go in for a bollocking off the headmaster.

She knocks. There is silence for a moment then 'Yeah?' comes a voice. 'Who is it?'

She stands there, unsure.

'Come in!' Sean calls.

As she pushes open the door, a light snaps on by the bed and Sean's eyes strike from the shadows. Jenny can't see past the light and she just stares into the blackness for a second.

'Simon?' Sean asks.

'No.'

Sean's pulled the duvet over himself and Jenny wonders if he's been asleep.

'You spending the night here, then?' she asks.

Sean nods. Then he realises she can't see him. 'Yeh. It's nice here.'

'Nicer than your place?'

'A bit.'

Jenny shuts the door and moves closer. She sits on the bed.

'I'm sorry we upset you,' says Sean. 'But—'

'It's OK,' Jenny smiles.

'I like you,' she says suddenly.

This is completely lost on Sean.

'Where *do* you live then?' she asks.

Sean hesitates. 'Oh, er,' he's vague. Then tries, 'That's a bit personal.'

'Don't be stupid!' she snaps. 'I'm not going to smash your windows or anything! Look, I really like you.' She stands up.

'I was going to piss off, you know. Why do you think I came back?'

Sean shrugs. He rather wishes she hadn't.

'Cos I *like* you. I want to *see* you again. Oh, please tell me where you live! Can I come and see you?'

Sean shrugs again.

So a couple of days later she turns up. Knocks on the door. And I answered, like I said, in my Valentine boxer shorts.

When she left I thought we weren't going to see her again. She thought he was fucking weird before but once she found out he was shacked up with some darkie bender – well, half-caste, or is that worse? – I'm surprised she ever came back. But I'm glad she did.

That all seems so long ago. She's stuck in my memory so vividly. Y'know you kind of remember someone's past as if they were a different person then. I just can't imagine her doing or saying things now that she did then.

Yeah, I *do* remember a different girl. And some songs or smells trigger it off. Just the smell of an air freshener, one particular kind that you never see anymore hardly, and it takes me back. I reckon smells are more vivid than, like, pictures and stuff. You know, they seem to remind me of her more than anything else.

With that straight blonde hair and her little girl face and pale lips. And her giggly voice and her way of looking at the world sometimes as if it was all a game or as if every little thing was magical and special.

She had this long light brown mac – well, grey or something, that had a *My Little Pony* badge on it and she even wore a Women's Rights badge.

Women's rights to be tarts, presumably. And I always remember those sleek black leggings that hugged her arse and thighs so sexily, and a pink woolly top that had three buttons at the neck that were always undone.

And she had a locket round her neck. It was empty though. She never put any pictures in it.

I don't remember where Sean was when she called round. It was morning, mid-week, Tuesday or Wednesday, and she left a number and her address at London Bridge.

I gave her a big daft grin and said, 'Look, if Sean doesn't come and see you, *I* will!'

It didn't go down too well. I offered her a cup of tea but she wouldn't stay. She said she had to be off.

So off she went. Sean didn't ring her or visit. I kept asking him about this bird, if he was interested and everything. He told me what had happened with McGurk. I pissed myself.

'Well, what did you expect?' I laughed. '*Course* she was gonna want a shower. She was bound to find him!'

'Yeah, we *knew* that,' Sean said. 'But by *that* time it didn't matter, did it? We'd done it.'

I laughed again. It looked like his sordid deeds were coming home to roost.

Karen was doing the hoovering just before *Top of the Pops*.

'Shut up that fucking row!' shouts Sue. '*Top of the Pops* is on in a minute!'

Her voice is lost in the endless whine of the hoover. She's watching her little black and white portable in the kitchen and carries a spoonful of coffee a couple of feet across the worktop to her mug. Silly cow! She *is* only *watching* it – cos she can't *hear* it!

Jenny sits on her bed in her bathrobe, her hair still wet from the shower. She lets the bathrobe fall open at the front and smooths talc into her breasts and stomach.

The phone rings. Streams of disco beat rattle in from the kitchen.

'Fuckin' hell!' shouts Sue, fucking annoyed.

Jenny lets it ring, staring down at her white powdered tits. She stands up and pats the powder puff on her muff and inside her thighs.

Karen picks up the phone.

'Jen! Phone!' she calls.

'Thanks!'

She puts her arms back into the bathrobe and ties it as she stands to leave.

The receiver lies like a giggling baby beside the cradle.

'Hello?' she tells the echoing hiss and the unknown stranger who could be the devil himself till he speaks.

'Jenny? It's Laurie. Laurie Fitzsimons.'

'Oh, hi!' She tries to sound nonchalant but she's uneasy. What the fuck does *he* want?

'Listen, can I see you?' he asks.

Christ!

'Er, when?'

'Tonight? I could meet you in a couple of hours.'

'Er . . .' she pauses. 'Why . . . why the urgency?'

He's silent for a moment.

'Is it about the job?' she asks.

'Yes.'

'I can meet you later on. About half-nine. That OK?'

'Fine. Where? In a pub?'

'No, outside somewhere.' Oh, God, she thinks. What am I doing? Do I really want this job still? And anyway, what the fuck's going on? He's got someone for it already.

'Er, let's see . . .' she says. 'Victoria Embankment?'

'Yes, OK,' Fitzsimons says. 'The Blackfriars end at the round-about. Do you know where I mean?'

'Yeah.'

'Half-past nine, then. I'll see you there.'

'OK, bye.'

She hangs up and sits staring at the wall, absently playing with the dial lock.

It's already getting dark at the Victoria Embankment when Jenny slips into the old red callbox and lets the door slowly creak closed behind her.

She lifts the receiver, drops in a few coins and dials.

Six rings and a voice says *Hello*.

'Hello, Mum. It's Jenny. Yeah, you alright? How you feeling?' She nods. 'Oh, not so bad.'

The lights begin to flicker into life, hanging in garlands along the waterside.

'Yeah . . . but what has the doctor said? Yes, he *does* know, Mum! He *does* know!'

Footsteps click past and on, up the slope towards the roundabout where the odd car chases its headlamps around the island and across Blackfriars Bridge. From outside the callbox the raised voice is faint and muffled.

'Look, you've been through all this before, Mum, and you know what he said . . . I'm not! It's nothing to do with whose side I'm on!'

The clouds roll low over the dome of St Paul's and huddle together above a pale pink horizon where the sun sat minutes ago bright and tired, ready for sleep.

'Mum! . . . Look, I'm not arguing . . . Oh, I can't talk to you when you're in this mood . . . Oh, don't be so pathetic!'

A dark shadow of a bird – could be a gull – swoops low over the water and almost touches it. Then it vanishes in the gloom.

'Don't *say* that! . . . No, you *know* I can't . . . Of *course* I do! I just know you're OK.'

Jenny listens for a moment.

'Look, you know you don't need me.' She's almost in tears.
'Mum, don't! I left because this was driving me spare.'

Jenny wraps the phone cord round her fingers nervously.

'I know! And she shouldn't let you tie her down either! You
shouldn't depend on her like that ... Mother, I'm only telling
you the truth! ... No, I don't! I'm going now ... I'm going
to hang up, Mum ... No, you needn't ... I'm not! ... I'll
write ... Tell me about it in a letter, Mum, I have to go ... I'm
going now ... Take care. My love to Alison.'

She hangs up and steps back out onto the street's cold darkness,
wiping her eyes.

Jenny walks along the embankment and pauses where the road
begins to rise up far above the water. A figure stands at the railings
by the subway entrance and he sees her in the dark, framed against
the flaring light bulbs strung between the streetlamps.

The two hesitate, looking at one another from a distance.
Fitzsimons waits till he's sure it's her then walks slowly down
towards her.

'Hello, Jenny. How are you?'

She nods and turns, walking on, and he follows and catches up.

'Listen,' he says, looking at his watch. 'Any time you want to
leave, just say – I don't want to keep you.'

'It's OK,' she says.

They walk on.

'Was it anything special you had to say?' she asks.

'It was, yes,' he nods, swallowing. 'It's about the job.'

'Yeah, you mentioned,' Jenny says unpleasantly.

'Are you still interested?' he asks.

'I don't know. I'm working at the club now.'

'The Edwardian?' he asks, surprised.

She replies indignantly. 'Uh huh!'

They are silent for a while.

'*She* didn't last long,' Jenny remarks indifferently.

Fitzsimons looks at her for a second, working out who she means.
'No,' he admits at last.

'How do you know I'll be any better?'

'Well, I don't. I'd just like to give you the opportunity.'

Jenny is pensive.

'I was keen that day. But I'm not sure now.'

'Oh, why?' he asks awkwardly.

She pauses, looking at him then out across the water.

'I wish I knew you better. I can't work you out,' she says.

'Am I *so* strange?'

She shrugs noncommittally.

If Fitzsimons had known how her crush on him had turned into a wet handshake he'd probably have found her difficult to work out, too.

'I'd like you to trust me,' he says.

She frowns. 'Look, I hardly know you – why the sudden interest? You didn't choose me for the job so what now? What's going on?'

He is silent and almost embarrassed.

'It wasn't until later that I realised I enjoyed your company,' he says. 'And that's very important to me. I find it difficult to get on with women for long.'

'Oh, thanks for telling me!' she adds sarcastically.

'Are you lonely, Jenny?' he asks suddenly.

Jenny is unmoved but she pauses to think and a tenseness crosses her face.

'Not really.'

He nods and thinks.

'I'm lonely,' he admits.

'You must be.'

'You can tell? Does it show?' he asks.

'No, I'm talking about the advert. No, *you* seem quite secure.' She looks at him. 'Not the lonely type at all.'

They walk on in silence.

'So that *is* why you advertised?' Jenny says. 'Cos you're lonely?'

Fitzsimons nods. 'Yes. I'm afraid so.'

She shakes her head. 'But you've got money and everything, you should be alright!'

He laughs ironically. Then his smile slips like dung off a hot spade and he takes a breath.

'It really makes no difference,' he says. 'Money doesn't help.'

'Oh, don't give me that,' Jenny says. 'All rich people say that. That money doesn't bring happiness. *I'd* still like to give it a try, mate!'

He shakes his head again.

'It just attracts rich people, Jenny. You know, you have to fit in – and rich people are generally poor in, I don't know, good nature.'

'Well, what else have you tried?' Jenny asks. 'Apart from the ad.'

'Oh, parties – agencies arrange singles parties in clubs, hotels, what have you. But the women put me off. They really depress me, those eager old women with their fingers still marked from wedding rings. They depress me.'

The two pass the phone box and Jenny looks into it, the L–Z Directory hanging torn and limp from the battered metal shelf.

'I *was* married,' Laurie explains. 'She left me.'

He looks out over the water and sighs. 'She said she couldn't stand my moods. Said I was mad – well, loopy. but I couldn't understand it – she had no one to go to – she must be lonely now, too.'

'What moods do you get into?' Jenny asks. 'You get depressed or something?'

'Sometimes. Bored really, I suppose. I tend to get bored with people. She called it misogyny.'

He looks at her desperately.

'But it's not true! I *love* women!' He pauses, thinking. 'But in time . . . after a bit I suppose I get used to people and stop respecting them. Familiarity breeds contempt. *She* said that.'

'And you want me to *live* with you?' Jenny laughs.

He sighs. 'I wanted to be honest.'

She nods. 'Well, that's what I asked for.'

They pause beneath Waterloo Bridge and look behind them. St Paul's is lit and stands tall behind the office blocks. Looking ahead the Houses of Parliament and Big Ben are solid above the shimmering water. They can't see but beneath the other end of Waterloo Bridge, the Bullring, are the cardboard bedrooms of the beggars. And a thick stink of piss.

'Do you like this city?' asks Laurie.

'Uh huh,' Jenny nods. 'It's OK.'

'Better than St Helens?'

'Totally different. Better in some ways.'

'I admire you, you know. Moving away from home to an unfamiliar city.'

She smiles.

'And I've been a prisoner of these walls all my life.'

Oh God! Jenny wants to tell him to belt up or to smack him in the mouth, he talks such shit sometimes! But she stays silent.

He looks at her, then at the puddles on the paving flags, and his eyes are sad.

'I trap myself,' he says. 'Have done since I was a child.'

A boat passes slowly by, the wake slapping against the bank walls and then the trusses of the bridge.

'But that was a long time ago,' he adds.

The boat lights fade as its engine echoes far across the gathering stillness.

'My mother, er . . . I think my mother was resentful of another man in the house.'

'What?' says Jenny in surprise.

'Me. Oh, I'm just reminiscing,' he says. 'Digging up the past.'

'I don't know what you're talking about,' Jenny admits.

'Just being bitter about my upbringing.'

'You sound like a psychologist.'

'Or a psychiatrist,' Laurie says.

They are silent for a moment.

'I talk such nonsense most of the time,' he tells her.

'No you don't,' says Jenny. 'You're just difficult to understand sometimes.'

They walk on. Some children pass, shouting.

'Are you working tonight?' he asks.

'At the club? Yeh.' She looks at him and smiles. 'There was a bloke in last night arguing with Mr Grant cos this guy'd spent six hundred quid and the girl had gone home without him.'

Fitzsimons smiles. 'Why? Didn't she like him?'

Jenny shrugs. 'It doesn't happen often. It was Maureen, y'see. And the boss doesn't mind cos she's his favourite.'

It begins to rain lightly as they step out from under the bridge. They look out over the water as the raindrops become more intense but are lost in the swelling of the waves.

Laurie puts up his loud golfing umbrella and offers his arm. She links him as they walk.

'So you never had children?' she prompts.

'No,' Laurence says wistfully. He laughs. 'I was going to say not *real* children.' He giggles. 'But what the hell does that mean!'

Fuck all, Jenny thought.

'I've got to shoot off to work now,' she says.

'Oh, can I offer you a lift?'

She stops and looks at him.

'I think it'd be quicker by tube,' she decides. 'But thanks anyway.'

'Come on. I'll see you across the road.'

They cross, clinging to one another tightly beneath the wide umbrella, and dash under the cover of Embankment station.

He sighs beside a peeling tube poster on the damp wall.

'I'm tempted to come with you and have a chat with Malcolm, but I'd better not.'

She's relieved.

'Well, do think about my request,' Fitzsimons says. 'The offer's still open. Take as much time as you need and I'll be waiting by the phone.'

She nods.

'OK?' he says.

'OK.'

Laurie smiles then turns and disappears into the drifting rain.

Jenny's eyes mist over as she searches in her handbag for her purse and tears pour down her cheeks as she walks towards the ticket machine.

Yeah, she did. She came back alright. The day after McGurk popped *his* head in.

'How're you doing, now, Sean?'

He sat and drank cognac with Sean and talked about his wine bar off Baker Street, golf and photography.

You're interested in photos, eh, Simon? What a surprise!

I was laid up in bed at Sean's cos I was getting flu but I went back to my Mum's the next day cos *he* was fucking useless at looking after me. He couldn't even cook.

'Oh, I saw your girlfriend last night, Sean,' McGurk laughed. 'I went back to the New Edwardian, so I did,' he added and paused for a reaction. He made it sound like he'd returned behind enemy lines or something.

'Oh, you mean that girl,' Sean said. 'Yeah, she came round here once.'

'I know, I was talking to her. It's Jenny, isn't it? She's got it bad for you, Sean, y'know. You ought to get in there – she's alright!'

Sean wasn't really interested in this conversation. He sipped his cognac.

'It's nice, this,' he said. 'Thanks for bringing it.'

McGurk waved his hand in dismissal and went on with his teasing.

'She wasn't too pleased to see me, I can tell you,' he grinned. 'I said she should come round again.'

'You what!' I croaked from my sick bed.

McGurk turned to face me.

'You've got a cheek,' I said.

'I told her Sean was eager to meet her again,' McGurk laughed. 'Didn't mention you, I'm afraid, Toys.'

'Cheers,' I told him.

'You don't mind do you, Sean?' McGurk asked.

Sean didn't mind. 'I haven't really got any business to do with her,' he said. 'So I don't really see the point. You're an arsehole sometimes, Simon!'

Sean's not annoyed. He's just inconvenienced.

The night drew in and McGurk seemed to stay forever.

He was talking about the States.

'. . . No, they love you over there,' he slurred. 'They take you in like a lost son if you're a harp. They love the authentic accent cos they can't do it themselves. They think they're all frigging Irish!'

'Do they?' Sean said.

McGurk nodded. 'But they're not! They're Yanks.'

'Some Yanks are OK,' I told him. 'There was this girl once—'

'Y'ever had a whisky enema, Toys?' McGurk asked me.

'What?'

'A few shots of Jameson's in luke warm water,' he giggled. 'Up yer bum and it's absorbed through the linings indoors. An experience *not* to be missed.'

'You tried it with cognac?' I suggested, holding up a glass.

His eyes lit up. 'Now there's an idea. In Boston one time some guys put cocaine in the water!' he collapsed in hysterics. 'Fucking *cocaine!*' he screamed through the laughter.

The next morning Sean called me a taxi and I stumbled down the stairs still wrapped in a blanket. I was stiff and sore and my head thumped, I felt fucking awful. I had this tight feeling in my throat and the tubes at the back of my nose were all tender and that.

'Peckham, mate,' I told the cabbie. 'Asylum Road.' *And don't fucking take the piss.*

'Hope you get better soon,' Sean said through the cab window.

'See you, Sean. See you soon,' I said and then noticed her in the wing mirror.

As the taxi started to move off I stuck my head out the window and pointed.

'Fuck me! Look who's here. Ha! Ha!'

The cab sped off and I could see Sean turn to meet Jenny, then I disappeared round the corner.

'What was that road again?' asked the cabbie.

I don't know why I laughed when I saw her. Nerves, I suppose. I didn't want him to see her, I was jealous. I wanted him to myself. And I was pissed off cos I missed meeting *her* again, too.

I'm back in a few days. My flu has turned into a cold.

We'd had a shit summer and it was freezing already – mid October. And I sniff my way up the steps, breathing sharp air through my red nose and clouds through my mouth.

I ask him all about Jenny's visit. They'd walked to St James's.

'That's a long way to walk! What did she say?'

'She said it reminded her of a park in Preston.'

'No, I mean about you. Why's she keep following you about?'

'Look, Toys. She's fucking mad, OK? She's like a kid. She don't know what she's talking about!'

I'm rattled by this. Jesus, that's about the most animated speech I've ever heard from him. What the fuck is needling him?

'Did she say she loved you?' I probe. I know I'm pushing it.

He looks confused.

'Yeah,' he admits at last. 'What a pile of shit!'

He strides off into the kitchen and I hear a bottle top being unscrewed and then that deep echoing gargle of a full bottle neck.

'You starting on that port already?' I shout to him. 'That another McGurk offering?'

He says nothing. I can hear him drinking.

I sniff loudly. 'So she fucking *loves* you!' I shout and walk to the window. My breathing mists the glass. I'm jealous – jealous and angry at Sean.

She says she loves him, but he doesn't know what that means.

'How long did she stay?' I call.

Sean appears at the kitchen door and leans on the frame, glass in hand. His face is a picture of dismay.

'All day. I couldn't get rid of her,' he says.

I look at his comical face and I melt.

'Did you *want* to get rid of her?' I ask and my face broadens into a grin.

He smiles. It relaxes his face and warms my heart. I walk to him and put my arms round his neck.

'Don't worry, babe,' I tell him.

But that's all I can say. My throat chokes on the words.

'How d'you think a brown nose would look, Toys?'

Eh? I looked up. Sean was looking in the mirror on the mantelpiece.

'Wanna stick your nose up my arse?' I suggested.

'No, I mean suntanning it! How would it look if I sunburned my nose, eh? I could mask off my face all except for the nose and then tan it on a sunbed.'

'Marvellous,' I said.

It was a huge white fireplace topped by the wide mantelpiece. Sean had arranged empty wine and brandy bottles on it, some pottery and his make-up and mirrors.

'Then if it didn't look any good,' Sean continued. 'I could mask off the nose with tape and tan the rest, eh?'

'Ludicrous,' I agreed.

'Coming out the *men's* toilets?' I couldn't believe it.

'Yeah,' grinned Sean, sipping his brandy.

'She broke her heel coming out the men's bogs,' I repeated.

'Yeah.'

Jenny had phoned early Saturday morning. It had been bright and I lay, half-asleep, listening to Sean. He stood at the door frame, the phone was just inside the kitchen on the wall.

'Er . . . ' he said into the mouthpiece.

'Where's she want you to go now?' I mumbled from beneath the covers. 'A fucking weekend in Paris?'

Sean stared at the phone dial, engrossed in what Jenny was saying.

'No . . . ' he said. 'It's just a bit soon, that's all . . . isn't it?'

So she persuaded him to meet in Hyde Park. It was overcast but not raining.

'Is parks all she fucking knows about?' I demanded.

'She seems to like 'em.'

'Tell her to fuck off!'

Sean looked at me. He could no more do that than he could turn water into wine. He was already turning wine into water – he'd downed half a bottle for breakfast. That'd stopped his hands shaking.

Beside the Serpentine he leapt up onto a bench and sat on the high back, his feet on the planks below him.

Jenny moved in and stood between his long thin knees, her elbows resting on them. And she reached up and pulled his face down and kissed him. He kissed her back but he didn't know why.

Jenny looked around. 'Just checking your Irish friend's not watching,' she smiled.

Sean laughed loudly.

And I heard them get back. She'd walked him home. She was giggling and I heard Sean's voice saying *Goodbye* and she was trying to arrange another meeting.

'You alright walking home like that?' I heard Sean say.

'Yeah, I'll just have to limp a bit.'

The stairs began to creak.

'I'll ring you then, OK?' Jenny said and Sean creaked up to the landing.

I was sitting in bed with a cup of tea, reading *Cosmopolitan*. I had my finger stuck up my nose to the second joint.

'What's she done, broke her ankle?'

'No, her heel broke off coming out the men's toilets.'

It was dark, it turned out. And she was scared to go on her own so she followed him into the men's and sat on the pan in the dark telling Sean to keep talking to her so she'd know he was still there.

'You're getting on quite well, then, aren't you?' I asked, still staring at the glossy pages.

I knew what she was going through. She'd tell him she loved him just as I had done. And he'd stand there, y'know, just as if he was waiting for the punchline or something. As if that wasn't the most final, end-of-the-world thing you could say.

I'm sorry, did you say 'I love you' just then or was it 'Have you heard the one about the Rawlplug'?

Sure, I told him how I felt. I'd insisted on spending nights with him and made myself a proper pain in the arse (in more than one sense) and he didn't object but never once did his feelings for me change. If he'd have told me to fuck off right from the start I could've coped.

It was cold in Regent's Park that day they stood beside the water. Sean had knelt on the stones beside the boating lake and splashed the water with his fingers to attract the ducks.

They swam away and now he stands, half smiling, the icy water evaporating from his fingers and cooling them more. They feel crushed and senseless with the cold but he smiles, almost, at Jenny.

She stands in the wind, her delicate blonde hair waving and brushing her grey mac shoulders and her little lips seem paler than ever. Her throat is warm and moist and trembling inside. Her stomach is restless and tears begin to form in her eyes.

She blinks and her face is so sad. The silence she feels is infinitely deep. There is nothing more to say.

'I love you.'

Words from a tender heart. Words she has never meant to sound so painful. She has never meant before.

'It doesn't matter what I say. You'll make up your own mind.'

Her eyes disappear into the rippling water surface and the white specs of feathers she sees blur over until she feels the first warm tears splash onto her cheeks. Her eyes screw into a mask of agony and she buries her face into her hands.

It's so painful and yet it's like sinking into a warm bath. There is something so comforting about abandoning yourself to sorrow, she could finally make real the tension, the confusion that had been feeding from her.

She doesn't have the energy to run away. She just wants to stand there in the cold wind and dry out her heart. But her head is already aching and the tears have grown cold on her cheeks.

She feels Sean's arms around her and those big brown Pierre

Cardin buttons are close to her eyes. He strokes her hair and holds her tight.

'Babe, why are you so cold?' she asks.

Sean tilts his head.

'Don't you want to be loved?' Jenny asks. 'Do you believe how I feel about you?'

She's looking at him, demanding answers.

'I don't know if you like being with me – I feel like I'm intruding all the time. You always treat me well but then . . . you always seem like you don't really want to see me again.'

'Well, there's no point, is there?' Sean says, looking across at the traffic on Park Road.

'What do you mean?' Jenny almost screams. 'If you think that, why do you see me at all?'

Sean looks down, his expression unchanged.

'Well, it's you, innit? You always want me to.'

Jenny's got a look as if she can't believe it. She looks hurt and indignant and she has to pull away. Sean lets her go.

She walks towards the road then stops and stares at the penthouse hotel suites high up with the clouds.

Sean kneels by the water and throws grass to the ducks. They dash excitedly for the grass blades that float in clumps, then stop and look up, confused.

They're scared by the gravel that starts to bomb the water beside them and they paddle away.

'Do you know how ducks mate?' Jenny asks. She's back and standing beside him.

Sean turns round and grins. It's like a fresh page – he's forgotten what they've just been talking about.

'Yeah,' he says. 'They gang bang or something, don't they?' then he turns back for another handful of gravel.

Jenny smiles with a brave face but her eyes are wet.

It seemed to take ages to drive to Wimbledon that Saturday morning when Fitzsimons picked Jenny up at the flat. She'd made it clear that she wouldn't move in with him but she didn't see any harm in spending a day at his place.

She was a little embarrassed at the idea of Laurie seeing where she lived but she'd agreed almost at once. She was desperate for someone to talk to.

Anyway he didn't stay long. Just enough for the girls to fuss around him excitedly.

'Thanks awfully but I'm afraid we must dash off,' he said when Karen offered him a cuppa. She didn't really know who he was. She still didn't know about the ad.

'I'm ready,' Jenny told him and they were followed to the door.

Jenny toyed happily with the electric seats and the lumbar support control in the Scorpio for a while then she grew bored and returned to her quiet, depressed self.

Fitzsimons could sense the tension but this wasn't the place to talk. He tried to chat casually about the club and his work but Jenny clammed up.

The tailback from the Wandsworth one-way seemed to reach to Clapham Common and they were held up, looking out onto the street where Cullen's faces Pollyanna's and the Battersea Wine Company by the bus stop.

Milk crates stood outside the launderette. The deadpan attendant stared out through the huge window-front with a pale, washing-powder face.

There was a sound like a James Brown trumpet section blowing as an Interflora van braked sharply into the tailback after rounding the west side of the Common.

An' I was cold, sitting in the bus station up at Victoria. I was beside an old woman with a sprouting chin and National Health thick framed black specs, the left lens frosted over so she looked like Marcie out of *Peanuts*.

She told me she'd worn her overcoat and wellies cos she thought it'd be poor weather but as how it was sunny now. Sunny but friggin' freezing.

I heard about her nail.

'I keep it in here,' she said, clutching her handbag. 'An', like, if I forget me key I use me nail to get in the door. And it helped me push a shillin' in a phone once.'

I nodded sympathetically.

'It's good for getting into things wrapped in plastic, you know. Sandwiches and stuff. It's useful is my nail.'

I said, 'Oh yeah, I always say it's handy to have a nail on you!'
She told me she's worried her eyesight's going.

'I can touch my eye without blinking,' she said. 'I never used to
be able to. People can't touch their eye without blinking. You're
not supposed to be able to.'

'Oh, don't worry,' I told her. 'That's nothing to do with it. It
don't mean you're going blind! Look, I can touch mine.'

And I put my finger to my eyeball and the delicate moist surface
at once detected this dry, dirty finger intruding on its clinical
sterility but I suppressed the blink easily.

'See!' I said.

She was fucking *well* pleased and she grabbed my arm and said,
'Oh, I'm glad I mentioned it to you, love. It's put my mind at rest,
it has!'

She asked if I was training to be a doctor cos she saw the word
'Doctor' on the book I was carrying. I told her it was just a novel.
It was Kerouac's *Doctor Sax*.

She went on. 'When I take my glasses off and look in the mirror,
it's all a blur. My face is all a blur with no nose or nothing. It looks
funny.'

The bus came later on. Things *really* got interesting after that.

Anyway they rounded the corner before coming into Wimbledon
village and Jenny looked across to Rushmere Pond. She'd hardly
noticed the huge wooded land that stretched back for a mile and
a half behind them.

'Ooh, what's that?' she asked, pointing.

'That's the Common,' Fitzsimons told her.

'Wimbledon Common? Where the Wombles live?'

Fitzsimons smiled. 'Yes.'

They passed through the tight streets of shopfronts showing
French dresses, bathrooms, pottery. And pubs and restaurants
standing grandly at the roadside.

'We can go for a walk there if you like, later on,' Fitzsimons
suggested. 'It's lovely down in the wood by the pond.'

Jenny smiled at him. 'I'd like that.'

They arrived at Fitzsimons's house and Jenny flopped down in the
lounge and switched on the TV.

The housekeeper had made a lamb Dhansak and frozen it so
Fitzsimons slammed it in the microwave and put some naan bread

in the oven. He defrosted some lemon rice and dug out a bottle of Muscadet.

'You ready for lunch?' he asked, leaning against the doorframe to the lounge.

Jenny kept her eyes on the screen.

'No, not really,' she said casually.

She turned to laugh at his face, hurt like a child.

'Yeah, I am really. Only kidding!'

Jenny insisted they watched the telly while they ate.

'I just wanna see this film,' she said and hurried back with her plate, still warm from the microwave.

It was *Whistle Down the Wind* and a young Hayley Mills was getting punched by some kid in the playground.

Jenny sat back in the huge armchair.

'I don't really like wine,' she smiled. 'But this is nice.'

'How do you like the curry?' Fitzsimons asked.

'Lovely,' Jenny mumbled through a mouthful.

There was a copy of *Time* on the sofa by the large windows that looked out onto a big garden and trees that stood some way off by the road. The house was well back from the Hill in its own little bit of land.

It was a lovely house. The ceilings were high with a fine cove moulding and in the lounge a decorated rose in the centre where a light fitting had once hung. It was plastered over now.

There were no longer any signs of a Mrs Fitzsimons. Not obvious signs, anyway, like her knitting bag that he said used to sit on the wooden chair beside the sofa.

Laurie had let the spice rack run dry and there was no longer fresh silk underwear in shining piles in the drawers. The bedroom didn't smell of perfume and the Lil-Lets box in the bathroom was long gone. And most importantly the bog roll seemed to last about five times longer.

But she lived on in the bedroom wallpaper and the plaster cherubs that she'd lovingly painted sky blue and put on the back of the door. And the water purifier that she had insisted they fit under the sink.

Fitzsimons had been glad she'd taken her Edwardian Lady flower prints off the walls and he'd replaced them with hunting scenes and a Cotman landscape and now he could put his golf clubs where he liked.

Fitzsimons is halfway through the *Times* crossword as Alan Bates is being taken away by the police and Hayley Mills's little brother is saying 'Will you come back soon, Jesus?' or something and then them two kids turn up and are pissed off cos they've missed Jesus before he was carted off to the nick. Then the credits roll up the screen.

Jenny sits with tears in her eyes.

'Oh, I love that film,' she says.

Fitzsimons looks up and nods without listening then smiles when he twigs what she's said.

'It's your part of the world, isn't it?'

She flicks off the TV with the remote and Fitzsimons drops the newspaper onto the floor.

'I'm stuck,' he decides.

'What? The crossword?' Jenny asks. 'Here, chuck us it!'

Fitzsimons passes the paper and Jenny stares at it.

'Oh God! I can't get any of 'em.' She grins stupidly at Fitzsimons.

'Try this,' she says. 'Five across: *gifted coin.*'

'How many letters?' asks Fitzsimons.

'Oh, I don't know. Oh, hang on. Er . . . six!' She looks up expectantly.

Fitzsimons stares back, thinking. 'Have we got any letters?'

'Something-A-something-something-N-something.'

'Oh – *talent!* Of course!' he shouts.

'Is that a coin?'

Fitzsimons nods.

Jenny looks impressed and scribbles it in.

'Right,' she says. 'That helps with two down. It's a long one – eleven letters. The clue is *When starlings whisper.*'

She looks up. 'Got it yet?'

'What letters do we have?' asks Fitzsimons.

'Oh God! you ready? M-something-something-something-something-R-something-T-something-something-N.'

'Sounds like T-I-O-N on the end,' Fitzsimons says.

'There's an explanation mark on the end. On the end of the clue.'

'What? An exclamation mark?' he asks.

'Yeah. Explanation mark.'

Fitzsimons laughs and Jenny joins in.

'What is it – "When starlings" what?'

'When starlings whisper,' Jenny reads again.

'I don't know,' Fitzsimons admits. 'Beats me.'

Jenny starts singing *When Doves Cry*.

'No. No idea,' Fitzsimons decides. 'Try another. Any more fit in with the one we just got?'

'Oh, I'm *bored*,' Jenny says. 'One across: someone who's completely bored of crosswords and wants to do something else!'

Fitzsimons laughs. 'Er, let's see. How many letters?' He leans back in his armchair and breathes deeply. 'You don't last long, do you?'

Jenny smiles long and luxuriously into Fitzsimons's eyes. She doesn't get that uncomfortable, embarrassed feeling you get when you look at someone for too long. She just enjoys it. Like a newborn baby staring at its mother.

'I like being here,' Jenny says. 'Shall I do the washing-up?'

'No, I've put them in the machine. The magic machine.'

'I knew you'd say that,' she smiles.

Jenny sighs and looks out the window, then her eyes wander over to the drinks cabinet and she says, 'Do you drink much?'

Fitzsimons follows her eyes and looks into the little empty key-holes. It's locked through the week when the housekeeper's around. She lets herself in the house but he doesn't trust a soul around his drinks cabinet. No, sir. No bleedin' one.

'It's funny, you know,' he says. 'I've been thinking about that myself recently. What with leaflets going around at work encouraging you to watch your weekly amounts, etcetera. I don't know if it's worth the bother, actually, I usually have a couple at lunchtime but only rarely in the evening.'

He leans forward. 'What about you?'

'No, I was thinking about a friend of mine,' Jenny says. 'I'm really worried, actually.'

'A friend? Why, what's wrong?'

She pauses, wondering whether to go on. But this was one of the things she had to talk about.

'Would you say it was too much to drink half a bottle of brandy in a day?' she asks.

Fitzsimons's eyebrows raise. 'Well,' he laughs nervously. 'I'd need a bit of a breather after that much, but I dare say I'd survive.'

'But that's every day. At least that much every day.'

'Who is this, Jenny?' Fitzsimons asks. 'One of the girls?'

Jenny shakes her head slowly.

'Are you really worried about this, Jenny?'

'Yeah.'

'Who is it?'

'A friend. I only met him a couple of months ago. He drinks like a fish. It's ridiculous, brandy, whisky, sometimes a whole bottle. Beer as well in the pub.' She stops and gasps.

'Have you talked to him about it?'

'I can't talk to him about anything!' Jenny snaps. 'You don't understand!'

Fitzsimons pauses. 'You should put him in touch with Alcoholics Anonymous.'

Jenny looks up like he's taking the piss.

'Now I *know* it sounds old hat,' he holds up his hands. 'But, really, they're the best. The people are good and the methods *work*. I know several colleagues who've benefited . . . Really, you should suggest it.'

'I will. I'll suggest it!' Her voice is strained as if she's just keeping her temper simmering. Her hands fall weakly to her side between the chair arms. 'But it won't do fuck all good.'

Fitzsimons has never heard her swear before. She doesn't even notice she has.

'He's called Sean,' Jenny says quietly. 'I met him in the club.'

Fitzsimons is nodding. 'Did he drink a lot there?'

'I thought people drank cos of emotional problems.'

'Yes,' Fitzsimons confirms.

He hardly hears her say, 'But he's got no emotions.'

Fitzsimons feels weak and useless. He can't seem to get inside Jenny or offer any comfort or anything just when she needs him.

He walks across and sits on the arm of the chair, reaching gently around Jenny's shoulders. She leans her head back against his chest and closes her eyes.

Fitzsimons stares blankly at the standby light on the video and beside it the LED time display glows softly in the mid-afternoon brightness.

He can hear Jenny's breathing like a hurt dog. That little nose pressed into the starched cotton of his shirt.

The paper's within reach and Fitzsimons picks it up. Now he can see the letter positions and it all fits into place.

-TIQN. What could it be? -ation, -ition, -ution. And the start? M-something. *When starlings* – the old chase slang! Of course!

'Murmuration,' he declares.

'Eh?' Jenny says.

'The clue – *when starlings whisper* – it's *murmuration*! A murmuration of starlings.'

'Oh smashing,' says Jenny.

So later they do go out and this is where she wants to be.

Out on Wimbledon Common with Fitzsimons, hunting for Wombles in the long grass.

The sun is high enough so you can see the layers of cloud beneath it begin to flow like the sweet-smelling chestnut fires of Oxford Circus in the winter time. But so low it sends spears of light between the trees and they are held fast like they're frozen in the icy air and they make shiny patterns around your legs and in the dry, flaky brown leaves covering the ground.

Jenny's thinking about those glowing braziers in the street that she'd slow down to pass and feel the warmth on her hands and face and smell that woody steam that oozes out every time one of the little brown nuts splits its skin and the hairs pop out.

There they sit, the chestnuts all huddled together and going black and crispy on the pan.

Jenny's cheeks flush red with the cold. There is no wind but the thin autumn sun barely warms her face as she hops along beside Fitzsimons, her arm through his with his hand shoved deeply in his cashmere coat pocket.

They had crossed the Common along the Horse Ride and past the golf course and now they're deep in the woods where the stream cuts its way through towards the lake.

'It's like . . .' Jenny's talking about the way love's so risky. Fitzsimons is watching where his feet are going, taking deep breaths that give the impression he's listening.

'It's like to see a rainbow best . . . you have to – you have to go outside with the rain.'

Small stones rattle along in front of Jenny's boots each time she loses balance and steps too heavily.

'Well, it's a bit like that,' she adds.

She blinks when the sun shines through between the trees and dazzles her.

'You know, originally there was only one sex,' Fitzsimons says. 'No men and women, according to Plato. Just one sex.'

'Sounds like just *no* sex to me,' Jenny frowns.

Fitzsimons smiles. 'No. Do you want me to tell you or not?'

'Not if it's up to your usual standard.'

'In Plato's *Symposium*—'

'The Fifth Symposium or the unfinished one?'

'—there are these beings called Androgynes. A mixture of the sexes. That's where the word *androgynous* comes from.'

'I heard someone say that about Grace Jones.'

'Yes. Anyway for some reason the gods split the Androgynes up into two bits – man and woman.'

'Oh good!'

'No, that's bad! They were fine as they were. Now they spend their lives, or *we* spend our lives, searching out our missing half. Our other halves.'

'And trying on everyone else's other half for size in the process!'

'That's right,' Fitzsimons laughs.

'No, that's quite a nice story actually,' she says. 'If it's true I think I'm after the wrong half.'

Fitzsimons spreads his arms like he's on the cross and says, 'Come on! Of course *I*'m your other half!'

'Not you, you clown!' She punches his chest. He looks hurt and his lower lip pouts out.

'Oh, baby,' she soothes and pulls herself up on his neck and kisses his cheek. 'Is ums upset, den?'

Fitzsimons sticks out his tongue and laughs.

'Oh, make me laugh some more, Laurie. I was dead depressed this morning but I feel loads better.'

He smiles and stretches his arm across Jenny's shoulder.

It looks like father and daughter together. As if he's taking her under his wing and dishing out the facts of life.

'It's Sean, is it?'

Jenny nods. 'The alky,' she says with a sigh. 'I think I love him, Laurie. I know you don't want to hear it but . . .'

'But he's not your . . . you know, missing half as it were?'

'Missing link more like. No, it's funny – he, er . . . he doesn't seem to care one way or the other. I mean, he doesn't say *no* when I ask him out but, then, when we're together he's – he never gets close, he just doesn't seem to get to care any more.'

'Could he just be using you?' Fitzsimons asks.

Jenny shakes her head. 'What for? *He* doesn't get anything out of it. It's like he's a little boy being dragged round a supermarket not complaining but not enjoying it, just taking it cos he has to.'

Jenny reaches up and disentangles a string of hair from her

earring. There's a sound of crows far off. Autumn crows deep black and bright and clear in the cold air.

'I seduce him sometimes cos I just *need* to have him close – I *need* him like that sometimes. And, well . . . the bodies fit together but I don't think the spirits do.'

She smiles suddenly. 'Anyway, you ratbag!' She punches his ribs. 'I thought I told you to cheer me up not depress me! Look – a womble!'

A grey squirrel shoots into the grass like a furry puppet on strings then reappears down by the waterside on a green log. They've come at last to the lake. The condemned lake where it's unsafe to swim.

Jenny sneaks off and tries to get nearer to the squirrel but it dashes off towards the path then stops, still in the grass but out of sight.

She's cooing to it, whistling, trying to make some sort of friendly squirrel sound. She's close now. Only a few feet and her hand's outstretched.

She steps closer still but it's off, across the dusty path, skipping over the tiny stones without budging a single one.

A last look back then he disappears between the trees and the thick leaves, the tail flowing behind him like Batman's cape.

Jenny herself skips back to her Dad – sorry, Fitzsimons. Same thing, anyway – that's how she thought of him by now. At last she had her dad back. It'd been a long time since her dad walked out but, well, better late than never.

'They've got fleas, anyway,' Fitzsimons told her.

'Do you reckon?'

'Oh yes.'

Jenny screws up her face in distaste. 'Cuddly though, aren't they?'

Fitzsimons supposes so. 'They can really screw up the trees though.'

Jenny stops and stares at him severely.

'Do you know what that means? *Screw up the trees? Fuck up the trees?* It makes it sound like sex really spoils and degrades someone. You wrap your car round a tree – it's *fucked*. You shag a girl – she's *fucked*!'

Fitzsimons looks at her in surprise. *What's brought this on?*

'Oh, come on – it's only an expression,' he says. 'Women use it too.'

'Not as much. If someone's been beaten up they've been *fucked up*. That's what they say where I come from. And if you get ripped off then you've been *screwed*. Why is that? Why is it always sexual, as if the sex act is such a bad thing? Girls don't think of sex that way.'

'How *do* girls think of it?' Fitzsimons asks.

'Oh, don't be funny!'

'No, I mean it. Why aren't women more aggressive about sex?'

Jenny thinks about it.

'They don't see it in the same way as men. Men take it as a challenge, a conquest. They like to think they've won something or got one over on a girl – *Oh, she's a mug, I laid her, y'know, she's an easy lay*. But women want to be loved. It's a comfort in a way.'

Here's Jenny trying to psychoanalyse why she's a screaming nympho!

'Oh, I think it's the same for a lot of men, too. We're just as sensitive deep down. Show me a man who can really live without love. I don't know, I just think you're making too much of the thing about the expression *fucked*. It's just a way of speaking.'

'I know, but it must have started somewhere. Everything . . . every word's invented for a reason.'

Fitzsimons nods sympathetically.

'I mean,' she goes on. 'Sometimes after a one-night stand I feel really used and dirty. But it's not always like that. It depends. It depends on the fella.'

'What, you mean how he treats you afterwards?'

'Well, partly. No, it's not how he treats you, it's just . . . you know, you can sort of *feel* how he thinks about you. It's a kind of an unconscious thing, these like invisible messages he's giving off. Some are like really off-hand and cold and others you can tell they're, they feel friendly kind of . . .'

'Yes, I know what you mean.'

'You know, they treat you as an equal, that's what I'm trying to say. Not like some piece of meat they've just used.'

They're standing by the lake now. Over the far side, up in some trees, is the warning notice. The whole lake's surrounded by woodland and it's getting dark now the sun's dropped out of sight.

'Let me tell you something, if you're interested,' Fitzsimons says.

'Another interesting fact?' Jenny jokes.

'Yes. Really. This whole thing stems from the time you're a baby. Feeding time.'

'What *whole thing*?'

'You know, the differences between the sexes. Man's aggressive attitude towards sex.'

'OK, go on.'

'Well, baby boys often have erections when they're frustrated during feeding time. That's how aggression and sexual arousal are linked.'

'What? Babies have erections?'

'Yes. Small ones of course.'

'Oh, of course!'

'When little girls feed—'

'Now don't tell me *they* get erections too!'

'No, but nearly. This is the interesting bit—'

'If you're into babies!'

'During normal, happy feeding, the little girl experiences anal contractions that are believed to stimulate pleasurable vaginal sensations.'

'Wow! Now that *was* quite interesting, Dr Fitzsimons! Where d'you get all this rubbish from?'

'Oh, books.'

'Books. And that's where it all starts, then – baby sex?'

'That's right.'

A grey blur sweeps across between the trees above them and the leaves shake a little.

'What about squirrels,' Jenny asks. 'Are they hung up on sex, too?'

'They must be. There's so many of them they're vermin.'

'Don't tell me, they screw up the trees, yeah?' and she laughs now when she gets the double meaning.

She looks up into the dark undersides of the last dry wrinkled leaves.

'I know they're vermin,' she says. 'But they're beautiful, don't you think?'

Fitzsimons nods.

They walk around the lake almost to the path that leads past the cemetery. There's a huge old tree trunk, split near the roots and felled cleanly with a chainsaw soon afterwards.

'Must've been killed in the storm,' says Fitzsimons. 'The storm of eighty-seven.'

'So they cut it down?'

Jenny's feeling sorry for the tree. 'Couldn't they have left it standing?'

Fitzsimons's face shrugs. 'I suppose it was unsafe.'

She's running her fingers along the smooth exposed surface where the trunk's been sliced through, almost trying to feel for the last faint trace of a heartbeat.

'Look at the rings,' Jenny says. 'So close I can hardly count 'em. Look how tight close they are!'

Fitzsimons touches the wood. It's hard and smooth under his fingertips. A brave tough old tree, reluctantly pushing out one more ring year after year so tight by the last one you'd hardly notice it'd grown at all since last summer.

There's a way up, through the woods, out onto the flat Common again where a path leads right past the windmill.

'It's gorgeous,' says Jenny. 'I've never seen a real windmill before.'

'They sell cardboard models of it in the library,' Laurie says. 'Build-them-yourself ones.'

Jenny grins broadly.

The sun is smothered in the wash of pink horizon clouds now. Long shadows from the trees down below stretch right up the hillside and form a deep dusk valley. The windmill blades look like they should always be like this, bathed in a cool pink of dying light. A fleeting colour is what makes it so special.

Jenny moves close to Fitzsimons, his back to the setting sun, and she takes his hand.

'You alright?' she says.

'You look so pretty with the light shining on you,' he tells her. 'I wish the sun could always be setting.'

Jenny smiles and shakes her head.

'There'll be other sunsets.'

6 WARM CARS IN THE RAIN

 Marco said to me one time, 'At the end of the day, women prefer men who are bastards.'

'Nah,' I said. 'I know women who say they only like their bastards in the morning!'

We were talking about women cos Marco wants me to be totally straight when I'm with him. Like that time down the airport.

In fact it must've been that bird down at Gatwick that gave, you know, *it* to me.

I just started noticing some pain when I pissed. Something had to be done so I went to see the doc.

He referred me to St Thomas's – Lambeth Wing, he said, Lydia Department. So I gave 'em a ring and asked for an appointment but the woman said no, it's just a walk-in clinic.

She told me how to find the place and everything. *OK*, I says, *see you soon* and I winked as I hung up.

That was a laugh, though, that day Marco said let's go down to Gatwick. To the airport.

'What the fuck for?' I said.

'There's always birds there,' he says. 'I used to go down loads with my brother. We used to pick up birds all the time. Then sneak through to the departure lounge and see if we could give 'em one in the satellite before it got to the runways.'

I just cracked up. 'Fuck off!' I giggled. It was a load of shit but it was funny. But once he'd got this idea into his head, he wouldn't let go.

'And there's always queues for standby tickets,' Marco said. 'They camp out in the ticket halls for days, I've seen 'em. Gorgeous birds heading for Italy. They're just crying out for attention. They love it!'

I was laughing again. 'No, they fucking don't! They just go down with their bags packed and if they can't get a flight they go home.'

'They don't all!' Marco almost shouted in excitement. 'Some do! One bird came down from Bristol – she was *so* pissed off cos she couldn't get home so I offered her a place to stay. Jesus, man, you can clean up down there. They're fucking desperate, I tell you!'

'Christ, come on then,' I said and dragged him out the door.

'What's this *satellite*, then?' I asked him. 'A shagging area?'

'No, you prick! It's like a little tube train that shoots you off to the planes.'

'Heathrow's closer,' I told him.

'Nah, it takes longer to fucking Heathrow! You get the Gatwick Express from Victoria – it only takes three quarters of 'n hour.'

'Yeah, but Heathrow's quicker. You just—'

'Nah,' Marco said. 'It's crap is Heathrow! It's the birds going to Europe you want. Not the old fuckers, fucking businessmen heading for the States. You know the kind of birds we're after. You ask 'em out once and they turn up with their overnight bag!'

'You don't know what you're talking about really, do you, Marco? Admit it.'

We got the train to London Bridge.

'You wanna get Sean?' Marco asked when we were out of the station heading for the tube steps.

'No,' I said. 'He's out.'

'With his bird?' Marco asked.

'No, one of McGurk's mates. Christ, that bloke's a goldmine for business. I reckon *all* his mates are benders.'

We took the tube to Stockwell and then got on the Victoria line.

Coming out the station there was this cellist – a girl, playing along to some Tchaikovsky on tape.

'Look! She's alright,' I grabbed Marco's arm. 'You wanna start here?'

'Come on,' Marco says. 'This ain't the airport.'

'Isn't it?' I said, grinning. 'Fucking hell—'

We went striding up the escalators past the stacked-up pile of bodies clinging to the right-hand rail.

'I never touch the handrail,' he told me. 'It don't move at the same speed as the steps. It's always slower going up and faster coming down.'

We caught the train from Victoria. It reminded me of a time me and Sean got a train at Waterloo and these two blokes got on, sort of middle-aged businessmen.

They sat in the next seat by this woman.

'Good evening, how are you?' one said. The other said, 'Good evening.'

They were obviously pissed.

The woman said, 'Good evening,' embarrassed.

Funny that. When you're nervous you can't think and you just repeat what you heard even if it ain't something you'd ordinarily say.

'Does this stop at Clapham?' one asked.

'Yes,' she said.

They sat there mouthing off about their work, sounded financial or something. And this went on for a while after the train had moved off.

Then they turned to us and one said, 'You boys are quiet!'

I looked at Sean.

'Oh, it's *them*!' I thrilled sarcastically. 'You know, the only two blokes in London who are so smart they can get pissed and then mouth off on trains. Cor, my heroes!'

Then I stared them out and they shut up after that.

I could see it starting to get dark through the dirty carriage windows and the ceiling lights were reflected back off the darkening glass. It was only about another few minutes to Gatwick.

Marco was reading a boxing mag.

'I'm waiting to see 'em misprint *uppercut*,' he said. 'Y'know, put an N between the U and the T.'

I had to think about that one for a second.

There was an article about Jack Johnson and the opponents he slaughtered. They fell and died like poor foot grunts on the fields of blood. Well, they didn't really *die*.

'I hope you've brought plenty of johnnies,' Marco said. 'You'll need 'em, mate. Give 'em a taste of what they're expecting from their holiday. A good-looking swarthy bloke like you shouldn't have any trouble.'

'More chance than you, y'ugly cunt!' I said.

'When we get off,' Marco leaned forward. 'At the plane station, it's the south terminal we want. That's where all the fit birds are.'

'OK,' I winked. 'At the plane station, right?'

It must've looked like I was taking the piss cos he slapped me round the head.

I wasn't arguing. Marco's Mum and Dad were Italian and he'd grown huge on tagliatelle verde and Bolognese sauce. Thick black hairs stuck out of his shirt into the hollow of his throat and his arms were like bunches of muscle stuffed up his sleeves.

He was short and always unshaven and the 'V' of his back tapered down into a small arse that I actually used to catch women staring at and then his bulky thighs that made him walk like a crazy little gorilla.

He used to get pissed then go down the gym, the weights gym not our boxing gym, and pump up so his arms stuck out from his body as if they were on strings. He always said he didn't feel the pain when he was tanked so he could train longer.

And when the fat old gym owner in his vest was locking up at midnight, he'd find Marco, the big hairy git, asleep on the tiles in the showers. It was a regular thing.

We got off the train, having to wait for a bloke to shift his cases and bags that'd been piled up against the doors.

Then through the ticket barriers and the station just turned into the airport. I felt like Dorothy stepping out of the black and white house into Oz and everything turned Technicolor.

'We must be over the rainbow,' I told Marco.

He pointed to the Dan Air stand. 'Let's try there first.'

It was hopeless. The place was packed with miserable, busy people, queueing for tickets and boarding-cards, sitting on luggage and checking they had their passports.

'You haven't packed it, have you?'

'Shit!'

'Where is it?'

'Right down the bottom.'

'Smoking or non-smoking?'

'Oh, non-smoking, please, love.'

'Arthur, do you wanna sit by the window?'

'Oh, fuck. What was the flight number again, Margaret?'

'Mum!'

'Shush, love!'

'Mum, do they have Two Thousand AD in Turkey?'

There weren't any gorgeous birds camped out in sleeping bags along the walls. No loose bits of skirt wandering around aimlessly looking for a pickup.

'Where's all the bits, then?' I asked Marco. 'Where's all the fine portions? Looks like they've gone. Looks like they've flown already!'

'Nah, man, you gotta look! You gotta keep an eye out for 'em.'

We wandered around the airport shop, looking at the books and magazines and chocolates.

'Where's the duty-free?' I asked.

'Oh, it's through in the departure lounge.' Marco pointed to the doors where the officials were checking passports.

On the chart overhead were the destinations and departure numbers that flicked over occasionally in a white blur then stopped, saying Crete and BA 8929.

'Do you wanna coffee?' I asked Marco.

He looked at me with big dog eyes. 'I don't think you can get one except through the lounge.'

'Oh, what! There's gotta be a Casey Jones or something out here!'

There were pretty girls in hostess uniforms at the information desks that lined the walls.

I kept ribbing Marco to go up and ask something stupid like who's the president of Zambia but he wouldn't.

'It says *information*,' I told him. 'Ask her what turns her on!'

I tried to stare out the girl on the Swissair desk but she ignored me and carried on typing at her terminal.

'Oh, we shoulda got pissed,' Marco said.

'Where do the flights come in?' I asked. 'The arrivals?'

'What, the passengers?'

I nodded.

'Oh, not here. They come out into customs somewhere then straight back into the railway station.'

'I want to find somebody coming off a flight from Majorca. Ask 'em if they're interested in a timeshare apartment in Peckham!'

Marco giggled then nudged my arm. 'Oi! There!'

I looked to where his eyes were fixed. There were two girls in green parkas, jeans and Doc Marten's. Their heads were shaved down to a number two except for little rat tails just in front of their ears.

We could see them begging.

'Mister, can you spare some—'

''Scuse me, sir, could you spare some change?'

'Excuse me, missus, but—'

Marco looked at me with eager eyes. They were beginning to look like a maniac's eyes.

'You're fucking *joking*!' I hissed. 'Forget it!'

He started singing *'Case her arse, her arse . . .'*

'Do me a favour!'

'. . . whatever will be will be . . .'

But he's walked up to them.

'I'm from security,' he said and flashed his gym membership stuck in his Travelcard wallet. 'Could I check you ladies' tickets?'

One tried to see the card again. 'Let's see that,' she demanded with an amused grin.

They weren't convinced. They clearly weren't as retarded as they looked.

'Oh, leave it out, mate,' the other girl said, the tall one. 'Can't you see we're busy?'

'Where you from?' Marco asked. 'Round here?'

'Yeah. Down by the church. D'you know it?'

'Er, no.' Marco flashed his card again at the giggling girl and shoved it back in his pocket. 'We're from up town. Peckham.'

'Where you off to, then?' asked the older girl.

'Eh?' Marco turned to me and waved his hand urgently like he was beckoning a dog or something.

'How do you mean?' he said.

'Well, are you flying or what?'

I started walking towards them.

'Oh. No,' he said. 'Er . . . Toys, what are we down here for?'

I stood next to him and looked at the two girls. They must've only been about fifteen and sixteen. I gave them a friendly smile and looked at Marco.

'You came here looking for birds to shag,' I told him and my bravado began to pump fiercely in my head.

The girls giggled at this and I felt my brow warming. I hoped I wasn't blushing.

Marco had looked away in despair and embarrassment and he shook his head. I felt like I'd just shat my pants at the kindergarten open day in front of my mum and the thirteen most important aunties in the universe.

'Is that right?' asked the taller girl and Marco looked back then at me.

'Our mother told us not to talk to boys like you,' the smaller girl said and hung her head to one side so you'd know she was kidding.

'I like the hair,' I said.

'Yours is nice, too. Who does the dreadlocks for you?'

'My Mum,' I told her. 'It's dead fiddly cos it's quite short.'

'What you called?' asked Marco. 'I'm Marco and this is Toys.'

The taller girl said, 'I'm Cathy and she's me sister, Mags.'

Mags looked at me.

'What you called? *Toys?*'

I nodded. 'Yeah. My name's Joseph Tortois so they call me Toys.'

The girls laughed a little too much for my comfort.

'You're *joking!*' insisted Cathy. 'Is your second name really *Tortoise?*'

I nodded. 'My Dad's from Jamaica.'

'Yeah,' said Marco, joining in the joke – he was loving it. 'Joseph *Dean* Tortois. Great, isn't it!'

'We live down by the church,' Mags told me.

'Oh, you must be the vicar's daughters.'

They looked blank and shook their heads. I decided not to laugh – we don't want to upset them.

They took us over to the wall and we sat on the floor.

'Are you in the Army?' Cathy asked Marco.

'Yeah. Marines,' he lied.

'I *thought* you were,' she thrilled. 'All those muscles!' She grabbed an arm and started feeling the bulging iron shapes. 'And *his* trousers.' She pointed to my combat pants.

With a tenderness that surprised me he reached the other arm across and stroked her neck behind her ear then leaned forward and pressed his mouth to hers and the two of 'em disappeared in a flurry of wrapping arms and squelching lips.

'She's always like that,' Mags told me and put her hand on mine.

She rested her head on my shoulder.

'Are *you* in the Army?' she asked.

'Couldn't even be a postman,' I said. 'Uniforms don't suit me.'

'It's the dreads, man,' she laughed.

She was quite pretty. The haircut didn't quite ruin her looks.

'Do you live at home?' I asked her then realised how stupid that sounded.

'Yeah,' she said.

'And does your Mum know you're out begging?'

'We live with Dad,' she said. 'He tells us off sometimes but at least we don't go hassling him for money. If we aren't begging we're down the railways sniffing glue.'

'So you're better off begging,' I said.

'Yeah,' she nodded. 'More money for glue.'

'Have you been sniffing tonight?' I asked.

She shook her head. 'Nah, not for days. Can't afford it.'

I leaned forward and put my arm round her.

'Reason I ask,' I said, 'Is – you know how it makes your breath smell?'

I kissed her quickly on the lips and then moved in again slowly and held on, her mouth massaging mine and our tongues beginning to meet.

I could feel motion in my boxer shorts and I was surprised. This little girl was turning me on!

'Does it smell?' she said. *What?* I didn't know what she meant for a second. Oh! her *breath*.

'Gorgeous,' I said. 'Just how it should.'

'Do you think I've got skinny legs?' She stretches out her legs along the dusty airport floor where trolley skidmarks thread like thin, dark veins. Her legs in new blue jeans, girl legs. Little girl legs almost but long and elegant ending in Doc Marten's. The thighs cut away high up like youngster's legs are – waiting for womanhood to fill them out, hormones stoking up the fat, working like sweaty fat-bellied navvies shovelling shale from a deep canal trench.

'Not skinny,' I decided. 'They're nice and slim.'

'Cathy says they're skinny,' she says as I run my hand down her thigh and then back up the inside, resting it on her crotch. I just rest my hand there like you'd stroke a cat's ears then leave your hand on its head. Just a reassuring presence.

Mags looked up with smiling blue eyes, her lashes were long and black without mascara. There was no make-up on her face but her lips still had that look of childhood, flushed with blood, fat and deep red and moist.

I kissed her again.

'Do you like my T-shirt?'

I looked at the Pripps Energy design as she pulled back her parka showing the loose T-shirt and those small swellings on her chest.

'Yeah. Nice tits,' I said. She giggled.

'Cathy says they're bee-stings.'

'Oh, it sounds like Cathy's got a bit too much to say. Why don't you tell her to get stuffed?' I looked across to Marco and the bird with a frown. They were still deep at it.

'Do you like Velvet Underground?' she said.

I don't know why she said that. She was trying to impress me. Talking about a band who were making records with Warhol before she was *born*.

Talking about a revolution. Almost drugged and brain-dead and living in the distorted mess music they loved even before she felt that first slap of air, real air, hit the back of her baby throat. Like a teenager's first drag on a ciggie.

Newborn baby lungs filling and coughing out that fluid. Sharp cold thick air whistling down her tubes and she just realising for the first time just what the fuck she was in for now. Christ, what can I do, I've got to join the crowds just smoothing a comfortable ride through life to get down safely into their graves with a sigh of relief that they've never had to suffer too much or leave any kind of mark, no significant mark on the world. No embarrassing achievements to grin off when friends ask them about it. Demanding an explanation as to why the fuck weren't you down the pub that time, in the safe crowd of anonymity in that smoky local, eh? instead of where you really were (how did you find yourself lost there?) in that place you finally made your name. Look what you've done to us, made us look pricks. Bastard! How dare you! Red face. Grin. Modesty. Think you can hide behind that, you shit! Judas!)

Did her mother, proud of her newborn baby girl, ever imagine what she would be doing in fifteen years' time in Gatwick airport? Probably not.

'I prefer Blind Illingworth,' I answered. *'Words don't sound right. Like I love you, I love you,'* I quoted.

I began to sing *Baby Hold Me Tonight*.

'What crap are you talking now?' Mags asked.

I laughed at her little, open face and pulled her close.

'Do you love me?' I said.

She scowled. 'Course not, you dickhead!'

'Come on, I want a piss.' I stood up and held out my hand to help her up.

'You're a real gentleman,' she told me and stood up, throwing her arms round my neck.

'I know. That's why we're going to the Gents.'

'Are we?' she said in a put-on little girl voice as I led her by the hand to the steps leading down into the little area where Men and Ladies stood at each end with a couple of video games against the wall.

'You'd better put up your hood,' I said.

Two women came down the stairs as I was zipping up the hood around her neck – they went into the Ladies'.

'OK,' I said. 'You'll get away as a little lad.'

No one saw us in the bogs. We went into one of the traps and I closed and locked the door.

She pulled down the hood and I stepped in and zipped it right down, putting my arms inside the coat around her slim waist and kissed her.

'Spends more than I earn. Don't seem right. Don't seem right,' I sang as I slipped off her coat and hung it on the peg behind the door.

I lifted the T-shirt up and her arms shot above her head in surrender as I passed it over her face and up over her slim hands. There was no bra.

What's she thinking, sitting on the toilet lid, bending over and untying her laces, little rolls of puppy fat appearing over the beltline of her jeans? Is she thinking about her Dad? Is she thinking how she's wasting begging time? Or about her glue and cider down by the railways? Or school?

By the time I'd taken off my shirt and shoes and camouflage trousers she was standing there in these white knickers.

I looked up to her chest and those small tits, barely casting a shadow beneath them but her nipples were alive and pert. I pressed her against my chest and the tits felt soft and delicate against me. I slipped down her pants and she stepped out of them on the floor and I stayed down there, sucking mouthfuls of flesh from her thighs and backside into my teeth and kissing her.

Moving to the front and nuzzling the brown mass of curls, waiting for the familiar smell to waft up so I'd know she was ready.

She put her hands on my head, standing there like a stained white-sheet statue, marbled with faint blue veins beneath the skin. I looked at her feet, the toenails painted with '17' Bright Lights ultra violet. Short but shapely toes, pink and naked and pretty on the cold, bare tiles.

Pretty and innocent on the tiles where lonely pubes lay, curled and dead, fallen from old railworkers' undies, and scraps of bogroll beside sparkling specs of piss.

I suddenly wished we were in a big bathroom like the ones you see sometimes in *House and Garden* or *Ideal Homes*, only the old-fashioned ones with huge cast-iron baths and loads of floor space and big windows spilling framefuls of glorious blinding Victorian sunlight onto the washbasin and bowl and ferns on a table of cast-iron curls.

No, not Victorian – you know how iffy they were. I heard it was more acceptable back then for a guy to sleep with a tart as a means of family planning than to use contraception on his wife! Incredible, isn't it! They even had legal brothels for the squaddies, to try and keep the clap under control.

She had me kneeling on the floor in front of the pan and she sat right on the edge, almost slipping off, and guided me between her legs.

I took hold of her hips and pushed myself into her then she let her weight take her forward and I felt like I was right up in her stomach. She must've too cos she gasped and gripped my neck.

We couldn't move much but it didn't matter cos it felt just fine.

'I'm on the pill,' she gasped. 'It's OK!'

It never even occurred to me. It never struck me I was leaving myself open to infection, either.

Marco grilled me about it on the train going home.

'I wasn't joking about the johnnies, you know!' he told me.

So about eight weeks later I got a taxi down to St Thomas's.

The cab driver dropped me off down by the car park and I climbed the bare stairs to main reception.

A sign by the lifts pointed to *Accidents & Emergencies*. Then I saw the signs by the stairs leading up. *X-Rays, Chest Dept, Ear Dept, Lydia Dept.* That was it. Lydia.

I began to climb the stairs, staring at the glass-fronted reception desk. It stretched right across one long wall of the reception area right down to the stores windows and together they enclosed the waiting floor with rows of plastic chairs.

Upstairs I passed the cardiac department then turned right down a corridor of large framed prints and came to a door saying *Lydia Male*.

There were a few guys sitting in there looking like the last thing they expected to see was someone actually coming through the door. A large print of the Royal Guard parading on the Mall hung on the far wall opposite the little booths that looked like the Social Security office.

I waited at the glass panel for a while and a black girl appeared on the other side.

'Er, I'd like to see the doctor about, er . . . something.' I realised how nervous I was.

'Have you got your card?'

I must've looked blank.

'Your appointment card.' Her fingers traced the shape of a card in the air just in case I didn't know what one was.

'When I rang up they said I didn't need an appointment.'

'Is this your first visit to the clinic?' she asked.

Almost as soon as I nodded she produced a white form and asked me to fill it in. She gave me a pen.

'Thanks,' I said.

She disappeared into the back somewhere and I looked at her arse shifting about as she walked in that tight-fitting white skirt.

There were files in blue folders stuffed just about anywhere they'd fit in that office back there. On shelves on the walls, in boxes on the floor and shoved under desks, you know, all over the place.

I had the form done in a few minutes and I was back at the window, tapping at the glass.

''Scuse me. I've done it!'

The black girl pulled the form and the pen through the gap at the bottom of the glass.

'What's the screen for?' I asked, pushing at the glass with my fingertips. 'You scared of catching something?'

'Certainly not!' She flashed an angry look at me. 'Would you wait there a moment, I'll make you out a card.'

I looked at her slender fingers for rings. No important ones.

'Do you get asked out much?' I grinned. 'By patients, I mean.'

She carried on writing the card with her black biro and her eyes didn't shift.

'I'd be surprised if you didn't,' I went on. 'You remind me of Neneh Cherry!'

I'm sure she smirked at that but when she looked up her face was ice. She slid the card under the glass.

'Please take a number and sit down,' she told me and tapped the box of numbers with her pen.

'Can I choose one I like?' I asked, flicking through the cards.

'Only if you want to be here till next week,' she said. 'Take the top one.'

'But it's only seventeen,' I complained. 'I wanted sixty-nine,' and I gave her a wink.

'Take the number, please, and sit down.'

'I'd rather wait here and talk to you.'

'I'm busy,' she said but she looked back before she disappeared among the blue folders.

I sat down and put my number, drawn in thick felt-tip on blue card, between my legs on the plastic seat. I'd worn a shirt and tie with my jeans and I felt a dick sitting there reading the notice board about a self-help HIV group in Battersea.

I read a *Nine to Five* then sat back and listened to the Gloria Estefan tape they were playing in the office. Neneh Cherry was still in the back there somewhere but I couldn't see her even when I craned my neck to see over the top of the desks.

I'd got there just before lunch time and it was starting to get busy now. There were blokes in suits that must've come in straight from the office, some going up to reception like me, but most walking straight through to God knows where.

I was about to go and check with Neneh Cherry why these geezers were just breezing through but I thought she'd had enough of me already. It's funny – I wonder how they subtly slipped out of the office at midday.

Oh, Dick. You coming down the Rosie for lunch?

Er . . . actually I must dash out and er . . . post this letter. Yes, that's it.

But Dick. That's your chequebook!

Oh! Did I say post a letter? I meant . . .

Why be shy? You weren't alone.

Lunchtime brought a drift of workers coming down out of the offices and businesses of Southwark and Lambeth. Printers and secretaries from the IPC buildings, data processing staff from Sainsbury's on Stamford Street and the engineers and post-production personnel from the London Weekend TV centre all drag their diseased arses down the clinic in a slow, syphilitic procession. Then roll out with their flies undone and their ties still stuffed in their shirts.

'Number seventeen,' called a voice.

That was me. I went to the desk but I could see it wasn't my Neneh Cherry.

'Would you go through and take a seat?' She indicated the door I'd seen the others going through.

'Thanks,' I said.

It was white in the other room. There was a huge long lab bench with technicians washing slides and checking cultures through microscopes. There were cupboards at head level and huge taps over deep white sinks.

There were three chairs against a wall and another small waiting room with wooden benches around a table of magazines. A few guys were waiting.

I could see into the consulting rooms when the doors opened. Just a little room with a desk and a tray of podophyllum and acid and swabs. And a pile of plastic gloves, stamped onto their paper backings.

I saw a woman doctor in one room and I hoped I wouldn't get her. But I did. I told her the symptoms and she nodded and smiled as if she had a nob herself and she knew exactly what I meant.

I felt a bit uneasy, her sitting there knowing all about a part of the body she didn't even have. She knew all about my dick and it made me feel naked. Not as naked as when I had to get my dick out and she gave it a good looking at and even felt my balls.

My tie was falling in the way all the time so I stuffed it in my shirt. Now if I see anyone with their tie stuffed in their shirt, between the buttons, it always cracks me up.

The lady doctor sent me out and I was taken into a little room by this Asian technician who whisked the curtain across. He stuck a swab down the end of my nob and then rubbed it on an agar plate. Christ, it fucking hurt, that! It really kind of tickled, only painful tickling. Worse than the burning when I pissed. Then he did it again, the wanker.

He took me into another place with urinals on the wall. The guy gave me two measuring cylinders and told me to piss in both.

'Leave them on the shelf there when you've finished. And wash your hands.' He pointed to the sink unit.

I came out the curtain and the guy said sit down again.

I started looking through some AIDS pamphlets and a couple on drugs then the doctor called me in again.

It's funny, but I hadn't given it much thought up till now. I started shitting it. Christ! What did I have? It seemed like ages walking to the door then going in and closing it. What if I had something serious?

She said there was an infection.

What? Syphilis? Was I gonna die? How bad is it, Doc, honest! Put it this way, is it worth looking forward to Monday's Far Side? *Who shall I leave my Otis Redding albums to – my Mum?*

'We treat it with antibiotics,' she told me. 'Take two tablets, two times a day, an hour before meals. OK?'

She smiled. She didn't seem concerned about my syphilis. I'd probably be a blubbering vegetable in weeks.

'What is it, then? What I've got?'

'Non-specific urethritis,' she said. It sounded pretty specific to me. 'It's quite common, there's nothing to worry about.' She was scribbling notes on my file. Then she looked back up at me.

'Avoid intercourse for the two weeks till you've finished your antibiotics. Er, is your girlfriend being treated?'

Shit, what do I say? If I tell the truth she'll probably make me track down Mags. I'll spend the rest of my life wandering round Gatwick airport.

I found myself answering, 'Oh yeah. She's alright.'

'And she *is* your regular sexual partner?'

I nodded dumbly.

'Have you had any recent sexual contact with anyone else, Mr Tortois?' she asked, picking up her pen.

'No, not at all,' I told her.

She made a note on my file. *RGF receiving treatment.* RGF? Regular Girl Friend?

She stood up. 'If you'd like to pick up your tablets from outside . . .'

'Do you want me to come back in a couple of weeks, check it's gone?' I said.

'No, it's not necessary. We don't bother re-testing. A week should be enough to cure it – we give two weeks' supply to be two hundred per cent sure!' She smiled clinically. She didn't give a toss about my v.d.

I wanted to ask her if she fancied a shag in about six days. A touch of Russian roulette!

I said thank you and walked out, back to the glass cabinets and a table of drawers with stacks of files on it.

The doctor gave my notes to the Asian technician and he dug out a bottle of Oxytetracycline. He read out the directions in a thick Kashmiri accent and gave me a dark, crooked grin.

'And *no* sex!' he added. I could tell he enjoyed his job.

I stuck the pills in my pocket and they rattled there all the way home. I could've sworn people knew what they were. Was it my imagination or were people really giving me dirty looks and whispering to each other?

'You know where *he's* just been, don't you?'

Anyway, I got the last laugh. As I was coming back out, through the waiting room, I shouted into the receptionist.

'Oi, Neneh! Neneh Cherry! Doc says I'll be cleared up in a fortnight. Can I call you *then*?'

We were in the Clipper at Rotherhithe with some of Marco's old mates off the sites. And, you know, when I'm pissed, I forget about fancying Sean – the world's just full of beautiful leggy girls. All red lips and lovely eyes and full-breasted blouses.

I stood there pissing into the long trough urinal in the pub, watching the fag ends gather with the floating blue soap squares at the grate end of the cracked porcelain bog. And my beer sighed deep inside me.

And I staggered back into the blue air saloon bar. Is it the smoke I can see?

I always feel like a fag after a few beers. Shit, no I don't, do I? I feel straight. Ha! No, I mean I fancy a cig. A fucking ciggie.

How pissed was I? I'd leaned my forehead against the tiles in the bog like a pissing ladder. People were walking round me 'stead of underneath me. Some people are *so* superstitious.

And of course the taxi arrived to take us up town. It was a long way from Rotherhithe to town – we were going to have a few in the Freemason's at Covent Garden then shoot off to the Alamo near Soho Square.

The first taxi picked up me and Gav and Paddy and we sat in the beat-up old estate with the dog bars up in the tailgate.

The cabbie was a crap driver. He was talking to his controller. A woman.

'Are they English?' came the voice, all crackles. She was talking about the second carload, still in the Clipper. The cabbie couldn't find them in there.

We laughed. 'Yeah, they're English alright! They're by the door!'
'What the fuck?' I said.

'Oh, there's a lot of foreigners around here. Come to work on the building sites.'

It just sounded so funny, y'know – are they English? No, they're friggin' Yugoslav trapeze artists!

We drove down Stamford Street and turned right onto Waterloo Bridge. The traffic was standing and people were all over the bridge.

'Fuck! What's going on?'

'Could be the Kingsway Tunnel closed,' suggested the cabbie. 'But I wouldn't think it'd matter at this time.'

'I thought I saw fireworks earlier!'

The voice crackled over the c.b.

'Seven!'

'Yeah?' said the guy into his handset.

'Seven. What's your position?'

'Just on Waterloo Bridge.'

The radio buzzed a bit.

'Where's One-Four?' the cabbie asked.

The answer crackled back. 'Don't know. He just left the pickup.'

'Tell him to avoid Waterloo Bridge. The traffic ain't moving.'

'Roger, Seven!'

We moved slowly and hung out the windows asking people what was going on. No one seemed to know.

'. . . says there's a lot of traffic on Waterloo Bridge,' hissed the radio.

One-Four must've asked where we were.

'He's sitting in it now,' the controller said.

We'd just passed the bottleneck actually and headed across the Strand.

We never found out what all the fuss was about. Probably Jenny throwing herself off the bridge as a stilettoed martyr to her undying love for Sean.

I thought she'd given up on him one time. But I was glad of it in a way. She'd been getting him pretty wound up and then she stopped coming round or phoning – giving him a rest probably.

He didn't even mention it. Never said *'Ere, that bird – whatsername – ain't been round for a while, has she?'*

Not even that. Not a peep. It was just as if she'd never existed.

I wondered what'd happened to her and eventually I had to say something.

'When you seein' Jenny again?' I said when I thought Sean was in a good mood. It turned out he wasn't.

Talk about wound up. She'd really been getting under his skin lately, you know. But not just that, it was all sorts of emotions. Sometimes when she rang he'd stand there with a kind of look in his eyes not like the bland one he usually wore. I wouldn't say it was exactly a smile but he was certainly more alive than I'd ever seen him.

Then other times he'd fly into a rage and slam the cupboard doors – the kitchen ones, smashing the steel pans around in the musty wooden darkness, and walk out the door and stay out in the cold all night.

I witnessed some strange things in that bedroom it seemed like the three of us shared. He was always so tender with her – he never flew off the handle with her there but I saw him suffering deep inside and his fingers would squeeze together in his lap, the knuckles draining and shining.

She'd cry and tremble, hanging onto the mantelpiece like it was the rails on a storm ferry in the wild deep night.

So I asked him – when you seein' Jenny again?

He looked at me with the firmest face I'd ever seen. His jaw tight and lined and his eyes open like the lights of Piccadilly. I could see the tendons stand out on his neck and he said 'Toys . . .' like he was about to give a huge headmaster lecture.

But the towlines melted away and his strength dissolved before me. His forehead collapsed into creases and the lips shivered as tears poured from the eyes.

Oh, Christ! My illusions fell over one on top of another at this miracle – like the face on the Turin Shroud, he sat and cried before me and I almost wept for him.

I went and held him but he didn't move – his hands were dead and buried between his knees. Only his eyes lived and his sobbing, trembling mouth.

'What's the matter, eh?' I soothed.

I backed off and looked at him. He didn't seem to know what was the matter.

'Are you missing her?' I said. I became very afraid. I felt like I was about to learn something that would hurt and destroy me.

He shook his head. I breathed again.

'Do you love her?' I tried, a little more confident.

He spoke like a five-year-old, in gasps.

'How – how can I, T-Toys?' he shut his eyes with the pain.

'Well, you feel something,' I told him.

'I've – I don't know . . . what it's – it's like, do I?'

'What do you mean, mate? You don't know what *what's* like?'

He couldn't answer because he didn't even understand what he'd said.

'*Love*? Is it love you're talking about?' I tried.

It would've been easier for him to walk out and let the stark, cold night see his sorrow and confusion, and dry his tears and calm his shaking throat. But instead he sat there, silent, almost unthinking. Blinking the moisture from his eyes until I got up and made us both a cup of tea.

Neither of us said anything else that night. I put on *The Song Remains the Same* and both our hearts churned to the lightning almost-blues breaks in *Dazed and Confused*.

If an electric light bulb can burn down and fade like a spitting old fat candle then the bulb in that room flared and died slowly and the room seemed to disappear into darkness and walls you couldn't see.

Jenny sat at home, staring at the mirror, smearing her make-up with bitter tears. She wanted a row of lightbulbs round the mirror frame, popping and going out, points of reflected light disappearing from the end of a plastic red clown's nose till she was left alone, in the darkness, still gasping from too much crying. You know when you cry too much and you end up with your stomach sort of spasming like hiccups and making a whimpering sound.

A line of light sat at the foot of the bedroom door and with the gentle draught came sounds of the girls talking, pots in the kitchen, a door closing, taps running, music from another room. The line of light, like a sick grin without teeth, leered at her from the straggly carpet where it disappeared underneath the bottom of the door.

She still clutched the tenners in her hand. He'd been gone about half an hour now, her client – the girls must have thought she was asleep. He'd gone in a bustle of discomfort and embarrassment but the last thing she cared about right now was upsetting a customer.

But what the hell was he *supposed* to think she was crying about. He has his face between her legs and she starts bawling! So he comes up with a grin thinking he's moved her to tears with his linguistic skills when she asks him to leave! Jesus, that was *not* the reaction he wanted. *Was I that bad?*

They say women think about the silliest little things during sex but when she's got a crazy rent-boy from Southwark Street on her mind, something's wrong!

She sat in the dark but something made her eyes sparkle in the mirror. The tears seemed to generate their own light as they generated their own pain.

She was far away, now.

She was still looking in on an empty room on a long, wet, shiny street. A room empty except for a piano against the wall and a small cardboard box on the floor. And she was crying cos she missed that room. It had warmed her through the Michaelmas term against a harsh Ormskirk winter of long cold nights and now she stood, looking in and sniffling with the chill and the sorrow.

Far off in the square the Union building looked down onto the steps and the library lights were still on, people shifting around on the top floor between rows of shelves. Two Africans crossed the square, their wide flares flapping in the wind.

This thing with Sean, it was bringing back all the old memories and feelings of college. Those bright kitchen evenings with the pans and steamed-up windows and all the girls sitting, chatting, laughing. With the night closing in all around but they were warm, and happy and together.

And in the bar – the excitement, wondering about the blokes. God, he's fit! And blinded by the disco lights on swaying stands, just a blur of bodies and music and the Bacardi haze. Giggling into the floating ice, *Do you think so? – Go on, ask him!*

And there's always a sick feeling when you see him leant against the speaker stack, his hands deep into the arse pockets of some other tart's jeans.

Those feelings and memories, indelibly fixed in her experience, impossible to describe, so painful to leave behind. No one else can understand what she'd felt there. And to look back on it all, realising it *is* really all over for ever, she could never recapture those huge, intangible times. Thought she'd be there forever. Thought she'd be a kid forever.

And Sean brought it all back somehow. He was a kind of a loss too. A loss of something she'd never had but wanted so badly.

She tried to make herself strong. To forget about him and turn to something new to live for. It lasted a while but she was too weak. She was just resting for the next assault.

I got one of those cards from the sorting office the other day. *This parcel could not be delivered cos you weren't in and it wouldn't fit through the letterbox*, that sort of thing.

So you have to go pick it up yourself from the Post Office.

They open bloody stupid hours – shut after about one o'clock weekdays, not open on Sundays. I was gonna go on Saturday and I knew it shut at half twelve.

My Mum was watching *Cagney and Lacey* the Friday night before, sitting in her pink quilted nightie and furry slippers. She sat sipping her cuppa and brushing straggly curls from her eyes, the curls that fell from between those coloured bendy foam things she had in her hair.

'When did you last put those things to the wash, Joseph? Them trousers?'

'Mum, they don't need washing! They're Army trousers! They're camouflage trousers – they're meant to be dirty!'

'I don't care. You give me them tomorrow morning, you hear? Only thing they'd camouflage you in is a muddy puddle!'

I put the mug up to my mouth and pressed my face over the steaming tea so the vapour dampened my skin. I looked at the screen where Cagney and Lacey were pissed off cos the little handicapped girl wouldn't accept the bike they'd bought her.

'Did you ask Skelly about them tapes?' I said.

'Yeah, he says he's got 'em, but he'll have to find 'em, alright?'

'Yeah, great!'

'I'll get 'em when I next see him, OK love?'

'Thanks, Mum.' I sat there smiling for a minute. 'Are you watching this, Mum?'

'Course I'm bloody watching it!' she laughed. 'What do you *think* I'm doing? Why, is there something you wanna watch?'

'No, I ain't seen the end of that video yet.'

'Well, wait till this is finished, I'm going to bed after that.'

So I sat through till the end and it was well after twelve when it finished.

'Don't forget to give me them trousers tomorrow,' my Mum said as she padded upstairs.

I watched the last bit of *One Flew Over the Cuckoo's Nest*, from McMurphy getting his electro shock therapy. And I felt sorry for Billy, the way Nurse Ratchett treated him, the old cow! I went to bed thinking about lobotomies and that shaved, scarred forehead.

I woke up at about ten the next morning when my Mum came in and started rooting through my clothes.

'Are you getting up, or what?' she said.

I groaned and turned over. 'No, I'm knackered.'

'Well, you'd better get up soon – I want them sheets to wash.'

She rummaged about some more then said, 'I'm taking these shirts and your trousers. Get some new ones out, alright love?'

Then she went and I drifted back to my dream about some girl at a party who was crying.

The next thing I knew it was ten past twelve and I had twenty minutes to get down to the Post Office before it shut. I pulled on a pair of boxer shorts and started looking for my combat trousers. Where the fuck are they – oh, shit! Mum took 'em. So I pulled out my jeans and put on a pair of trainers – no time for socks. I dived into a T-shirt, grabbed my card and stuff and dashed out the door down to Peckham High Street.

I didn't have my watch on but I must've made it cos there was still a queue. There was this large clock on the wall and it said twenty-five past.

Some bloke was pissing me off, grumbling all the time as how there was only two people on the counter. I felt like hitting him.

At half past the black girl came through the door at the side of the counter and collected the cards from everyone in the queue then closed the big wooden doors to the street. I was next in line to be served by this time.

Anyhow, they found my parcel in the log book and the bloke was looking for it on the shelves.

The girl was talking to the bloke behind me.

'If you don't have any identification then I can't give you the parcel.'

That's a point. They hadn't asked me to show any i.d. Oh, well.

'Oh, come on,' he said. 'Don't give me a hard time.' His voice was quite posh but he looked somehow mad. Like one of the guys from the ward on *Cuckoo's Nest*.

'I'll open this letter, then,' he said. 'That'll prove who I am.'

'Letterheads aren't valid identification,' the girl said. But he carried on tearing open his letter.

The other bloke behind the counter took up the cry. 'Letterheads aren't valid identification,' he said. 'There's a list here,' and he pointed to a little poster in the glass counter window.

'I'm under instruction not to give out anything unless–'

'Bullshit!' said the bloke. 'That's bullshit!'

But he took his letter and left.

I got my parcel and headed out. The black girl noticed another woman had joined the queue and she said, 'We close at twelve thirty.'

The woman just stood there, thinking if she waited and ignored this everything would be OK.

'I'm afraid you're too late,' the girl said again. 'We close at twelve thirty. It's now twenty to one.'

'I was here just before twenty to one,' the woman said.

'We closed at twelve thirty.'

'I was here at twelve thirty.'

'Well, I collected the cards at twelve thirty. You're too late.'

I got home and tore open the big package. I knew what it was. That gardening book I'd sent for – it was my Mum's birthday in a couple of weeks and she loved reading about gardening.

I just hoped it had a section on growing weeds in the concrete cracks of a crumbling Peckham backyard.

She came back. Well, she phoned. Said she wanted to meet Sean in a pub up town. The Dog and Trumpet on Great Marlborough Street.

I told you about that before, didn't I? How Sean used to hang around up there in some kind of daze. You know, perhaps she wanted to get back to old times.

'You going then?' I said. 'This is what you've been waiting for.'

Sean shook his head. 'I just can't say no to her anymore.'

'What do you mean? You never did say no to her!'

'I never used to care one way.or the other, Toys. Now I want to say no, I can't.'

'That's the way it goes, mate,' I said. 'What did you tell her?'

'Christ, Toys! Can't you come with me, eh?'

He looked desperate. He wanted me to go along and stop him falling in love with this girl cos he was afraid of something he'd never known. As if I could do anything. He knew as well as I did it was on the cards.

'Yeah, alright,' I said.

I felt really sick suddenly. This was something I'd been pushing out of my mind for so long. Christ, he's straight so sooner or later he's gonna fall for a bird. But no, I just kept ignoring it and putting it off cos after all it *was* Sean. I mean, he's a spaz, isn't he?

I felt like a kid come to the end of the long summer holidays and I still haven't done my project. What a sick, panicky feeling. My little brain-dead bum chum was going off to marry his sweetheart.

Sean looked as scared as I felt all the way to the pub. He sat on the tube staring across at the heater grille between my feet and I kept looking down to see if he noticed the dangly velcro straps on my Hi-Tecs.

Every time the doors opened he looked up as if she was likely to be getting on and his eyes rolled round, scared, like some old-timer cotton picker.

It was packed as usual in the pub and Jenny looked horrified when she saw me.

She hissed to Sean, 'Why'd you bring *him*?'

'What's the matter?' I said. 'Don't you *like* me?'

She snorted in disgust and I laughed at the sound.

'I like *you*,' I said.

'Come on, Sean,' she said and guided the lamb to a table up above the steps by the wooden rails.

There was a glass roof in the centre of the ceiling and it looked like a greenhouse dome with the huge pots of plants hanging beneath it but still high above the heads of the drinkers queueing at the bar.

I heard staff from Top Shop across on Oxford Street talking about how they closed the bog cos someone crapped on the floor and how the internal auditors bollocked them for the sloppy fire drill cos the upstairs accountants could be trapped. I thought that was the whole reason they designed it that way!

Down the Dog and Trumpet, eh? Where the contract cleaners meet to give tips on the best offices for ripping off quids out of drawers. Some of those places – anyone could get past the guy at reception no problem and get away with about a tenner and a nice new jacket.

I sat down next to Sean and put my two pints on the table. Jenny was at the bar buying Sean a drink.

'What's she getting you, an orange?' I said.

'Yeah. What else?'

'That bird,' I said in despair. 'Here y'are, mate.' I pushed a pint to him.

'Thanks, Toys.' He took a long gulp and his mouth smacked when he stopped. 'Listen, you hang around, alright?' he said, holding onto my chair.

I nodded and my nose almost touched the lager froth up to my mouth.

'You bastard!' Jenny spat at me, standing there fresh from the bar. It sounded so much more aggressive in her accent. She thought I was poisoning her lover-boy with my filthy beer.

'Hey, who said *I* got it for him!'

'Oh, fuck off, Toys! No one asked you to come here so why don't you just piss off?'

'I don't want to drink orange,' Sean said.

Jenny sat down and sighed.

'Why don't you just try?' she pleaded with Sean.

Sean shook his head. 'I don't want to.'

'You mean you *can't*!'

I knew I was pushing it but I said, 'Look, can't you take a hint, doll? He doesn't want your crummy orange—'

Christ, I thought she was gonna have a stroke the way she went red. She was standing up screaming at me and dragging Sean off his chair, just dying to get him out of the place away from me.

I just looked around at the embarrassed staring faces until the words started coming into focus and making sense.

'—at all! You fucking wanker! Why don't you just leave us alone?'

Sean wasn't moving and Jenny just screamed, literally.

There's a mad old woman walks down Stamford Street in the early morning some days and screams blue murder at the traffic in her hilarious pantomime voice. Then other times you see her perfectly normal. Jenny reminded me of the old woman in her manic morning phase.

She grabbed my pint and it went straight into my face and down the front of my T-shirt and I just gasped and stared.

'You bastard bummer boy! You fucking queer!' She was crying now. 'If you touch him again I'll fucking *kill* you!'

I've had this sort of thing before but this was worse. The voice was straight out of a bad playground drama and the face she was pulling was ugly.

'Just piss off and bum some filthy little pervert who wants you, not Sean. Fucking *leave him alone!*'

No one else in the room was speaking. They'd all turned off to look at this hysterical scouse bird bawling her head off.

Jenny was still trying to drag Sean to his feet to get him away from me.

'What are you staring at?' she screamed. 'Fuck off!'

The chap from behind the bar had come round and he was trying to talk to Jenny, his hand out to hold her.

'Get off, you cunt!' She shook her arm away even though he hadn't touched her and she actually stamped her foot like a kid in a tantrum.

'Sean, come *on*! I don't want you with this wanker!'

I was so embarrassed for her I'd almost forgotten to breathe and my heart was beating excitedly.

Sean got up eventually when the landlord appeared – a silver-bearded fat old cockney who ordered us all out shouting almost as loudly as Jenny had done.

'We can do without your sort!' he said. 'Bloody hysterical cow!'

She must have blown it now. You know, blown her chances with Sean. But outside she pressed herself into his wrinkled raincoat and whispered to him.

'Oh, Sean, I'm sorry! I didn't want to show you up. It's only cos I care so much about you.'

I leant against the railings and looked at the wet, black street. Sean was telling her it didn't matter.

'I'm going home,' I said.

'No!' said Sean. 'Come on, let's go to the Hansel.'

'Sean – I'm wet and cold and pissed off. I don't like being shown up like that in a pub!'

'Come on, Toys—'

'*She* don't want me around.'

Sean put his arm round my shoulder. '*I* do,' he said.

We started moving off but Jenny hesitated a moment, glaring at me, then she came along too, her face a picture of hatred.

She was quiet in the Hansel and I insisted on buying the first round. She didn't say a thing when I put a pint of Foster's in front of Sean.

My T-shirt was sticking to me with the wet beer that spread through it and it began to smell.

'So,' I said to Jenny. 'Where you been lately?'

She looked at Sean like she was saying 'Why is this creep still around?'

'How've you been?' asked Sean.

She reached across and put her hand on Sean's.

'A bit lonely, Babe. I've not really been getting on with Sue very well. It's been a bit miserable in our house you know.'

'What you been arguing with her about?' Sean asked.

'Not me again, I hope,' I said. 'You know you girls really must stop fighting over me – you can't *have* me, OK?'

This time Sean scowled at me. I wasn't going down too well tonight – maybe I should've stayed home or counted the early trains down Queen's Road.

'They won't put the heating up,' Jenny explained. 'Sue's so fat she can't feel the cold but I want it turned up and Sue says it's a waste of money.'

'She'll turn it up when the pipes freeze,' I said. 'What else?'

'Do you *mind*?' Jenny snapped at me. 'I'm trying to talk to Sean, not you.'

'Hey, let's not start this again, doll,' I said. 'What do you wanna do, get us kicked from one pub to another all night? That may be your idea of fun but it fucking ain't—'

'Toys,' Sean said in a calm tone. 'She wasn't starting.'

'Babe, why do you live with him?' Jenny asked Sean.

'Who, Toys? He's me mate.'

Well, that was another new one. Somebody once asked Sean about me. '*Is he your mate, then, that black kid?*' down the pub or somewhere and I was so shocked when he said *no*.

Sean was the same way with everybody. He was good to everyone and he never expected anything in return, especially not love.

It just reminded me again of the way I'd treated him and it made me hurt so I shut up.

I wanted to shout *'No, I don't do that to him anymore. Haven't for about ten months – before you met him, you slag!'* but I just kept quiet.

'I had an awful dream,' Jenny said. 'It was wartime and my room was this brick tunnel underground and it was really badly lit and dusty and the floor was littered with broken bricks. I was in there doing something and there was this sleeping bag on the floor and I remember dreading having to sleep there that night. And every time a bomb exploded outside, little bits of brick and dust fell down from the rounded ceiling and I was afraid the whole thing would collapse.'

'You must be really worrying about that place,' Sean said.

'No, I just get depressed there sometimes.'

She was picturing her room and how she'd taken to hiding away in there with the lights off. She used to lie in bed never wanting to leave it and just stare frightened at the strip of light around the doorframe.

It seemed the world had grown too big and painful for her and now she was writing off friends one by one – she'd thought they were something else, it's funny how people let you down and show their true light sometimes.

But it was fucking depressing. No one to love her and running out of mates and now even doubting herself. She just couldn't bring herself to sleep with anyone else these days and her boss, Grant, was beginning to notice.

'Jesus, I can just sit and talk if I want!' she told him when he took her aside.

'Yes, that's fine,' said Grant. 'But—'

'What do you want me to do, go off with every—'

'That's not necessary, Jenny. But it's bad custom to turn down business. You're refusing to leave with *anyone* recently, and although I don't mind you living off hostess fees if you can manage . . .'

That was the thing about the bar - old guys who just wanted company in the club. If she'd have been working the streets she'd have starved by now. Who wants to stand beneath a dripping rattling gutter outside the bookies', talking to some grubby-faced bird about the liberation of Romania? And then pay for the chat! No bugger, that's who!

'Are you managing to pay the rent and everything?' asked Sean.

Jenny nodded. 'Yeah. I'm making enough money. Just about.'

That was the first lesson Sean learnt. No matter what you have to do, you need money. For housing, food, clothes, and that's about it. Oh, and in *his* business, for making yourself look attractive. It wasn't vanity – he didn't understand that – it was just sheer common business sense. He'd learnt the survival lesson cos of his Mum.

After the divorce she'd had to work up the school kitchens and sweeping up at the pubs around the area and then she'd invest the family's bread money by blowing it down the Granada bingo or on the fruit machines in the pub.

Sean's mate used to go with him sometimes when he went gobbling big-bellied blokes in the estates behind the school for a few quid pocket money. But the mate got sick of it.

This other kid started showing off to the trainee male nurses walking on the road bridge over the lines to work.

He'd jump off the canopy at New Cross Gate station onto waiting trains. And then jump back before they set off, or stay on for a bit and surf them. He died, still laughing, when he bounced off one time and broke his neck on the tracks beside it and they couldn't get him off in time before the train heading the other way smeared him all the way to London Bridge.

Yeah, the mate got sick of it. Perhaps he should've stuck to it. Sean never stopped.

''Scuse me,' Jenny said. She nervously pushed the Tia Maria and Coke away from her before she stood up. 'Just goin' the loo.'

I leaned back on my chair. 'She means going *to* the loo,' I said and made no secret of watching her arse waggle round the bar to the Ladies'. She had her tight black leggings on and the arse was nothing short of magnificent.

'Fuck me, them buns of hers,' I said. 'I'd just love to go up behind her and – you seen her when she's playing pool? When she bends over and sticks her arse out! Christ, that arse! That fucking arse!'

I was ranting and Sean couldn't have brought me out of it more rudely and painfully than if he'd slapped my face.

He said, 'Is it as nice as mine?' and I felt his pain severely in my gut. My stomach knotted and I felt sick. (Is this what period pains feel like?) I knew *then* if I didn't know before that he was changing. He'd never be the same again.

Jenny was gettin' slowly more relaxed and more pissed. There were stars in her eyes and the beermats grew wings and flapped around her head.

She kept crossing and uncrossing her legs and I was fascinated by the way her fingers wound around the thin stem of her wineglass. She could wrap each finger about three times round.

I was leaning on the table, staring across at Jenny, wondering how close I could get my head to hers. She was talking fast, seizing on every breath and her eyes wandered from Sean's face to the four corners and almost in my direction.

I could see the cornsilk dust on her face and the eyes, highlighted with liner and flashing thick black lashes, and if you looked really close the lashes were irregular, small lumps of mascara clinging to the shafts like a leaf splashed with droplets of dew.

And she'd forged herself cheekbones high up with blusher and her lips leapt out of her face, curling back sometimes from her clear white teeth, those lips so sharp and red and vivid she looked like a 3-D picture.

She thought she was clear and dry. She felt she could run a straight mile but I laughed when she stood up and flopped back down telling her 'We're all going to Brighton' joke.

'Why do they put milk bottles up above the door down your street, Jen?'

'*Above* the door?' Sean said.

'Yeah, y'know. Like on the top of the door frame,' I said.

'I haven't seen 'em,' Jenny said.

'Yeah, you have! The milkie leaves 'em on the shelf above the door. There's like a glass half-moon panel over all the doors 'n he leaves 'em on the shelf.'

'Why do they do that?' asked Jenny.

'I *dunno*!' I said. 'That's what I want to know.'

'Stop people nicking 'em,' said Sean.

'It'd only stop *dwarfs* nicking 'em!'

I'd been down that road millions of times on my way from Sean's to London Bridge. Lamps sitting there with baking soda fires constantly burning in them, I could never figure it.

And my shadow would stretch out further and further in front of me as I walked away from a lamp and it would fade into a huge giant shape of me then disappear.

And a shadow from the lamp across the street would rush by me

to my left across the terraced wall and windows and I'd pass under
another lamp, the hot orange bulb buzzing, and my shadow would
return from between my legs. A head at first then growing, rushing
ahead of me, shoulders, back, legs and then it too would fade and
disappear.

The rain used to be so cold and I flinched each time a drop hit
my eyelashes. And warm cars passed. There was the smell of warm
cars in the rain.

I was starting to drift, myself. I slid my empty beerglass around in
the rings of beer that shone on the table.

''Nother one?' offered Sean.

'Yeah, cheers,' I said and he got up and Jenny followed him to
the bar.

I dunno whether she wanted to be near him or shot of me. This
pub was alright. Quite posh – no contract cleaners in here.

I rubbed at the beer rings and smeared them across the table,
trying to dry them out. All they did was soak my hand and I wiped
it dry in my hair.

I was getting dog tired and I could feel my cheeks sagging down
below my chin and dragging on the carpeted floor.

'Course it's cold enough for a hat!' someone said on another
table.

'Yeah, I want one with a feather in—'

'Oh, shit! My Grandad had one like that!'

I remembered great feathery hard hats in the war museum,
looked like they had a dead chicken on 'em. And some kid's
cigarette case inscribed *To Billy Jones, good luck in the war –
don't get shot!* and the silver finish all tarnished and scratched
and a big jagged bullethole straight through the middle of his
Woodbines.

By the time they got back from the bar I'd painted a Mona Lisa
in beer on the dark varnished table and Leonardo was leaning over
my shoulder telling me he was sure the Giaconda never wore an
acid house badge.

Get your hand off my arse, Leo, I said.

I woke up in my own room the next morning. I was surprised not
to be in Sean's room cos I usually stayed there Saturday nights but
it was the Peckham birds that sang outside that Sunday and made
me flinch and the sick pain behind my eyes got worse. It sounded

like someone had an oil drum over my head and they were at it
with a road drill.

Yeah, *that's* why I'm here, I thought. I remembered Jenny having
a quiet word with me. That was quite clever of her – not making
a scene about it. So I reluctantly agreed and pushed off and left
them to it.

After the pub Jenny'd insisted we visited McDonald's cos she was
'starving'. She wanted some chicken nugget things.

I stood outside refusing to move.

'I don't go in McDonald's,' I said. 'You must be fucking stupid
helping them! You know what they're doing to our environment,
don't you, cutting down the rain forests.'

'Oh, come on, Toys,' Jenny said. 'You soft git. They don't do
that. Haven't you read their leaflets?'

'Oh what! Come off it! You mean you believe that? Jesus, if
everyone was like you—'

They went in and I followed through the heavy glass doors still
moaning.

'You'll be sorry when you're gasping for breath when all the
oxygen's gone! Them forests make our oxygen, you know. You'll
be sorry – bet you won't be dying for a Big Mac then, will you!'

We sat upstairs in the kids' section where they have that big
plastic train and the mural with Ronald McDonald in a world where
cheeseburgers grow on plants and there are milkshake rivers. It's
enough to make you puke!

Course Jenny couldn't resist the fucking useless paper hats the
staff wear.

'I want a hat like that!' she squealed like a five-year-old.

'What, a fucking Happy Hat?' I condescended.

'A Happy Hat! I want a Happy Hat! Sean, get me one!'

I could've smacked her one but I looked at Sean. He seemed
unmoved.

I sent a bird a tin of prunes once. *That* moved her.

Anyway I was at home and bored. I watched *The Waltons* and
John-Boy was hunting around town looking for a word processor.
No, a typewriter, really!

There wasn't much to do. I wandered round the house until my
Mum made me put the hoover on. Then she sent me down the
shop for some eggs and hairspray. I dunno what she was cooking!

I got back and made a cuppa. I kept thinking about Sean. I really wanted to go round but I didn't know how long *she'd* stay there. I didn't want to catch them at it, you know what I mean.

Skelly was round at our place. That's my Mum's boyfriend. I say *boy*friend but he was about fifty. He'd started losing his hair about ten years before and finally gave up trying to hide it and had all he had left shaved off.

I thought it looked really smart but my Mum nearly took a fit when she first saw it.

Skelly knew my Dad. They used to work on the fork-lifts together at Dixon's. Sometimes my Dad used to come round to the school in the afternoon cos if they got their work done by about two or three they could knock off. So he used to see us at afternoon playtime and chase about in the yard.

I love that big guy. He lives in Pitsea now, married. Married to some bird with her own pottery business or some crafty thing. I used to love his thick accent the way he got his words the wrong way round. Try as I might to copy him I still came out talking like this. Like a friggin' cockney. I could never figure that. I'd insist I was Jamaican. Diluted Jamaican.

And it don't bother me that I'm illegitimate. Never has. I still call someone a bastard without thinking. So what difference does it make? I don't blame him, I'd do the same myself. But people say *Oh, it's the kids I feel sorry for*. Bollocks!

And I loved his deep blackness. He looked so sleek and brand new when he got out the bath, dripping and still with shaving foam in his ears and I used to laugh with joy. But I wanted to be as black as him and I never was.

I miss him now cos I don't get to see him that often. And when I do he just tells me to get a decent job. What, like *you* did, eh Dad?

I really wish they'd stayed together, him and my Mum. They did get engaged once but I don't think my Dad was serious about it. It was just after a rough patch they'd been going through and Dad wanted to calm the waters.

At about five in the afternoon I thought it was probably safe to go and see Sean. I'd been stopping myself all day.

At Queen's Road the clouds broke up a bit but it was still quite cold. Sunlit strangers gathered on the platform's grey concrete flags, whispering to absent trains.

I dug my hands deeply into my coat pockets. The rails looked ice cold and they began to hum and rattle when the train grew near. A high whine and everyone looked at the carriages pulling in, not cos they were interested but just cos they didn't dare look anywhere else.

I did. I was looking at the fat guard hanging out of the door with his panel of switches and buttons.

It's always empty on Southwark Street on weekends. The few shops are closed and the metal screens pulled down over the glass fronts. I know it was Sunday, but I mean, I've seen 'em on Saturday an' all and it's just the same.

It was getting dark when I arrived at Sean's. There was no answer when I knocked and I waited there, agonising about whether to let myself in or not. He might be still in bed with her!

Finally I got out my key and banged it about on the flat brass surround of the Yale lock as a last futile attempt to wake him up before I went in.

I wasn't ready for what I saw.

'Fucking hell, Sean! Are you alright?'

He couldn't hear me. He was sitting up in bed with his earphones on, plugged into the stereo and I could hear the music squeaking out of it from across the room. It must have been deafening.

And he was shivering and his face was pale and blue and shiny like a squid. God, he looked so ill I couldn't believe it.

He saw me and took off the headphones as I sat on the bed beside him. They fell to the floor still calling out in that tinny voice and he grabbed my hand, making it shake along with his. It felt like a washing-machine on full spin.

He spilled tears down his face along with the sweat from his brow and I pulled myself away and looked at his poor crumpled face.

Then it dawned on me.

'You haven't had a drink today, have you?' I said.

He tried to talk but his lips and teeth were trembling too much. I could feel his legs thrashing about under the covers and I saw the terror in his eyes.

'You been sick?' I said. 'Hang on, I'm gonna get you something.'

If he could've spoken he'd have saved me the trouble. All the bottles I found in the kitchen were empty and the sink was splashed with brown droplets. Christ! I sniffed the plug hole. It was brandy.

Or whisky. Or both. Jesus, what had she done? Chucked all his fucking drink away!

I started panicking. Were the offies open yet? Fuck, where's the nearest pub? He was sobbing now and I was almost having a coronary dashing round checking all the cupboards for cans.

'You had about eight cans of lager in there,' I shouted to him, dashing back in the room. 'And there ain't no empties! What happened to 'em?'

Sean was trying to point to something, his arms waving wildly.

'Did *she* take 'em?' I screamed.

His head shook. But that didn't mean anything – it was shaking all the time! My legs collapsed under me. I felt frightened and sick and I was sure he was gonna die before I got him some alcohol. Oh Christ! My heart was palpitating and I was getting dizzy.

I dashed back into the kitchen leaving him to gasp, trying to say something. I had an idea.

I tore open the cupboard under the sink and the Ajax went flying as I shoved in my hand and started madly twisting the knurled collars on the U-bend. I got one off but the other one was lower down and brown water started seeping out and dripping onto the shelf. It stank something awful of filthy drains and stale whisky.

The tube came out and I held it upright so I didn't spill any and carried it up to the draining board.

There was a mug with some tea dregs in it and I slopped them down the sink and they shot right through onto the shelf beneath. *Oh fuck!* I gently poured the disgusting contents of the U-bend into the mug.

It was mostly alcohol but there must have been a fair bit of stagnant water in there. And hairs and a wet, fluffy gunge. It'd probably kill him but at least I'd tried.

I dashed back into the room and sat by him. He was lolling his head and his arms were thrashing. He was delirious, I was sure, and I grabbed his chin and held his face towards me, sticking the mug under his nose.

'Sean, come on mate! Drink this, good lad.'

The fumes probably brought him round. I just hoped his sense of smell had been knocked out cos it stank!

I think his system must have recognised the alcohol cos he gulped it down quickly, stopping every few swallows to cough violently. He finished it and I sighed exhaustedly and let the mug drop to the floor.

He lay there still quivering and shaking for about ten minutes and I sat by him until the shaking slowed down and he passed out. I must've given him about ten or twelve measures of spirits there and I thought that'd be enough for the moment.

I phoned a taxi and he took me across the bridge to an offy on Cannon Street. I could just afford seventy centilitres of Teacher's so I got that and dived back into the taxi and back to Sean.

He woke up at about ten o'clock and told me where the cans were. Jenny had thrown them in the dustbins outside so I went down and rooted through in the dark till I found 'em.

I put them next to the whisky on the draining board.

'That should do you for a bit,' I said.

'Oh, get us a glass of that Teacher's will you, Toys?'

'You owe me a tenner,' I said. 'For this and the taxi.'

He gulped down the whisky and smiled at me.

'Thanks, mate,' he said and grinned. 'I've had a pretty rough day, you know.'

'What the hell happened, Sean? You wanna tell me why your fucking medicine ended up in the sink?'

Sean shook his head and thought back to the previous night.

'Yeah, we got arguing a bit and she told me she'd stopped sleeping with other blokes and she thought I should pack in working myself.'

'She what? Christ—'

I remember thinking, I suppose she thought if they didn't keep up the payments, she could repossess her virginity.

'Yeah, I know. I thought it was a bit of a liberty so I told her I had no intention of giving up. I mean, what the fuck else can I do? I can't exactly work in the City.'

'I hope you told her to fuck off . . . What, then she threw away your juice out of spite?'

'No, she said I ought to give up drinking after that. Said she was worried about my health—'

'Oh, yeah! Look at you now! Fucking—'

'So I agreed to pack it in.'

'What? Just like that!'

'Yeah. I was OK this morning when I woke up. I almost had a glass to stop my hands shaking but she saw me and said *Hey, remember what you said* and I said yeah, OK, I'll throw it all down the sink so I won't give in.'

'You fucking arsehole! You should've known you can't just do that!'

'I thought I could.'

'So *you* chucked it down the sink?'

'Yeah. And I was alright when she left this morning. Bit shaky and everything but she said *ring me if it gets too bad.* She didn't know what was gonna happen. She don't understand – she's just a kid. So I got her to throw out the cans as she left. She said *now don't you go looking for 'em else you'll be in trouble.* I didn't have the strength to look for 'em when it got too bad.'

'Why did you have your headphones on like that?'

'Dunno,' Sean shrugged. 'I was just trying to take my mind off it, I suppose.'

I sat back on the armchair and let out a deep sigh.

'Let me ring her, Sean,' I said. 'And tell her what she's done.'

'No, don't—'

'Oh, fucking hell, man! She *needs* to be told, the stupid little prick!'

He shook his head. 'No, don't.'

'Why not?'

He shrugged slightly again. 'It wasn't her fault. She's right anyway, I should stop drinking so much.'

'Stop drinking so much? You'll have to stop completely or nothing, man! You're an alcoholic. Alcoholics can't cut down!'

He looked at me in surprise.

'I ain't an alcoholic, Toys.'

He really believed it. It was as if he was saying *I ain't from Mars, Toys. I'm British!*

I checked on him a couple of times the next week. He wasn't in either time. It wasn't until Jenny phoned me at home that I realised he was missing.

It never occurred to me to ask how she'd got my number at the time. I still don't know. Anyway, she was frantic – she said she'd been over every night that week and he hadn't been home. She'd rung hundreds of times and let it ring for hours but no answer.

I said I'd meet her at Sean's flat that night – Friday, and we let ourselves in.

The clock on the mantelpiece had stopped and I cursed it for not having a date on it.

I checked the fridge. There was a carton of milk with a layer of rancid cheese floating on the top but no clues there. I wanted to find out when he'd last been in the flat.

'I last saw him Monday morning when I left,' I told Jenny when she asked. 'He was OK. Just a bit tired.'

'I only saw him that Sunday morning when *I* left,' she said.

'I know,' I nodded. I hadn't told her about Sunday night's episode yet.

Then I saw it.

Christ! The U-bend was sitting on the draining-board right next to my fingers as I leant on the sink unit. It hadn't been put back yet!

Shit, if he hadn't even used the sink he can't have stayed around much longer than *I* did. He probably left on Monday.

I had to explain the reasoning to Jenny and then about Sean's toxic withdrawal on Sunday night. This was all getting too much for her.

'Christ, Toys! You fed him the shit out of the plughole? I don't *believe* you sometimes!'

I had to make a few phone calls before we reported him missing. Simon McGurk hadn't seen him for weeks. Ravensknowle, a tart who used to take him up Madame Jo Jo's, didn't know where he was.

'Ooh goodness,' he simpered. 'I *am* worried about him, dear, aren't you? You *will* let me know the minute he turns up, won't you? Listen, I'll get in touch with some friends see if *they* know anything . . .'

In the end I phoned his Mum and then wished I hadn't. She went apeshit. Moaning on about how he lived and who he mixed with and she *knew* it would end in no good. She told me to clear off out of his flat and stay away. Said she was gonna ring the police. Then she hung up.

'She's phonin' the police,' I told Jenny.

She took the receiver from me. 'I'm ringing them an' all,' she said. 'I want them to contact *me* when they find him.'

'Give 'em *my* number as well,' I told her. I didn't want to be left out.

They rang his Mum and Jenny when Sean was finally located. Not me.

Sean rang me from home at his Mum's and explained everything.

He'd got smashed on the cans and whisky that Monday morning, then gone out with his stockings and a short skirt on and the works and ended up in town getting more and more pissed and wrecked.

He tried to tell me what he'd been doing all week but he wasn't too clear on it. He'd been absolutely brainless constantly and he just said he never found his way home.

He stayed at some bloke's house that first night. He'd met him up town but he got bored of Sean and kicked him out.

He remembered sleeping outside a lot and one time him and this tramp nicked some bottles out of a supermarket by going in with a carrier bag and just walking out with them.

'You did all that dressed in a skirt an' everything?' I said.

'No. I ended up buying some clothes from Oxfam. That was quite a laugh. I got changed in the shop. I didn't have any undies tho'. Well, I just kept the knickers on!'

In the end a couple of coppers found him wandering around outside an offy looking for a way in and they arrested him.

He was out of it, of course, when they read him the Notice to Detained Persons and he was too incoherent to ask for anyone to be notified of his arrest. He didn't have a brief and as for consulting a copy of the Codes of Practice – he'd have probably thrown up on it!

They kept him in a cell overnight and the next morning sent him, shivering with the DTs, to a de-tox centre. Before he could get out of there back to the offy, his Mum had turned up, tipped off by the coppers, and taken him home. They dropped charges.

She made him a cuppa, gave him a square meal, then he went out to the pub to get wrecked.

'When you goin' back to the flat?' I asked.

'Tonight. I was gonna set off in a bit, actually.'

'Does Jenny know where you are?'

'Yeah. She was round here today but my Mum told her to clear off.'

'You had a lot of people worried y'know, pal.'

'Yeah, I know. I'm sorry about that.'

'Oh, shit,' I said. 'I've got to ring Ravensknowle, he'll be worried still, the old dear.'

The Friday night before Guy Fawkes Night (which was on the Sunday) there were bangers and rockets going off already. I hadn't seen many kids asking for a penny for their crappy guy sitting in a knackered old push-chair. The time they did try it on I literally didn't have a penny on me. I had a tenner.

Marco used to do that. Just give 'em a penny, just a one pence piece. That used to piss 'em off. *Well, you said penny for the guy,* he'd tell 'em.

There goes another, don't know what it is, whistling out of the sky then exploding far off in the darkness and a dog barks at it frantically. Then two more muffled cracks even more distant.

It's like a lightning storm, you just sit and wait for the next flash and crack. What a combination that'd be – if they had a fireworks display in the middle of a thunderstorm. Great glowing blue arcs of power discharging onto a squadron of sky rockets hitting a cloud and blasting them into a flurry of rainbow sparks and drifting iridescent points of light like millions of methane pond fires.

Most of the bonfire parties were gonna be on the Saturday night. There were a few on the Friday and some on Sunday the fifth. I just hoped it was gonna *feel* right not having it on the proper day.

There was one at Blackheath, I saw it in *Time Out* and I asked Sean what he was doing that Saturday night. He'd already been roped into one with Jenny. She wanted to go see the one at Battersea Park.

'Why's she wanna go there?' I said. 'It's miles away!'

'It ain't that far. It's about as far as Blackheath is from your place.'

We sat and watched the weather forecast. They were vague about tonight.

'Well, is it gonna fucking rain tonight or what?' I shouted at the telly.

'They don't know,' Sean said unhelpfully.

As I was coming home I saw a woman pushing a twin push-chair but there was only one kid in it. I wondered what had happened to the other one. Had it died? I'm really morbid, ain't I? And was she reminded of the loss of her baby every time she looked at the push-chair? If so she ought to trade it in for a single one.

I was going to go and mention it to her. I wondered if widows or widowers felt that way when they looked at their double bed.

Anyway the sky cleared up later on and it was even bright for a bit so I was quite confident it'd stay clear when it got dark and I couldn't see the clouds anymore.

My Mum went out with Skelly to her charity bonfire do. For Multiple Sclerosis.

I asked her if she wanted me to come with her. I knew what she'd say.

'Not if you don't want to, love. Anyway, I thought you were going out with Marco.'

'Yeh, I am. I was just being polite.'

Marco turned up at the door grinning.

'I've bought some fireworks,' he announced. 'They cost six quid! D'you wanna let 'em off in your back yard?'

'Oh yeah,' I said sarcastically. 'Better still, what about the front room?'

The back yard *wasn't* a good idea so we took 'em down to the rec' and spent half an hour shouting and laughing at them like kids. They weren't very spectacular but we savoured every spark. There was a skyrocket in there along with Silver Zodiac, Fire Fly, Dragon's Crown, Jack-in-the-box, Emerald Shower and Retro Jet. There was a volcano one as well.

So that was our bit of warm-up excitement.

'Got any bonfire toffee?' Marco asked when we got back. 'Or any baked spuds or parkin or something?'

'Cup of tea?' I offered.

'That'll do.'

My Mum used to make parkin when I was a nipper. I don't think they have it much down here but of course her being a northerner it came natural.

'We've got some sports biscuits.'

'Oh great! Give us one with the football pitch on – they're the biggest!'

I laughed and put the kettle on.

'Hey, we'd better get a move on,' Marco said. 'It's half-six already.'

'We've got time for a drink.'

'Watch it, you'll be pissing yourself all night,' he said. 'You know what your bladder's like.'

He was right actually. We got there about seven-thirty, the time it was due to start, and the fireworks were going already. The field was wet and muddy in places.

'Come on, let's find the bonfire,' Marco said. 'See if they've lit it yet.'

'Hang on,' I said. 'I'm dying for a piss.'

He laughed and came along too. 'I'd better have one, I s'pose.'

We sneaked past some coppers and into a driveway by these four big houses and slashed up against their fence. I'm sure someone kept coming to the curtains.

The huge cracks in the sky made the ground seem to shake and my chest rattled with each force and the sound and colours echoed from the buildings all around.

The sky was already a cascade of light and colour, and from nowhere balls of blue-tipped crimson flares shot out in every direction, millions of them, and they filled the sky and warmed it.

It was incredible, I never knew fireworks could get so big. The MC crackled over the p.a. calling for everyone to clap in accompaniment to each bang. He said the rockets reached a height of six hundred feet and they burst apart a hundred yards wide. A hundred yards! Christ, an' it looked it, too! They were beautiful.

We stood by the warmth of the hotdog stand and watched the incredible display. I realised I had an idiotic grin on my face and when I turned to look so did Marco. And I loved him at that moment, the little Italian twat. Like you do when you realise why someone's your friend – cos they think the same way *you* do.

There were balloons everywhere and some kids had those glowing bands round their heads that are passé any other night of the year.

An ambulance stood ready, its blue light flashing and the MC announced lost kids at the green tent. They were gonna raffle the unclaimed ones off at the end.

The noise was absolutely incredible; frightening really, and when a bomb burst it filled your vision. My eyes were blurred with emotion.

The last firework sent two huge orange columns into the blackness, burning and standing bright and strong, then each tip exploded into millions of tiny orange sparks that seemed to hang in the air forever.

The MC thanked everyone for coming and warned us not to fall in the ditches.

'What ditches?' Marco asked me.

I shrugged.

'Is that it, then?' he said. 'What about the bonfire?'

'Looks like they ain't having one.'

He looked so disappointed.

'Come on, there's still the funfair,' I said and pointed over to the glowing area of lights by the road. The Ferris wheel stood huge over the fairground that throbbed and flashed and spun wildly.

Walking past the ambulance we saw a little black kid in there sitting with a kidney dish of water up to his face and the medic was squirting water into his eye.

We didn't stay long at the funfair cos we were off to a party nearby on Humber Road. And when we were leaving I noticed some toilets.

'Shit, we could've gone there, look,' I said to Marco.

I thought about the bonfire. Perhaps the Council wouldn't allow it, you know there are some pretty heavy preservation orders on that land cos of the plague victims buried under there. You go digging that place up and the black death's back in town and they still don't even know what caused it. Not exactly, anyway.

Oh, I've *got* to tell you about this party. Well, first of all, I wasn't even invited. In fact not only wasn't I invited, I was told *not* to come or at least I heard through Marco that Clare didn't want me there. So I thought fine, I'll go to the bonfire and that'll be OK. But cos the fireworks and stuff were over so early, I decided to come with Marco and crash it.

I thought sod it, anyway. Why can't I go? You know, she only hates me cos I'm loud and obnoxious. That's no reason.

I was already pissed when we arrived cos I'd bought this quarter of Napoleon brandy from the offy – the cheap stuff. Christ, I hoped I wasn't getting like Sean!

We dumped our coats in this bird's room, in her bedroom, and I saw these shoulder pads fall out of her wardrobe that was open with all clothes and stuff piled up in the bottom of it. I held 'em up to my chest and laughed.

'Look, falsies! Tit pads,' I said.

I was only joking but from what this bird said that's exactly what they were. I held 'em on my shoulders, then shrugged and pissed off downstairs.

Danny's mates were there, an' Graham looks just like George Michael. Well, *I* think he does, anyway.

'Oh, Georgie boy!' I was saying. 'Oh, y'know, I love that one you did, what was it, *Freedom*?' And I started singing it to him.

There was loads of lager an' stuff in the kitchen and, like, washing-powder cups to drink it out of. I was talking to these hockey players – they were chucking beer all over the kitchen floor. I was trying to show them how to drink it.

'What sign are you?' one guy says. He says, 'Are you Cancer?'

'Yeah,' I said. 'I am.'

He said, 'Are you? So am I. I was reading in the paper, it's a good week for Cancers, this week, for making love.'

So I said to this girl, 'Here, d'you hear that? This is a good week for me an' him for making love.' She looked a bit funny at me. 'Anyway,' I says, 'I've made loads already this week, so go have a word with him!'

My laugh was getting louder and more forced and I felt like a crappy game show host. But I was loving it. Danny's mate Paul was trying to get himself out of the shit he was in. He was talking about Paula's tits and how big they were. They *are* actually quite enormous.

'No, I bet girls with big tits get really selfconscious an' all that.'

And Paula was saying, 'Only when people keep going on about them!'

An' Paul just tried to talk himself out of it but he just got deeper and deeper in it.

'I'm Ian's brother,' this kid said to me. Ian is Clare's flatmate. I hardly know him.

'Oh, *Ian*,' I said. 'Yeah, he's me *best* mate.'

I kept stopping strangers and talking to them. Well, how else do you meet people?

'Alright, mate,' I said. 'You brought the beer?' This bloke was just coming into the kitchen.

He caught on. 'Yeah, it's outside on a lorry,' he said. 'Eight crates.'

I kept making as if to go then coming back.

'Outside?' I said.

He nodded.

'On a lorry?'

'Yeah.'

'OK.'

I opened the front door and looked around. It was nice to get a breath of cold air. Oscar's bird saw me from the landing.

'It's out here, is it?' I asked her.

She just laughed. 'What?'

'That beer, it's out here, is it?'

'What you talking about, Toys?'

She was waiting for the loo.

'There's one upstairs,' I said.

'I know, I'd better go and find it,' she giggled. 'Or I'll have an accident.'

I went into the bedroom again and waved out the window at next door's having a barbecue in the garden.

'Yoo-oo,' I shouted.

Christ, does the whole street have their parties on the same night!

They made wanker signs at me so I kept on waving.

'Hey, throw another cat on the barbie!'

I told a bloke in the kitchen about them.

'You don't care, do you?' I said. 'They were making rude signs at me and you don't care?'

'I can't even focus,' he said.

I said, 'Danny, give us a fag, mate!'

And he had his hands full so he motioned to his top pocket with his head. I took the packet out and there was only one left.

'No, Danny, it's your last one. I couldn't take that.'

'No,' he says. 'It's alright. I'll get some off of Paula later on. Go on, have it!'

I says, 'No, I couldn't take your last fag. I'd rather be rogered by a two-foot pigmy with drawing-pins in his condom!'

It was really dark in the lounge and everyone was dancing away to *Black Box* on the stereo and I was singing along really loud. Jo kept grabbing my arse and my dick so I grabbed her back. Her backside. I should've grabbed her tits.

They were talking about Sean and Jenny in the kitchen as I drifted past.

'Weren't they supposed to be here?'

'Eh? Who?'

'I thought Sean was coming,' someone said.

'No, he'll be shagging his bird.'

'Give 'em a ring!'

'No, you tight bastard!'

Someone phoned them later on but there was no answer. I didn't think anything of it at the time.

'They must be out still.'

'What! It *is* three o'clock.'

This bloke was talking to me about tarts and slack birds an' all that. He was getting on my tits.

'Yeah, I like Mersey tunnels,' he was saying.

'Me too,' I said. 'Great for getting from Liverpool to . . . wherever they lead to. The Wirral.'

'Oh, sorry mate,' this hockey player said. It was Jason. He'd knocked me and spilt his beer on me. I had a wet elbow.

'Here,' he said. 'Have my pint.'

'Thanks,' I said and took the can. He looked surprised. I don't think he really expected me to take it. Or perhaps he changed his mind.

He called it a pint.

'It ain't a pint,' I said, looking at the can. 'It's only four hundred and forty millilitres. A pint's five hundred and sixty-eight millilitres if you've ever looked at a milk carton. Or six hundred and fifty-eight or something.'

I was feeding rice to the blokes in the kitchen. There was loads of stuff on the table but most of it had been polished off. Actually there was only rice and coleslaw left but I was getting hungry so I was troughing it and offering it around. I was spoon-feeding anyone who'd have some.

'Here you are, Margaret, there's a good girl, have some rice.'

'No,' she said. 'I want some coleslaw.'

OK. So I fed her that.

'That's it. Your Dad *will* be pleased. Good girl!'

I don't know why I was talking to her like that. Oh yeah, cos I was feeding her like a kid.

Someone started up *You've Lost that Loving Feeling* by the Righteous Brothers and we were all bawling it full volume, standing on the soaking kitchen floor with rice falling everywhere and the swing bin on its side full of fruit and leaking punch onto the work surface.

'Here, I've got a good game,' I shouted. 'I'll say a quote from a famous TV programme and you have to guess what the programme is. Here goes.'

I put on my Del-boy accent and said, 'Rodney, you don't *live* here no more!'

'*Magic Roundabout*,' someone said.

Anyway, Marco was saying he was off so I said I'd get a taxi with him back to Peckham.

'Oh, we'll walk,' I said.

'Fuck off, it's miles!'

I was walking round all the rooms saying *thanks for having me* and shouting goodbye to everyone. Saying *thanks for a lovely evening, I've really enjoyed myself* and all that over-the-top stuff.

All night whenever Clare saw me she just said, 'Fuck off, Toys, you're a wanker.' And she meant it, I could tell.

But now as I was off she came and she was alright at the door as I was leaving.

I told Marco in the cab.

'She was alright, Marco. She loves me!'

'Nah, she's just being sarcastic!'

'I've got to get up early Monday morning,' Marco said to me that night just before he went home. 'I've got that job starting.'

'Oh, yeah. On the bins, innit?'

'I don't think I'll be able to get up, I'm a right lazy cunt in the morning.'

'Oh, you'll be alright.'

'Nah, I always turn off the alarm an' get back into bed.'

'I know what you do, then,' I said. 'When your old man's gone to bed, right, put a sign on the kitchen table saying *Fuck off, Dad, you wanker* and then go to bed. That way you'll have to get up before him to shift the sign else he'll kick the shit out of you!'

Marco pissed himself. 'What if he got up in the night for a drink or something?'

'Nah, it'll work, I bet you,' I said. 'It's a good idea!'

I couldn't fucking believe it. She rang me *again*! Why the hell does she keep ringing *me*? Christ, don't get me wrong, I wanted to *know*. But I just didn't get it. Why me?

'Oh, Toys,' she said. 'He's gone again.'

I wanted to say *I'm not really surprised, love.*

She'd said something at the bonfire that triggered him off and he'd gone, just walked away, angry she said.

'An' you thought he'd come straight back, did you?'

'I went to his flat,' she said. 'I thought he'd be there. I heard the phone ringing so I knew he wasn't.'

That was probably them at the party phoning.

'And he's been gone all day yesterday?' I asked.

'Yeah.'

It was Monday. The sixth of November. I'd meant to call round on the Sunday but I never got round to it. It was weird, why did he keep shooting off like that? He never used to. He wouldn't get his money's worth out of the rent if he kept this up.

'I left messages on the door an' everything,' she said. 'And called round loads of times but they were still there.'

'Who were still there?'

'The *messages*.'

'Do you want me to come round and let you in like last time?' I said.

'Yeah! Will you?'

'Oh, what the hell's the point, Jenny? What do you expect to find, a suicide note?'

'You bastard! Who do you think you are? It's me who should have that key, not you! It's me he loves not you, you bent—' The rest was lost in tears. Her tears, I might add, not mine.

Sean phoned me the next day and told me where he was. He'd been staying with Al Irving, a tall blond transvestite. A mate of Simon McGurk's.

Al was from Boston in the States and he used to run clubs over there. He had a place near Regent's Park now, and a few wine bar sort of things in north London. He was quite a laugh was Al – loud and camp and he really did have his own long, blond hair. Everyone called him Alison. Alison Irving.

'You phoned Jenny yet?' I asked Sean.

'Oh God, don't mention it,' he said. '*I* didn't ring her but somebody did. She had the police out looking for me and everything.'

'Christ, I'm surprised they bothered, with all the fucking work they go on about having piled up.'

'Well, it's cos of last time, I suppose. They wanted to make sure I wasn't out smashing offy windows or anything.'

'What did Jenny say?' I asked.

'Well, she was none too pleased to hear I was shacked up with this blonde Alison Irving bit.'

'Fucking hell,' I laughed. 'Who told her that?'

'I dunno. Simon, probably – you know what a shit-stirrer he is.'

'Well it wasn't me!'

'No, I know it wasn't you, Toys.'

'Here,' I said. 'You ain't been trying no giving-up drinking business again?'

'You're joking! I'm drinking more than ever. Nah, I just got pissed off with Jenny, that's all.'

'What did she say to you at the bonfire?'

He went quiet. I couldn't even hear him breathing. I was just about to say 'Sean?' when he said, 'I'll tell you later, Toys.'

'Anyway,' I said. 'So if you disappear again I've not to worry, is that it?'

'Oh, I'm sorry, Toys. Listen, I'll ring you straight away if it happens again, OK?'

'Yeah, OK mate. Thanks for ringing this time.'

'Thanks for answering the phone.'

I laughed.

It did happen again. But I wasn't at home. I was at Sean's with Jenny. He'd been gone about three days and Jenny had been staying at Sean's flat so she'd be there when he got back. I'd even let her have the keys.

I stood and looked out the window then at the flaking paint on the window frames. There was mould at the bottom of the glass, just a thin layer, and all covered with dust.

'I'm missing *The Waltons*,' I told Jenny.

'Well, fuck off and watch it,' she said. 'I don't want you here.'

I looked at my watch. 'I'll not get home in time now. It's the one where Jim-Bob's smoking crack and going to acid house parties.'

She shot me a filthy look.

I'd seen these Turks on the train on the way there. They were rattling off a load of Turkish then finishing each sentence with *You know? Alright? You know what I mean?* It sounded so funny.

The phone went and Jenny got to it before I did.

'Hello?'

The voice said, 'Hello, can I speak to Joseph please?'

'Is that Sean?' she said sharply.

Christ, I thought, she oughta be able to recognise his voice by now.

Anyway, he said, 'No.'

The dozy get!

'Oh, Sean, where are you, Babe? I'm missing you!'

'Can I speak to Toys please.'

She went fucking mad.

'You bastard! Are you with that blonde fucker?'

'No.'

'Oh yeah? What happened to her, then?'

'A lot happened to her,' he said. 'We had a really good time together but I blew her out cos she was getting too clingy.'

Course he was just saying this to get her wound up but I think he overdid it.

She was crying and sounded on the verge of hysteria.

'I don't believe you!' she screamed and collapsed into sobs. I felt sorry for her.

She slammed the phone down and had her hand to her mouth. I'm sure she was almost sick, she looked so pale and shocked. I think she was sick into her mouth a bit then probably swallowed it. I was dead scared when I saw her face, I thought she was gonna die she was so shook up.

She was still shaking, sitting on the bed when Sean phoned up again and I stood there talking to him for a bit.

Jenny took the receiver and Sean said, 'Stay there, Jenny. I'm coming home.'

'Stay here?' she said. It was the first time he'd ever actually shown he wanted her around. It was a landmark and she knew it. When she hung up she was crying more than she had been a minute ago.

It was cold in that room, waiting. I was expecting Jenny to tell me to fuck off any minute but she was too wrapped up in her thoughts. I just wanted to see Sean, make sure he was OK, before I left.

Well, I wanted to see just what the fuck had made him say that to Jenny. I was scared, I really was. I felt like my control was just slipping away, you know, she was winning the game. The same game I used to run, I used to rig, but a game that I never won.

I knew the tramps were shivering on the embankments and under bridges that stopped the cold as it fell but somehow it crept its way up through the ground, through the cardboard and into their hearts.

'Can you spare some change, mate?'

I'd stop and grin at him if I was in a friendly mood.

'I'll give you a quid if you tell me a joke,' I said once.

He just stood there and stared at the gold coin breathing its own steam of wealth into the air and he was dumb.

Should I have given it him anyway? The quid? I put it back in my pocket and walked off.

I'm glad I thought of that. *I'll give you a quid if you tell me a joke.* What's the matter, don't tramps know any jokes?

And on the train a guy nervously looked at his watch just for something to do. I just *knew* if I asked him the time he wouldn't know it. He'd have to look again.

So Sean came home and he broke down in tears to both of us and said he was gonna pack in drinking, but properly this time.

'I'm off to the AA. I've been once already.'

What? He hasn't even got a car!

And pack in shagging blokes. 'What did I do it for, anyway? I'm not even queer! Sorry, Toys! No, really, I'm changing my life. I've just, you know, realised – I can just see my life now as it really is and it's time to change, you're right, Jenny.'

It's time to change alright. And it takes time to change. Anyway, he'd taken enough time up till now so I guess changing overnight was OK.

7 SOME DUSTY TERRACE

'Mock me, mock me, I don't care!' I said one time. 'We will!' said McGurk. 'Don't worry. You don't have to *invite* us. We're gatecrashers at the Mocksville party!'

Everyone laughed even more after that.

It's foggy tonight. Been like that all day. They're at it on the radio – . . . *freezing fog patches all over town so if you're driving anywhere tonight, leave in plenty of time so you're not in a hurry.*

There's scaffolding on one of the houses down our street cos they're having a new roof put on. Anyway, there's this ladder lashed onto the scaffolding overnight, but high up, out of reach so it ain't nicked, and it's really long, shooting off into the air and it's so long it disappears like Jacob's Ladder into the fog that hangs low over the roofs.

So I hit the town after Sean got back. I was miserable, he didn't want me around anymore – said *course* I could keep my keys but he was getting a new set cut for Jenny. Oh, well, I ain't gonna use 'em no more. It's plain he don't want me around.

Marco told me about what he did Sat'day night. He was sitting on the pan in some club and he was about to be sick but he couldn't get up in time and he leaned over and threw up in his trousers!

They're doin' work near the Rosie, laying huge black plastic waste pipes for the new office block that's being done up. All down the length of the road there's a trench newly filled with concrete and the flashing lights seem to dance in the gloom like fairies among the piles of earth.

By Waterloo station I stood outside the Wellington Tavern, a Burke's Free House, and looked at the bright signs hovering in the cold dark air. They could sell beer on their own. Heineken, Warsteiner and the jolly Murphy's Irish Stout sign.

I stood with my back to a phone box, breathing hard and darting my eyes like a trapped deer, desperately wanting to go in and phone Sean. That kind of breathing hurts your throat and my heart hurt my chest and I trembled and felt ill. Felt so weak and alone. Scrabbled with nervous fingers among the fluff in my coat pockets.

Fuck it, I'll have a few more beers an' I'll be OK. I can't ring him anyway, I can't disturb him now.

Does he believe all the things she told him now?

'I'm shit.'

'No, Sean, you're not! You're a wonderful person, you've got to accept that. You *do* deserve love. I love you and I want you to believe you can be loved.'

'Nah, it don't feel right. I ain't never had that before. I'm just shit.'

'Baby, you're worth something. You're special, you're not rubbish, it's just the way people have made you feel!'

Plead with him! Plead! Plead! Try to get those ideas into his poor abused skull. Yeah, it looks like he believes it all now. I think she's broken the spell.

And that leaves *me* out of it. Well out of it.

I don't mind drinking alone. I can think – no one talking to me an' me having to nod and mutter *yes, how interesting, oh* do *go on. Piss off!*

I can hang around and watch the buskers, hear the rough twang of guitar strings and see the singer's fillings and his two days' growth. And hear his voice echo down the tube tunnels, fading off in wisps like smoke.

It's dark in the hairdresser's window, big hairdryers line the walls. But most of the other shops keep their lights on all night – racks of jeans and flatchested dummies in fucking awful lycra dresses.

I got tired as quickly as I got pissed. An old guy talked to me. He kept his watch in a waistcoat pocket that opened out like a drawer in a Dali painting. He was pulling my eyelids closed. Boring old twat.

I looked at the hairs sprouting from his ears – Christ, his brain was sending out shoots! He had hairs on the end of his nose, old guys do. *You'll be an old guy like me one day, son. No, I'll be an old* gay – *there's a difference. There aren't so many about, we tend to die young.* The way I felt right now I could've died that night.

There was a quiz on in the pub.

The quizmaster said, 'Right, the next category is TV. Question one – what is the full name of the painter and decorator in *Cheers?*'

'Norman Peterson!'

'Correct. Next – Sam Malone from *Cheers* used to play for which baseball team?'

'Red Sox!'

'That is correct. In *Cheers* what is the name of Rebecca's rich English boyfriend?'

'Er . . . '

'I'll have to hurry you.'

'Oh, shit. I *know* this!'

'It is in fact Robin Colcord.'

I went up to the quizmaster at half time and bought him a pint.

'So you watch *Cheers* a lot, eh?' I said.

In the second half, 'OK, folks, next category – Geography.'

Moans from the contestants.

'Here goes. In which East Coast city is *Cheers* set . . . ?'

Across from the Wag, stuffed in Gerrard Street's mouth, there was the usual hot dogmeat stand and a dark Italian who revealed his bottle of Smirnoff each time he opened the little hatch to get at the bread buns.

I saw Leroy from *Fame* going into the Wag once. He wouldn't get me in, just looked round when I called, then ignored me like a girl in the morning. He was carved between two birds. He's a bit of a sculpture. But he's straight. What a waste.

The old guy was telling me about professional trivia game machine players when I said, 'Here, it's just struck me!'

That shut him up anyway.

I said, 'You know how good Sean is at shagging an', you know, just generally foreplay and all that?'

He obviously didn't.

'Well, now that he's doing it cos he wants to and not as a job, is he gonna be better or worse, eh? Could swing each way, couldn't it? What do you reckon. We'll have to ask Jenny.'

What's the matter, you silly old git, don't you know what I'm talking about?

I couldn't wait for April Fool's day. It's the day you go out and say *Give us your money or I'll smash your face in!* then say *April Fool!* to their horrified faces.

He was with me at Shaftesbury Avenue. Or was it some other old geezer? Larry Olivier's ghost. I queued with the middle age bellied northerner coach trips down here with the bowling club and dressed in their awful brown suits and coats that look as if they've been scalped off a dog. Why don't you wear a decent colour. Christ, a nice dark suit would look better.

No, he can't wear black, you know. It makes him look ill. Skin's too pale, you see.

They'd been out since six, from the black smile of the Novotel cleaning lady by the revolving doors and off to a department store coffee shop. They'd smoked enough and drunk enough in the pub beneath high carved ceilings where alabaster scrolls coax in the smoke rings and absorb their brownness. And now they were queueing to sit down and see a show – fat white pudding arses getting fatter and whiter as the cast make pricks of themselves and act down parts in last century's commercials.

'Come on, mate,' I said to the old guy. 'Let's go down to Gatwick, there's loads of birds down there. Me and me mate go down all the time – we *always* get a shag!'

A voice seemed to hiss to me, 'There *is* no tomorrow.'

Did you know there's *two* Shepherd's Bush stations? They're on different tube lines and they're *miles* apart. One at each end of the one-way system – Central and Metropolitan lines.

I can't remember whether it was me but someone was working the queues trying to sell independent financial advice for the price of a pint of Foster's.

We should've stayed at the Wag. We'd have heard Public Enemy's rap rattling out through the toilet air grilles round the back. They were just one of the refugees from the postponed *Biology* event.

Later on they'll pile out the Wag, heads still thumping from the woofer beat. Scarf-headed like pirates and even brocade on a brushed cotton jacket with shiny buttons, bright pennies in the nightbus sun.

'I'm sorry, I didn't quite catch the, er, telephone number,' to a fit bird.

Could be you, one of the clubbers tottering out, still acid sugar grains on the fingertips. It's times like these you wish there was an A–Z tattooed on Bernie's arse.

'Come on, mate, get your pants down – we've got to find the tube!'

The ghost-of-the-London-cabbie crawls out, wreathed in mist, from the throat of a duffelhero bus-spotter.

'Where do you wanna go?' he whines. 'You got Leicester Square just along Charing Cross Road for the Northern line. Live in Clapham, eh? Balham? No? OK, what about Piccadilly Circus down Shaftesbury Avenue for the Bakerloo and Piccadilly lines. Live in Wembley? Elephant? Ealing? No?'

'Fuck off – this is the only chance we get to look at Bernie's arse! Where's Wardour Street? Oh, typical – it's on the crack!'

Legs tired, almost shaking, and the sweat clinging to your back from all the fierce dance frenzy inside freezes in the cold December air but you don't feel it cos you're as pissed as a President.

What was the matter with that bird anyhow? Don't she like having her arse felt or something? That's how we do it in Leicester! *So why don't you fuck off back to Leicester, then, an' do it there?*

Anyway here she is – 'Are you a bouncer?' she asks and grabs his nuts to find out.

I remember Marco sitting scribbling in felt tip all over a fiver.

'Who you gonna give *that* to?' I asked him.

'Oh, some cunt.'

'Ere, don't the clocks go back tonight?

Yer what, Tony? In December? Oh, shit, if I get eight hours' kip I'll miss The Waltons.

It's OK. It's only the one where Elizabeth starts hanging round transport cafés.

Yeah, young guns looking for action and they'll be out in the riverside pubs again on Sunday when they open at high noon. Well, it's OK if you're shooting straight.

Something made me think of it.

It's so embarrassing in the dole office when you're just signing on for the fortnight, you know, subtly dressed in your black bike leathers with **City Bike Couriers** in fluorescent orange all over the place, an' your handset starts having a fucking barney – shouting away to itself about jobs and deliveries and everything. And the dole officer looks at you just a bit suspiciously.

'Christ,' you say. 'This Walkman's never worked, you know. Stupid thing!' banging the handset on the desk. 'Where do I sign?'

It's like the bird with her new boyfriend in the house and the old boyfriend's ringing up all the time, crying to her on the phone and she's there shrinking away in a corner with her head down, not knowing what to say. Just listening to the great long silent stretches on the phone and sobs. Silence can be pretty expensive. And the new guy wants to know who it was.

Oh, just, er . . .

Through the shrill static lines stretching across frosty furrowed fields where birds sit and crap down onto the brittle grass blades she still hears his weak voice. Almost like a whisper from the floor of a deafening choral Mass he squeaks, 'I'm not mad *with* you, I'm mad *about* you!'

Sick-making, isn't it?

You can see all sorts from the train – broken windows looking in, rusty old air flues on factories, scaffolding, peeled paint boarded-up window frames. Some dusty terraces, low brick castles in built-down areas.

Windy Burns Night, nineteen ninety. The storms came again, remember? There were twice the number killed as in the great hurricane of eighty-seven.

I'll tell you what, Chichester didn't look much in 1766. You wouldn't have needed an *A–Z* to find your way round that place. Just looking at this poster of Chichester in the library foyer. Then I'm off home.

My Mum must've been out cos the door was double locked. I put the kettle on and watched a bit of the Leonard vs. Duran fight I had on video.

An' when I went to bed I couldn't sleep, just couldn't relax. Kept thinking about those old playing fields at school and the long grass down by the river and jumping over the river where it grew narrow and climbing trees over the water and rope swings and coal tips and wet, filthy jeans and cold hands in front of hot fires and scarves and hats and freezing noses and that bird Jenny with my Sean. Where I should be.

Remember that time she bawled me out in the Dog, she went fucking mad! Well, now she's got what she wanted – what I wanted. I just hope she's happy. Some Christmas!

I got up and sat in the front room with the curtains still open and a car moved about now and again. Sloshing anti-freeze around in their water jackets. It was minus six these nights. Tyres would freeze to the roads, wiper blades would freeze to the glass. Fuel would freeze in feed lines. In Alaska.

In fact that night I was sitting just where I am now. And my cheeks were wet with tears just like they are now.

I was crying for Sean then and I'm crying for him now.

I touched Jenny's hand today. In the pub. We sat by the open fire and she told me all about it with her sad, damp eyes and I put my hand on hers and held it there just for a second. What would Sean have said?

I stared at the blue and green flames hanging like a halo over the coloured print of the Grolsch beermat I'd thrown onto the black coals.

And my eyes followed a curling fern on the green wallpaper – thick, padded and plush and I looked at the copper spoons and the bed-warming pan hanging in the bar.

I wanted a shit, actually, but I couldn't say anything.

'Jenny, this is fucking serious! You've got to go. You've got to get this sorted out!'

'But I don't like the doctors at my surgery.'

'If you're pregnant *I want to know!*'

She just puts her head down like a stubborn child. Sean shakes his head in exasperation and shoots to his feet pacing out a route to the door. Then turns and stalks back.

She farts and looks up with a smile.

'Go to *my* doctor then, for Christ's sake. I dunno, change your doctor, don't you wanna know?' He puts his head down close. 'You know this won't go away if you try an' forget it.'

'I *am* trying to forget it.'

'Well *don't*! You're like a kid sometimes. Fuck!'

He picks up her pink top lying on the bed, stretches it between tight knuckles and throws it down like a smelly dishcloth.

She's sitting in her bra and she takes the top and climbs into it.

'I don't like blood tests,' she says.

'Fucking get a home test kit!' He realises what she said and double takes. 'You don't need a blood test! Christ, wait here, I'll get a fucking test kit from Boots. Fucking hell, they're only a fiver!'

It's funny cos a couple of weeks later Sean had a blood test. If you can call it that. You know, before you give blood they prick your thumb and take a drop of blood to test for iron.

Yeah, he was kinda celebrating Jenny not being pregnant by doing his bit for National Blood Transfusion.

They also tested his blood pressure an' that nearly busted the friggin' meter!

He told Jenny.

'I went to see the doc after that,' he told her.

Hmm, hypertension, the doc thought. *Let's see, what conditions could be producing such a symptom? What disease are we dealing with?*

'Tell, me, Mr Cuddell, do you drink at all?' Best safe to eliminate all possibilities.

So Sean told the doc just how much he *did* drink.

'Good God! That's anything from a hundred to one-fifty units a week! I'm hardly surprised your systolic is so high. This is a very serious problem, Mr Cuddell.'

Yeah, and Sean was underestimating.

'Do you have a problem with drink?' the doctor asked.

Yeah, it's so fucking dear!

'I *am* attending self-help groups,' Sean said.

Self-help groups! What's that? Sounds like you're shown the drinks cabinet and you help yourself!

Oh, ha ha, doctor! You're not being too helpful, are you?

'Come on, Sean. I'll take you to a nice restaurant I know.'

Well, it was lunchtime and I got him into the works canteen at the place I was delivering to.

Steak and Guinness pie or fried plaice? I couldn't decide. The other choice was liver and bacon and that was out of the question. I went for the pie in the end and Sean followed me. Oh, got to have the caulie cheese – it's absolutely delicious here, the cheese going brown and toasted on top and the soft cauliflower florets melting on your tongue and mixing in with the gravy and the lovely Guinnessy chunks of steak.

And green beens.

So we sat and munched on the crispy crust, brittle like shortbread but moist and delicate and the taste of the Flora on the brown roll licked my lips and my tongue.

I had Manchester tart for my pudding.

'I knew a tart from Manchester once,' I said to Sean rather predictably.

A fat old bird walked past and she fucking stank of horrible old perfume, I tell you she must have had *no* sense of smell. It nearly made me retch.

A couple of girls got up on another table, picking up their plates and smoothing down their suit skirts onto sheer brown stockinged thighs, firm and full and shapely and my eye followed the flesh down to the knee, so sexy and hard, and then the gorgeous calves encased in that shiny erotic fabric. And heels, high, raising the legs up and forward and completely changing their shape like elegant deer legs.

'Watch this,' I said to Sean.

As they walked past I dug my spoon into the hard crust of the tart that sat against the plate, beneath all that thick yellow custard. And I pushed into it as hard as I could and when it finally gave way with a huge crack as the spoon shot through and hit the plate, the wet custard and jam and crust flew off and splattered onto the girl's skirt and dusted pieces of desiccated coconut down into a shower onto her lovely knees.

'Oh! Excuse me!' I shouted, jumping to my feet. 'Oh, Christ! I'm sorry, I'm really sorry!'

I wanted to brush it off her skirt but she backed away and looked appalled.

Her mate was saying, 'Oh, Kerry, it's ruined! Make him pay for it!'

'Did you do that on purpose?' she demanded.

'No,' I said. I handed her a couple of serviettes off the table and she was rubbing frantically at the stain. Sean sat there with his mouth open, he just couldn't believe it.

'My name's Toys,' I said, holding out my hand. 'I was just delivering some stuff here. I'm a courier, y'know. Well, a boxer really. D'you wanna come for a drink tonight, eh? Bring your mate an' all if you like.' I turned and winked at Sean.

So she looked at me as if to say no.

And then?

Then she said no.

Well, she said, 'You must be fucking joking, mate! Look what you've done to my suit! I'll have to get it dry-cleaned now. Look at it, Melanie!'

'I know. Make him pay for it!' Melanie said again.

'No, he says he didn't do it on purpose.'

'Leave it out, Melanie,' I told her.

'You bastard! Who do you think you are?'

Jesus, that's exactly what Jenny said to me.

So I guess I struck out again. I dunno, perhaps I ought to rethink my strategies.

'Where did I go wrong?' I asked Sean later.

'The Manchester tart,' he said. 'Remember?'

'Yeah. Cheesecake next time.'

'Definitely.'

'This really is a marvellous example of first-century porcelain.'

Some bloke off the *Antiques Roadshow* was handling this woman's vase.

'Is it valuable?' she asked.

'Oh, yes, I should say so! It's a beautiful piece. Quite exquisite, very rare.'

'What's it worth then?'

'Oh, I should say you're looking at – Oops!' The vase slipped out of his hands and smashed on the floor.

He levelled a cool look at her. 'Oh, about a fiver.'

I started going back to the gym more after Sean changed.

That's the way I demarcate that period. The time *before* Sean changed. And the time after.

And the time after was when Jenny started going round with a Cheshire cat grin on her face she was so happy. It really made a difference – she had a reason to live now.

She'd wrote a few poems when she was a kid and she showed them to Sean. Now she had a real reason to write and there was no stopping her.

Back then first class stamps were only 18p. She bought a Danielle Steel book of poems and she used to copy them out too and give him 'em.

But this was the first one she wrote him herself –

If the whisper of a song once forgotten
                brushes you gently like a kiss,
If it reminds you of me and the love
                we shared let me know.
Hold the thought dear to your
                heart and treasure its power.
Bring me to life, don't leave me in
                the cobwebs of your memories.
Let the still of the night light up
                your memories of someone special,
Then let me back into your life to
                hold you forever,
Let me love you to madness and love you through pain,
Then once the pain eases, let me love you again.

Not bad for her, is it? I must say I really wasn't expecting anything so articulate from such a foul-mouthed little girl. Still, she is a college girl.

I dunno who the *someone special* was. Did Sean say she reminded him of someone he knew? Someone *special*? I doubt it somehow, but who knows.

It's funny, after she'd hooked Sean I suppose she forgave me for whatever it was I'd done to make her sore. I met them in the pub and I was having a go at her for her poetry.

'Ah, it's a puff's game,' I said.

'Oh, and you're such a hard boxer,' she mocked. 'What have you got against writing?'

'Well, I wouldn't say I was against writing *per se*,' I said. 'That was a good expression wasn't it? *Per se.* I picked that up in—'

'Are you afraid to write? Afraid of creating something that'll outlive you? Is that it?'

'No,' I sighed. 'I already said I wasn't against writing, if you listened. It's just this romantic poetry stuff.'

'Oh, just cos you've never felt that way,' she said. 'I've got Sean doing some poetry an' all.'

I looked at him.

Sean wiped his mouth. 'I've written a bit, yeah.'

'Oh, you great jessie!'

'What did you say earlier?' Jenny said smugly as if she was Sherlock Holmes with some incredible revelation. 'You said it was a puff's game.'

'Yeah.'

'Well, *you're* a puff for God's sake!'

'Not for God's sake. For mine really.'

'Anyway you are!'

'Yes, well, thanks for that little pleasantry, Jenny. I must say Sean's company is having a great effect on your manners.'

'Thanks,' she grinned.

I've seen all the poems and letters they wrote to each other. It's trash, the lot of it. She used to write him loads of letters even though she only lived, like, about less than a mile away. She said she used to feel lonely and she could feel more close to him if she was writing to him.

She had this funny word she used. When she wanted a cuddle she used to look at him all babyish and say, 'Nuggle me!' An' he couldn't resist her when she said that. Soft git!

> I just woke up without you
>> With an empty bed to hold.
> I rolled over to love you
>> But found silence, empty and cold.

What would her Mum have said? *Mum, I'm missing him and feeling randy. Go an' have a wank then.*

> I just woke up without you
>> With only an ache to nuggle.
> When I woke up without you
>> My day became a struggle.

Yeah, anyway, like I said I started going back to the gym quite a bit, you know, get back into the boxing and everything. Well, I didn't have nothing else to do, did I? Anyway it was a great idea to get Sean out of my mind.

There's nothing better than totally absorbing yourself in a new interest to forget someone.

There were a load of new faces down there and Christ, my sparring was a joke! I was totally useless and kept getting twatted left, right and centre. I already had a flat nose but this was taking the piss!

You ever been in a changing room an' there's always one guy goes to the shower with a towel round him, you know? An' everyone thinks, Christ, what a puff, what a jessie! You know, what's the matter with him, no one wants to look at his pecker anyhow so why's he covered up like a Mummy's boy?

But it's funny cos, seriously, if you *are* gay, it *does* matter. How would you like to get changed in front of a whole bunch of birds? I bet not many blokes would just let it all hang out, no sir! Cos that's what it's like. If you're gay, other blokes are kind of the opposite sex, and it's natural to be coy. So if you ever see that, don't take the piss, cos it could be the truth that he's a puff. And, hey, we have enough trouble without jokers an' all. *I* know.

Speaking of which, there was this new guy down there, Chris. The first time he spoke to me he said, 'Here, someone said you was gay. Is that right?'

'Yeah.'

'Brilliant!' he said.

I said, 'Why, are *you*?'

'No. It just means someone else to take the piss out of.'

Great start.

He was flapping round the punchbag one time and I walked up and said, '*You* don't mind making a dick of yourself, do you?'

But we have a laugh down the gym. When we're not punching each other's heads in, that is. Big Jim has this mug with **STEROIDS** written on it in massive letters. That always cracks me up.

Jim shaves in the sauna sometimes, with this little cup of water sitting by his arse.

'Don't throw your water on the coals, this time,' said Marco. 'It fucking stank last time.'

'Why was that?' I said. 'Cos it's dirty?'

'No,' Marco said. 'The hairs burn, don't they.'

Marco would light up a fag in the sauna sometimes. Not when there was anyone else in there. 'Oh, I only smoke in the sauna,' he'd say. 'It's good – it cools your blood, you know.'

I took his word for it.

When there's lots of us down there, there's always a queue for the showers cos everyone piles out the sauna and round to the swills.

I was waiting one time and these revolting retching and spitting noises came from one of the showers.

'Bagsy not getting *that* one,' I said to Marco.

Chris used to reckon he offered money to beggars if they'd spar with him so he could practise his streetfighting. But he was full of shit most of the time. He lived in the pub next door – the local for some of the lads. It was quite clever, actually, they called it the 'Duck and Diver'. It took me ages to figure that one out. They could've called it the 'Bob and Weaver' an' all, I expect.

Me an' Marco were at the gym one night, last thing, and Marco was looking at the Nescafé jar.

'It says here you can make a hundred and eleven cups of coffee with this jar,' he said. 'Come on, let's try it.' He started cracking up at the thought. 'Millions of cups of coffee all over the place when everyone comes in tomorrow!' he giggled.

'Nah, we ain't got enough cups,' I said. 'There's only seven.'

'You're right. We'll have to borrow some from next door.'

The Boy Cuddle was a writer now! Christ, he couldn't write a shopping list before he met her. Now he's better than e. e. cummings.

> I want to be with you always,
>   Bathing in the warmth of your love
> That hides me from the world's cares and troubles
>   Like the caresses of a dream.
>
> I want to nuggle you
>   Until your feather-down touch
>   Sends me to sleep.
> I want to nuggle you
>   Until my fears and pain
>   Have left me.
>
> Never leave me alone inside myself
>   Locked away in a misery that never speaks
> And cannot express itself
>   In poems of here and now and the way I feel.
>
> So that's why
>   I want to nuggle you
>   To let myself know you're still here.

    I want to nuggle you
      To give you some idea
        Of how close I can be
          And of how I always will be.

Actually it should be Boy *Nuggle* now!

'We're gonna have to be careful now, after that scare,' Sean said.
    'I know,' she said. 'Every sperm is lethal.'
    'No, the opposite of lethal. Life-giving.'
    I dunno what it was about sperm. They never stopped talking about it.
    'Blood's thicker than water,' I said once.
    'But sperm's thicker than blood,' Jenny said.

Sean said once, 'It's weird, innit?'
    'Yeah,' I said, running my finger through the frosty condensation clinging to my chilled Sapporo. 'Weird. It goes down smooth but it's really got a kick when it hits you.'
    'Nah, I mean Jenny.'
    I looked at him.
    'I mean, think of all the people you meet in your life or even just on the street and you just pass 'em without a word. Or a nod or anything.'
    'Yeah, weird.'
    'But Jenny is someone I kiss and hold and love, you know she's so different from the strangers. There must be something really special about her.'
    I could feel a poem coming on but I put my hand over my mouth and managed to make it to the bogs in time.
    When I got back he was talking about their first kiss in that hotel room. I couldn't help laughing, I was picturing the two of them on *Mr and Mrs* in twenty years' time.
    How did we meet? Oh, this Irish guy wanted to see us on the job. That was Simon, I remember. He was our best man, wasn't he, darling? Hm, of course that was back when you were a pro.

'Are you coming to Amsterdam?' Marco asked me. It was about the first thing he said when I walked in the gym.

'Eh?'

'Ron's arranging a trip to Amsterdam to see the Muay Thai.'

'Who the hell's the *My Tie*?'

'It's the Thai boxing, innit? Kickboxing. What do you reckon?'

'I didn't know you were into martial arts. Who else is going?'

'Oh, Ron can get us a cheap coach trip, that's all. We're all goin'. It'll be great. Come on, we'll be able to go down the red lights and everything. They have cake with dope in it! It's legal over there.'

'Don't tell me, they've got an airport full of fit birds!'

'Probably. You coming?'

'Yeah, alright, it sounds like a crack. How much?'

'Ron reckons he can do it for less than a monkey each?'

'A monkey?' I said.

'Yeah.'

'How much is that, then, Marco?'

'Fifty quid.'

'No it ain't, you twat. A monkey is five hundred, alright? Don't use that slang if you don't know what it means, mate. You just end up looking a nob.'

Marco looked totally embarrassed for a second then said, 'You're gonna wish you hadn't said that when I get you in the ring, you little shit.'

'No way. Sorry, pal, I ain't sparring outside my weight starting today. It ain't healthy.'

We were one short for the coach. The gym manager, Ron, had a word.

'Look, lads,' he said to us. 'Ask your friends, see if anyone's interested. If we can fill this last seat it'll obviously be more cheaper for those that are going. An' this is a really good trip, it's educational and it'll be a lot of fun so ask around.'

I asked Sean. He'd never been abroad and he jumped at the chance. Then he thought about Jenny and had second thoughts.

'Come on, mate, it's only three days you'll be away,' I said. 'You won't miss her that much.'

'Yeah, alright. But I'll have to see what she says.'

He asked her and she bowed her head like a martyr.

'I'll miss you, baby,' she said. 'But I want you to be happy so you've got to go.'

So that was it. I told Ron and we all paid our money then waited excitedly for the departure in mid February.

It finally struck Jenny just when we'd be away.

'Oh Sean, you won't be here for Valentine's day!'

'Oh, yeah,' he said. 'The fourteenth.'

We'd be away the Tuesday, Wednesday and Thursday and the fourteenth was on the Wednesday.

'Back out if you want,' I said to Sean knowing he wouldn't.

'No,' he said. 'It's OK. There's always next year.'

Christ, talk about philosophical! Aristotle couldn't shake a stick at him!

I'd forgotten about St Valentine's day anyway. Until I bought a couple of pints of milk that said drink before the fourteenth. How romantic – your milk will turn to smeggy cheese on Valentine's day!

Jenny had asked Sean to keep a diary while he was out in Amsterdam. She said goodbye to him as he climbed on the coach outside the gym in the pale light.

'I'm gonna miss you around here,' she said.

He grinned. 'I'm gonna miss you round here, too,' he said pointing to his groin.

She slapped him and watched as we sat down, everyone grinning excitedly. Then we were off.

The coach took us down to Dover in the early morning and we hung around in the ferryport for a couple of hours before we could board the boat.

Me and Sean had to get one of them yearly passports and it was quite a thrill going through customs getting 'em checked.

We stood on the cold deck and watched the white cliffs growing smaller as the sun rose.

Then, when we landed in Belgium, the coach took us across the flat irrigated fields to Holland. There were millions of canals and windmills but it's basically very boring flat land. The odd cow.

There was a removal van from Cornwall on the motorway with us.

We got to Amsterdam sort of early evening and headed for the hotel.

In the street I saw CND posters in German. We passed a motorcycle accident and I looked over to where a pigeon was disappearing into a hole in the wall.

It was Dutch TV in the rooms. There was a Dutch bible. No, I thought the hotel was really good, apart from the bogs. They're a different shape so you don't crap into water but onto the porcelain then your turds slip down into the water if you're lucky. Perhaps the Dutch like looking at their turds.

In the toilets downstairs you can buy nobbly Durex for three guilders. It's about the same price as back home. And there's English graffiti. Most of it disgusting but it reminded me of something I saw in the bogs at the old brick bus stop I used to catch the school bus at.

> Here I sit, broken-hearted,
> paid one pence and only farted.

I noticed everyone seemed to be in couples in the streets. I felt really out of it walking round on my own but I stuck with Sean most of the time.

We found the porn shops the Wednesday. It was a laugh at first but I tell you, after those couple of days there wasn't one of us who wasn't thoroughly sick of the sight of erect pricks going up arseholes and dogs or donkeys getting sucked off by pretty girls. There was one picture of a fist up an arse and this sort of thing was being shown on video screens up on the ceiling all the time.

So we wandered about looking at the huge dildos and the chinese love eggs and Chris said there was a porno cinema where you paid sixteen guilders and you could stay in all day.

'Come on, it's only a fiver,' he insisted.

Most of the lads were with him but me and Sean decided to go and visit Anne Frank's house. I told Sean I was sick of the porn already and he agreed.

'Fucking hell, man. You get *all day*!' Chris said again. He had a way of drawing out words to accent them. He was a Brummie originally but he spoke like a Londoner cos of public school. He stood there in his shades with his flick knife in his pocket as we later found out.

'Yeah?' I said. 'You reckon you can beat your bishop that long!'

Anne Frank's house almost made me cry. We were taken around by a guide and then in the last room there was a display with loads of information on boards in all different languages.

I'll never forget those photos of bone-filled trenches. But when

I looked close they weren't bones, they were people, but so thin they hardly looked real. Then to totally depress you it finished off talking about racism in Britain and France, how it was on the increase with neo-Nazi groups.

We were both really quiet after that walking back to the hotel. But we did stop off to look at some paintings and antiques in a few shops. And of course all the time Sean was looking for something to take back for Jenny.

We passed the diamond houses that all invited you in to look around at how they cut and work the stones. We thought we'd give that one a miss.

Back at the hotel we met the others in the bar. They told us they'd found the proper red light district and seen the tarts in huge windows like a shop front. And how pimps were approaching them offering dope and stuff.

We talked about how everyone spoke English over here and how easy it was to spend the money cos it was like play money. And the trams nearly knocking cyclists over all the time. They'd taken a tram but not paid.

The beer was expensive in the bar, everyone had halves. Amstel beer was really nice and we'd got some bottles of Grolsch from the supermarket for about thirty pence a bottle. They were up in the rooms for later.

So that Valentine's night we spent in the bar, everyone moaning how they wished they had their girlfriends with them.

Sean said, 'Jenny told me I hadn't to play that game where someone pays for a tart, someone else shags her, then someone else claims he did.'

Everyone laughed. It was quite a romantic mood in the bar even though we were all blokes. Some of us were trying White Russians – a Black Russian, only with cream too. I can't resist Tia Maria anyway. And I had a cocktail stirrer which Jenny calls a kiss catapult. She kisses the flat round bit then fires it at someone.

Sean had a postcard to send to Jenny. He asked at the hotel reception how much a stamp to England was.

'One guilder,' said the girl. 'Do you have the postcard?'

He held it up.

She took it. 'Give me the guilder and we'll send it in the morning.'

'You'll be back before it will,' Marco said.

'That's not the point,' Sean told him.

We decided to shoot out for a pizza. There seemed to be more pizza places than anything else in Amsterdam. But I said we'd meet them there cos Sean had to get some money changed. I went with him.

We ended up at the railway station after passing the sex museum on the way. There was a band outside the station, busking and I stayed and watched them while he went in to try and change some cash.

He was ages and when he came out he showed me what he'd written in his diary.

> I'm on platform 2b of Amsterdam Central Station.
> Let me tell you a few things. Today I got up and showered just in time for breakfast which should finish at 10 a.m.
>
> It was great – loads of food. Anyway, then we came into town and had a good look round. It's a really nice town actually and I could spend days wandering round the shops.
>
> Well, it took me ages and ages to decide what to buy Jenny. Lots of things occurred to me including jewellery, a pewter goblet, books, clothes, etc. Anyway I finally went for a frilly blousette sort of thing.
>
> Now I've just been round all the exchange places trying to get fifty guilders with my Access card. I ended up here at the station and had to get three hundred and fifty guilders minimum.
>
> The toilets on the platform are closed so I paid twenty-five cents for the privilege of going into a portable cabin type men/women's toilets. An old bag on the door. I think you're supposed to drop your twenty-five cents on her plate when coming out.
>
> So I'll head back now. We're having a pizza tonight. At least I've got loads to spend now. Over a hundred quid. If I don't get back (which I will) tell Jenny I love her. Thanks, little diary, for being here. I'll copy this up when I get home. OK? Bye.

It was late when we crawled back to the hotel rooms. The meal was great and we'd gone on a bar crawl afterwards. Then up to the rooms and the Grolsch. Rich and Chris were laughing and passing round their donkey mags they'd bought.

One by one people disappeared to bed. Then we remembered Ron. We were supposed to be turning up at the Jaap Eden Hal to see the kickboxing. He'd been raving about it all the way here. How it was a new kickboxing TV show being beamed to a satellite audience and we couldn't miss it.

He was probably back and in bed by now. He'd bollock us for sure.

Anyway, me and Sean went back to turn in. The two of us were sharing a room.

'Oh, I can open my card from Jenny now,' he said. He looked excited like it was Christmas.

This was his Valentine card from Jenny. There were two little verses on the envelope, surrounded by red kisses and hearts.

> I wrote this out with a golden pen,
> But I scrapped it and started again,
> Because I know that gold is cheap,
> So I send you my love to keep.

> If you think anything of me and the love we share
> Leave this closed until Amsterdam, and open it there.

It was incredible, she must have spent hours writing the card. It opened out twice and was covered in writing.

> Darling Sean, I love you
> Even though you swear,
> Darling Sean, I love you
> When my clothes you wear.
> Darling Sean, I love you
> Though we get stuck in showers,
> Darling Sean, I love you
> Though we stay in bed for hours.
> Darling Sean, I love you
> Though you call women *birds*,
> Darling Sean, I love you
> Though your mates are all nurds.

Darling Sean, I love you
Though you smack me in the mouth,
Darling Sean, I love you
Though you are from the south.
Darling Sean, I love you
Though you take up all the bed,
Darling Sean, I love you
Though curry is all I'm fed.
Darling Sean, I love you
Though you brush your teeth all day,
Darling Sean, I love you
Even though you make me pay.
Darling Sean, I love you
Despite all I've said,
Darling Sean, I love you
Let's go to bed.

Forget the jokes, forget the rhyme,
I love you my valentine.

x
LOVE YOU

Boy Cuddle,
This card is too small for my love to fit,
Stay with me forever, in hard times don't quit.
Let's try to make a life together,
I promise I will love you forever.

LUV
U
4
EVER

I think I'd better warn you,
Boy are you in trouble,
You make my knees weak
And my heart's in a muddle.
You see I think I love you
Now don't be alarmed!
We don't have to get married,
There, are you calmed?
You don't have to love me,
Just like me will do.
But no matter what
I'll always love you.   x

There was more. Five pages. Course I didn't see all this at the time. He just smiled and put the card away.

And there was only one day left in Amsterdam. The coach would be picking us up outside at noon the following day and we knew we wouldn't get any peace from Ron about the kickboxing all the way home.

The last thing me and Sean did that night was have a wanking competition, see who could shoot first. Quite romantic for the occasion.

'So when did you write this, then?' asked Sean.

'When I got home from that first time I came to see you,' she said. 'After we met in the hotel.'

Sean read it some more.

'Not very good, is it?' Jenny said.

'I like it. But you've done better.'

'I wish I'd met you in college,' Jenny said.

'Yeah, I wish I'd met you earlier. Definitely.'

'Before I had chance to do all those things I regret.'

'What like?'

She paused. 'You know,' she said shyly.

'What, sleeping around an' that?'

Jenny nodded.

'That's alright,' Sean said and looked away again.

'No, I'd like to be a virgin again for you.'

He laughed. 'Give over!'

She wasn't laughing.

'Anyway,' Sean said. 'It's all up here.' He tapped his head. 'If you really do regret all that then you're as good as a virgin.'

'Do you think so?' Jenny asked, grinning excitedly.

'Course.'

Jenny gave her notice in to Grant at the club. Without being too rude he said he thought it was for the best anyway. Sean turned down all the business McGurk and Ravensknowle put his way and he never went up the Piano Bar again. He did pop into Madame Jo Jo's from time to time, though, to see his old mates. But the place was starting to fill up with straights.

They never thought twice about leaving work, it had to be done, though neither of 'em knew how to do anything else. Anyway, even if they'd starved to death it would've been a small price to pay for love.

'When I was a little kid,' Jenny said, 'there was this boy I used to play with a lot. One day I said to him *do you love me, then?* He said *will you keep it a secret?* I said *yeah, I promise* so he said *yes.* Then I went round telling all my mates!' She giggled.

'Do you regret that relationship, then?'

Jenny laughed. 'I was only six!'

'An impressionable age,' Sean grinned. 'Toys told me a story 'bout when he was at school and one of his mates was taking this sixth form girl out one night.'

'How old was his mate?'

'Oh, fifteen, I think. Anyway, his mate bet Toys that he'd shag this bird that night and Toys bet he wouldn't. Anyhow, this girl found out about it and she was really pissed off cos she never intended sleeping with the bloke but she didn't see why Toys should make a tenner out of the fact.' Sean starts laughing.

'Go on,' Jenny says. 'So what did she do?'

'She went to Toys and threatened to sleep with the guy so Toys would lose his bet.' Sean held up his finger. '*Unless* Toys gave *her* the tenner stake.'

'But he couldn't win either way.'

'Yeah, but if he let her do it then his mate would win the cash *and* get his end away too.'

'So he paid her?'

'Yeah. And guess what she did? She ended up shagging the bloke in the heat of it and Toys had to shell out again!'

They both cracked up.

'Hey, you didn't have a bet on with McGurk that time in the hotel, did you?' Jenny laughed.

'Nah. It's a bit of a safe bet that a prostitute's gonna shag you, innit?' Sean smiled.

Jenny looked hurt. 'That sounds horrible. Is that how you thought of me?'

'It's what you were, babe. Come on, *I* was too! But it ain't how I see you now, I've told you, it's a new start, you've got to feel that too!'

'Yeah, I do.' But she still looked cut.

'Come on! We're both virgins again. Remember the Madonna song?'

That time she thought she was pregnant and Sean went to get a test kit, remember? It showed positive so Sean persuaded her to go down the doctor's to have a proper one.

'They *always* indicate positive,' he said.

'So what's the point in them?'

He laughed. 'You're always relieved when the doctor says the kit was wrong!'

'This is not funny, Sean!'

He knew and he went with her when she took her urine sample down to the clinic in a kind of milk carton they'd given her.

The strain broke when they were coming home and she smiled wearily. 'I was so embarrassed when it started leaking,' she said.

Sean laughed and pulled her close.

'Come on, babe, we'll be alright. Nothing can hurt us now.'

'I know.'

Sean had an interview with British Airways out in Feltham that next morning. It was where the computers were and that was something he fancied though of course he didn't know sod all about 'em.

Anyway they said come along for an aptitude test and everything so he set his alarm early cos he had to be there for nine thirty.

Jenny cooked him some scrambled egg while he got out his only suit. It was the one McGurk bought him that time he met Jenny. He was excited.

'Hey, Jen. I wore this suit when I met you. It should bring me good luck.'

'I hope so, babe,' she said.

'I'll be able to buy loads of suits when I'm working.'

They both sat up to the kitchen worktop on stools and Sean started on his egg and toast.

'I've got something for you, babe,' Jenny said and put a little envelope on the worktop by his plate.

He smiled and opened the envelope. There was a tiny hallmarked silver *S* and a poem.

> A little silver S more precious than gold,
> A little silver S puts my love in your hold.
> A silver S of love sent from my heart,

Just to let you know we will never part.
Don't take me for granted just because I care,
Stay with me forever, be always there.
Take this present now to hold within your grasp,
Hold this silver S and have my heart in your clasp.

x

To Sean,
Love you
Jenny
x

PS   Good Luck

He leaned across and kissed her.

'Thanks lovergirl,' he said. 'I'll take it with me.'

'I know you will!' she joked.

He slipped it into his pocket and sipped his tea.

'Have you taken your pills. Your vitamins?'

He nodded, face still stuck in the mug.

'And your royal jelly?'

He smacked his lips. 'Yeah. Course. I need my energy.'

'Does it make a difference, d'you think?' Jenny asked.

'Don't know. Haven't noticed a difference.'

'You have to take it for about three months before it has an effect, I think,' she said.

Sean nodded, chewing his toast.

'There must be something in it,' Jenny said. 'They've done trials and . . .'

She paused as if she'd finished.

'Tribulations,' said Sean.

'Mmm,' she nodded, absently.

Sean cracked up and she laughed when she realised what he'd said.

He took the piss. 'Tribulations – mmm,' he mimicked.

She held his arm and giggled and they smiled.

Sean reached down and kissed her long and luxuriously. They parted and Jenny's eyes were shining.

'I could kiss you till the cows come home,' she said.

Sean picked up his tea. 'Roll on cows,' he said.

Jenny smacked him.

'Roll on deodorant.' He smiled and sipped the tea.

They'd left plenty of time to walk down to Waterloo. Jenny was coming with him as far as the station to say goodbye.

'Right, got my letter, my umbrella, my suit and tie.' Sean was checking everything off before they left. 'The cooker's off, windows shut, got my key. That's everything.'

They set off under an overcast sky.

'The results come this afternoon, don't they?' Sean said.

'Yeah. You've got to ring the doctor.'

'*I* have?'

'Yeah. I daren't.'

'OK, I'll ring when I get back.'

'What time is it, love?' Jenny asked, a little out of breath. 'We seem to be going a bit fast.'

'I know. It's getting a bit tight, we'll have to hurry.'

They cut down Union Street and were halfway down when it started raining. Jenny giggled and clutched him tight beneath the crackling umbrella.

Then Sean stood still and his face went white. Jenny's heart almost stopped for him and he reached for his back pocket knowing he'd find nothing.

'Oh, no,' he said.

It was just the most crushed little noise she'd ever heard. Sean's world had collapsed and his plans and excitement poured away with the rain down the gutters.

'I haven't brought my money. Have you got any? The ticket's about a couple of quid.'

She shook her head. 'Where was it? Your money.'

'In my cheque book. In the little pocket.'

She looked at him helplessly.

Then he blew up.

'Christ Al-fucking-mighty!' But that was all he could say. He went red in the face and stamped about.

'Oh baby, let's just go back and get some. It'll be alright!'

'Course it won't be all fucking right! How's it gonna look turning up late for my interview? It won't exactly make a good impression will it?'

'Come on, we'll go back and you can phone them. Then get a taxi to the station and you'll not be too late.'

He bowed his head and followed her back without a word.

They were alright about it on the phone and said they'd expect him later on.

'Thanks, Jen,' he said. 'I don't know what I'd do without your sense.'

I was at his place later on.

'I felt so fucking useless, Toys,' he told me. 'I was sweating in this suit from rushing and it was raining and I'd made a right cock up, you know?'

I nodded.

'And I thought Jenny was pregnant,' he said. 'Christ, even the rain wouldn't touch me.'

'Anyway, at least she ain't pregnant,' I said.

Sean shrugged. 'I was having mixed feelings about it. Jenny was scared to death about the idea of having a kid. She says she can't even look after herself never mind a nipper.'

'So that's it, then, is it? No more tests?'

'No, it's definitely negative.'

Sean had a dream a few weeks before that. In it he was lying in bed beside Jenny and she had a TV set resting on her stomach.

It was kind of like an X-ray machine and through the screen he could see inside her. Inside the swollen womb he could see male sexual organs growing from the red walls. One was circumcised, one not. Then there were a baby's arms growing from the flesh inside, their hands clasped together.

He felt disgusted and sick in the dream and he pushed her away and rushed out of bed. He was trying to tell me about it but no one would believe him. He didn't want to make love to her if she had those things inside her.

He finally told me what had caused the dream. Jenny had taken a morning-after pill and she'd signed a thing that said if she turned out to be pregnant she would abort the baby.

Someone else told Sean why that was. The chemicals in the pill would have meant that the baby would be horrifically malformed. It probably wouldn't survive birth anyway. That's why being pregnant scared Jenny half to death.

He sat for a long time after that and told me how he felt when he knew he had to kill his only child.

'But it would've been disabled, Sean,' I insisted. 'Deformed.'

'Yeah, and why was it like that? It was my fault for not taking precautions.'

I couldn't say anything. I knew he'd stop blaming himself in time.

He told me about the first time she told him. They'd sat and hugged and Jenny cried her eyes out. They knew what they had to do but it was really fucking Jenny up. She went home to her Mum's in St Helens but she couldn't tell her, she just sat and cried and her Mum wanted to know what was wrong all the time.

Sean phoned her from the pub the Saturday night. He was really missing her and wanted to make sure she was OK. She wasn't but it was a relief hearing his voice.

When they were saying goodbye she said *I love you*, and he said *Love you too* but the line was lost. And then he didn't see her until the Sunday night when he went to meet her at Euston. But a day is a long time when you're in love.

He took the tube from London Bridge north with the piano chords from the Elton John on the radio. He had to go pick up his little girl who'd be lost and afraid in the huge station with all the punks.

I was in Euston one time and there was this old guy sitting there talking to himself. Bald guy with a beard, happy looking. Sitting on one of the plastic moulded seats against the wall and mumbling away quite cheerfully when this punk walks up and kicks him in the face.

'Shut it, Grandad!'

The wall thumped when the head hit it and the old guy fell down with blood all over his face. You should have seen the eyes of the strangers, watching. The disgust, the disbelief. *Bring out the dogs.* But he was gone. Laughing.

Sean was tall on the escalators. You see someone striding up the moving staircase way down below you and if they catch up and stand taller on the same step then you really feel how tall they are.

Age makes you bend. Bend over right down to the ground like a tree in the wind. What is it. Gravity. It pulls you down all your life. Breaks the back of the old. Sends a baby plummeting from a table to crack its head on the tiled floor. Sucks planes out of the sky like a broomstick and smashes them on a hillside.

It pulls you down all your life. It even lowers you into your grave.

In March he wrote this.

LOVE YOU TOO

But the connection had already broken
And the cold machine echoed my own words
Mocking, into a tender ear.
You've gone. I'm alone.
Cold.
And alone.

Remember the smiles?
How the careless games of youth are always embraced
Without caution.
But our trust has betrayed us,
She has turned away from our outstretched arms,
And bright, laughing faces.
Left us, let down, our worlds crashing around us,
To cry like a child with no mother
Or a mother with no child.

I remember when Jenny read that. There were tears in her eyes. He never showed it her until the scare was over but she remembered clear enough and it hurt her. They didn't make love for months after that. It nearly broke them up.

Chris and Big Jim were sparring. Spitting and panting like dogs. Grunting as they ducked and leaping forward with the punch. You could almost smell the heat of the lights and the roar of the crowd. And the lines of grease above the eyes and along the nose glistened in the bright spots.

There was almost a disco beat from somewhere, it was like a Rocky film. If only they could have seen themselves that night. I was on such a high, so glad to be alive, to belong to this club. I smiled broadly at Ron but he wasn't looking.

Marco was on his back on the floor by the ring, his little feet in the air pedalling away and every time he stretched out those brown legs as if to push a pedal away from him I could see the muscles in his thighs separate into three heads and I sighed.

I looked into the mirror and pulled up my shirt looking at my belly. I strained the rows of muscles into line and saw how they were shifted out of step like a zipper. My Dad's were like that, I think a lot of black guys' are.

Ron was showing a kid how to dodge the stand punchball – it was fast and powerful, that spring could throw the hard leather ball into your face and knock you out as surely as Big Jim's size-eleven fist could. And then Ron was saying don't just lash out, wait for the ball, follow it, measure it, wait, then punch fast. But the kid kept missing, thumping air and jumping out of the way like a kitten.

I stepped from one foot to the other and slipped my finger behind a tendon in my arm. Just where the bicep inserts into the forearm, if I bent my arm I could get a finger behind the tendon and trap it when I straightened out. It was tight, felt like the lines lashing a stack of roof trusses on the building sites when I was a kid.

Big Jim got a punch home. Chris's eyes stared at him in shock and he rocked on his heels, you could almost see the stars. The knees dropped and he almost fell but he caught himself and stepped away, spitting confidently and nodding as Terry, the ref, checked him out.

'Yeah. Yeah, alright, Terry.'

Terry's arms went up and axed down together in front of him, and Jim stepped back in close, his guard high.

On the racks by the mirror there were skipping ropes hanging, ancient and painted red, peeling and cracking close up in the glass like broken teeth. Once they shone and felt smooth in the palm, red – blood-red or sex-red. Red like a swollen eye, all bloodshot veins and puffed-up dark socket.

Ron kept saying he'd get us some weights machines hooked up on the walls one day. When the club could afford it.

Where the balls of fluff and dust gathered in the corners – a bench press machine. Where Marco threw his toenail peelings, behind the curling plastic floor tiles – a high pulley. And a low pulley, Ron, for rows. Yeah, there where the blue flakes of paint fall from the walls onto the carpet, rotting and stinking from spit and snot.

The mirrors were whole – no breaks. But they were dirty. Stained and spotted like a bathroom mirror from years of toothpaste sprayings and shave foam and squeezed spots. It needed a clean with a rag and Vim cream.

Ron had stacks of *KO* and *Boxing* magazines. In one of the *Knockouts* there was still an old Charles Atlas advert with the dude himself standing there with his leopardskin trunks on back to front. And this was Winter '89! Mind you, they are old reprints in *KO*.

They're all American, them boxing magazines. I dunno why he bothers keeping 'em here cos no one ever reads 'em.

By ten o'clock p.m. the gym's hot and starting to smell. I managed a few rounds with Marco, taking it easy cos he's a junior middle, heavier than me even though he's shorter. Then we troop into the showers, someone farts.

The water's hot and steaming and it melts into my tired arms and smooths down my ribs, easing that bit of tightness where Marco's punches knocked in my chest. I watch the water run in rivers off my skin and disappear into my pubes. And the soap suds snake off down the grids and into the hole.

'What you doin' now, Marco?' I said. 'Poppin' next door?'

'Yeah. Quick one, though. I'm supposed to be seein' Shell.'

We dried quickly to the buzz of hairdryers. A lungful of Mycota spray and I coughed. Little flaky toes and pale arses everywhere and laughter and pointing fingers and missing teeth grinning.

'I'm talking about *him* in Amsterdam!'

'What?'

'You fucking *know*!'

'She weren't as bad as Mickey's bird, fuck me!'

'I ain't talking about Mickey . . . '

Outside I squeezed past a Manta parked close to the wall, lucky the offside wing mirror was missing. And shot into the Duck with Marco and some of the other guys.

I asked a mate from school something quite recently. I said, 'You don't think of me as black, do you?'

He looked relieved – *well* pleased that I'd shown I understood.

He said, 'Yeah, you're right!'

He was chuffed with himself, proud that he could actually treat me as normal even though I was a half-caste. It was an achievement to him. But why did he have to congratulate himself for something like that? Why didn't it just come naturally?

I tried not to blame him but it's hard to be close with someone who's basically prejudiced. Specially for us coloureds, cos we're rejected by the blacks as well. Poor cunts, we've got no people but ourselves. Now that's what I call a minority. How many half-castes are there? Count 'em on one hand.

Then I tried the test on Sean. I said, 'Sean, you don't think of me as black, do you?'

He said, 'Course I do!' as if I'd said *Sean, you don't think of grass as green do you?*

That boy's so innocent it's unreal. Of course I'm black! Grass is green, Toys is black. So what? Don't offer the grass a job! Is that it? That's the way he saw it. He wouldn't know racial prejudice if it came up and stuck a bottle up his pretty white ass!

So finally I asked Marco. I said, 'Marco, you don't think of me as black, do you?'

He said, 'Oh, fuck off, Toys! Don't give me this persecution complex crap. I get it for being Italian, y'know!'

So I packed in asking after that. I guess that told me.

Sean talked about him and Jenny as the moon orbiting the earth. Sweet, ain't it? It's how he saw the two of 'em. But who was the earth, green and rosy like a big blue apple – with red bits – and who was the fucking dusty old grey moon trolling round forever in orbit, all covered in craters and little green men? I'll let you guess.

No, he did loads. Poems. Some of 'em weren't too clever, I hope he don't mind me saying that, but they weren't. They started getting like hers, all rhymes and soft scouser drivel.

You know how two lovers are often called, like, just two halves of one person. You know, if you get one of 'em on their own, they're just totally vacant, aren't they? Totally nuts and thinking about their other half and everything and it's just not worth being with them. Mind you, if you get 'em together all they do is suck each other's faces . . .

Anyway, about the thing where they're just one person really, the two halves thing, Sean didn't mind, he even wrote about it.

You and I are one.

You and I are one of the kind of people
Who are quite content to be alone.

You and I are one of the kind of people
Who talk to themselves on the phone.

You and I are one of the kind of people
Who take far too long making up.

You and I are one of the kind of people
For whom the hardest part of the day
                              Is waking up.

I thought that was quite good. You have to think quite hard to get it, at least *I* did. The *making up* bit isn't about them falling out, it's about women's make-up, lipstick an' all that cos Jenny used to take ages so Sean said.

One of McGurk's mates worked in the Houses of Parliament. Made the tea, I think. Sean used to ring him up and they'd say '*Will you hold please*' and instead of crappy music they'd play a tape of the Tory MPs being cruel to children or something.

That's what he said anyway. No, he didn't! That's in quite bad taste, actually, I've just remembered what happened to Sean as a kid. It's funny how you say the wrong thing sometimes, isn't it? Anyway, lucky I never said it to him. I just made it up.

Jenny went home again a couple of times, back to St Helens. Her Mum wasn't too good and she went back to help her sister out with the kids and the old lady.

Sean went to pick her up from the station the Monday night. He never got the job with BA.

She had another poem for him.

'I missed you, you slag,' he said and grabbed her close.

'Slut,' she said. 'I love you.'

They sat on the tube and Sean held the little piece of green writing paper between his fingers hoping everyone else in the carriage would see that his little girl loved him and was clever enough to write him poetry.

I was with them one time and Sean said, 'She mentioned you in one of her poems.'

'Hey, thanks,' I said.

'Why not return the compliment?' she said.

'What, write a poem and mention you? You're kidding!'

'No, why not?'

'I couldn't write a note to the milkman,' I said. I thought that was rather good and I laughed for ages.

'Try writing a poem to the milkman,' she said.

'Nah, not our milkie. He'd take it the wrong way!' Christ, I was making gay jokes now!

Marco had put a cheque through our letterbox when I got home. My Mum said she thought it was really funny and Skelly had laughed an' all. It said

Pay Mr J. D. Tortois   A massive, massive, massive, massive pair of tits

and there was a drawing of a pair of tits in the box where you put the amount in figures.

I laughed my tits off!

He'd even dated it the forty-ninth of April. How stupid. Everyone knows there's only forty-seven days in April.

I went out with Sean around Peckham and we passed this Indian shop, Hindu or something and there was this picture of an elephant thing with six arms.

His eyes lit up. Thinking something dirty probably.

'That'd be handy!' he said.

'It would be round here,' I said. 'You need six hands to walk round Peckham without getting something nicked. One in each pocket.'

There was a dog, crouched by the roadside grate, being sick and spitting the last lines of gob from its yellow teeth. It was outside the sandwich bar.

We looked at one another and laughed. 'It don't say much for the sarnies!'

It got dark and we went home. I made him a cup of tea and chucked my *Penthouse* collection on the bed.

'Here, dive in,' I said.

He laughed. 'Is that an offer?'

I had to treat him like a mate now. Everyone had conveniently forgotten I used to be crazy about the guy. Now I was supposed to change overnight. *Oh, Toys, stop being so* gay! *Stop fancying him for God's sake!*

So when he joked *Is that an offer?* I was supposed to laugh and slap my thigh, God what a laugh, *imagine* if I really *had* meant that, what a bummer I'd be! Ha ha!

But instead it hurt me. Christ, if only I could *dare* to offer something like that. Yes, go down on me, it'd be a dream come true! To have him do it cos he wanted to and not cos he was torturing himself like he used to do.

But not only that, to just take me and hold me and kiss me and say *yes, Toys, you're the guy for me. I only want you and I'll be around forever, whenever you need me. We can spend all our time together, laugh, joke, talk, cry, and love. Everything!* But it's a joke, isn't it? And that's the way I remember him before he went into the hospital. Like that, sitting on my bed with his broad grin, waiting for me to laugh. *Come on, join in the joke, Toys!*

He went home alone that night. Jenny was in St Helens. I wanted so much for him to say *Come on, Toys. Come back with me. Like old times, eh?*

But I knew I had no right there anymore. Where was the key, anyway? I'd stuffed it down the bottom of some old box somewhere.

So when Jenny rang Sean's place on the Sunday to ask was he going to meet her at Euston, I was as surprised as anyone to find myself there to answer it.

'No, Jenny,' I said, 'Sean's in hospital. But he should be coming home tonight.'

Then came the screaming and hystericals down the phone and I had to explain everything.

'Is he a member of that hospital, then?' Jenny asked a few days later.

'A *member*? You don't have to be a member, for God's sake! You know, there aren't requirements for getting into hospital! You don't have to know the Queen or anything. It isn't known as *Guys Hospital for people called Christine!*'

The hospital had phoned me about three o'clock early Sunday morning.

'Do you know a Sean Cuddell?' they said.

'Yes, what's happened to him?'

'He's in Emergency at Guy's Hospital,' she said. 'He's asking for you. Can you come?'

Christ, it felt like the alcohol withdrawal all over again. But he didn't drink anymore! I nearly passed out with shock. I was almost sick.

I saw him. Lying in bed all quiet and helpless like a drowning worm. His skin looked like a dirty puddle and the face was swollen. His breathing was short and fast. He looked ill. He must've been drugged up cos he wasn't conscious.

I talked to the nurse. She didn't seem real. A pale face with shocking black hair poked out of a stiff dark-blue uniform.

'His kidneys have stopped working,' she said. I couldn't take it in, I just couldn't believe it.

His kidneys have stopped working. Stopped working!

'What do you mean?' I demanded. 'Is he dying? How can they stop working, he'll die!'

'No, he won't die, it's something we can treat.'

She held my arms. I was shaking and kept darting my eyes at him. I wanted to cry, I wanted to hold her and have her tell me it wasn't happening.

She took me aside and sat me down.

'Has he had problems before, any serious illnesses recently?'

'I dunno.' I couldn't think. The only thing I could remember was . . .

'Yeah,' I said. 'He gave blood and they said it was too high, his blood pressure or something.'

'His blood pressure. Are you sure it was that?'

'Eh? Yeah. Yeah, it was blood pressure, definitely. The doctor said it was cos of his drinking. He used to be an alcoholic but he's OK now.'

'Does he drink at all now?'

'No, not for about three months. Is that what it is, the drinking? Will it be OK now?'

'We know about the blood pressure. It—' She looked at me. Then said it again. 'We know Sean has very high blood pressure, it was doing a lot of damage. But we don't know if that caused the kidney damage or if it was the other way round. We've given him something to lower the blood pressure and we'll dialyse him. He should be able to go home this evening.'

Wait a minute! 'What's that you said, dialyse?'

'Yes. What we have to do is clean out the blood because the kidneys can't do it themselves. We use a machine, the process takes about five hours.'

I knew I looked confused. I didn't understand enough to ask questions.

'He has a little trouble breathing at the moment,' she said. 'It's called pericarditis – crystals of urea form around the heart and inflame the heart lining. It'll disappear when we dialyse him.'

'And he can come home tonight? He'll be OK then?'

'He'll be a lot better by then, yes.'

'And they'll be working by then? His kidneys?' I was starting to smile.

'We don't know. This is acute failure. Kidneys usually do recover if the failure has been caused by a serious illness but if the kidneys are too badly damaged then they may never recover. You will have to face that possibility.'

I didn't *want* to face that possibility. I wanted her to fuck off and get someone who knew what he was talking about. How could Sean's kidneys stop working, for God's sake! He was OK, he wasn't ill. He'd walked round Peckham most of Friday. He was alright.

'Why's he breathing like that?' I said. It was shallow and he seemed to be gasping.

'It's the pericarditis.' She looked at her watch. 'It disappears very quickly after dialysis, don't worry. It *is* alarming but it will stop.'

He was out that night with strict instructions from his doctor. He wasn't supposed to drink hardly anything, had a special diet and he had to go back to hospital all the time. For that dialysis thing, three times a week.

Jenny had him to herself for a few days then I took him out and Christ, did he look ill! He was weak and he kept scratching himself.

I got as many brandies down him as I could and I'm sure he looked better after that. It got rid of the taste in his mouth, anyway. His breath did smell pretty bad. I could smell it from where I was standing. It was a bit like piss.

He showed me the scar on his wrist where they'd operated on his arteries and things.

'What was wrong with them?' I said.

'Nothing, it's something for the dialysis. It's a fistula so they can put a needle in and take out the blood to clean it.'

'Oh, right.' I was feeling sick.

'I don't piss anymore, Toys,' he told me. 'It's weird.'

'You'd be great at a football match,' I smiled. 'You'd never want to go!'

He laughed a bit. I could see how dog tired he was all the time.

Jenny told me he had trouble sleeping. He couldn't lie still on his back cos he got short of breath. And he'd fidget all night then be tired the next day.

He drank his brandy and rubbed at his arms and legs.

'My bones just feel – they *ache* all the time. And I itch something chronic, Toys. 'Specially on me back where I can't reach. I'm always asking Jen to scratch it but she says you're not supposed to. She puts baby oil in my bath.'

I sat and put my hand on his. Nothing funny, and he didn't take it that way. He knew what I was feeling. I was on his side. I was with him all the way.

Marco was talking to him one time when Jenny was there.

Marco said, 'Do you have to watch what you eat?'

'I have to watch it, yeah,' said Sean. 'Else it'd crawl off the plate. 'Specially with her cooking!'

Jenny slapped him and giggled.

Sean phoned me.

'Do you know Monica?' he said.

'One of Jenny's friends, ain't she?' I said.

'Yeah. She phoned us up the other day, said she was doing a ouija board thing tonight. D'you wanna come? I thought you'd enjoy that!'

'Yeah, alright. I never done it, though, have you?'

'Nah. Don't worry, she says she does it all the time. Her Mum and Dad used to let her do it at home.'

'Anyway, how you feeling, mate?'

'Oh, can't complain. I've got my scrubber here looking after me. Apart from that, OK. I get tired at work but I manage. They understand.'

'How's the cramps?'

'Oh, I just get 'em a bit at night after my dialysis. It's alright, I've got used to 'em. It's only like when I used to go swimming. I always used to get cramps in my calves all the time.'

'Listen, Sean. I don't know where this bird lives.'

'Right, I'll give you her address, you find it in the *A–Z*.'

Sean was on dialysis three times a week now, four hours a time. He used to drag himself to hospital along his own Via Dolorosa to keep himself alive.

He had a huge fat vein like a deformed blue snake in his forearm from the operation on his wrist and he used to needle it himself to get the blood out.

The worst thing, he said, was the fluid restriction. He was allowed only five hundred millilitres a day, about a pint. He didn't drink like he used to but he still used to go over the limit.

The nurses slagged him off for it. They said he'd have to stay on dialysis for longer to get back down to his dry weight.

One Saturday after dialysis Sean was in the Bunch o' Grapes for his lunch and a brandy and he met Jenny in there. She walked in as he was finishing his beef sandwiches.

'Hiya baby,' she said, kissing him. 'Thought you might be in here. How do you feel?'

He smiled. 'A bit tired. You want something to eat?'

'No, it's alright.'

Sean chewed slowly. He looked in a daze and he stared at Jenny's chest.

'You looking at my tits?' she laughed.

'Sorry. Just staring into nothing.'

She looked down. 'I don't call *that* nothing.'

Sean smiled.

'I was waiting for you in the flat,' she said. 'But I thought I'd find you here.'

He put his hand out and took her fingers. 'I'm glad. I was missing you.'

'I know,' she smiled. 'I can't keep away.'

'Are you staying tonight?'

'Course I am. If you'll have me.'

'Yeah, you know I want you to. But I won't be much fun.' He looked around and leaned close. 'I'm sorry, Jen, you know I love you but . . . '

'Oh, Sean,' she said. 'Stop worrying about it. Do you think I only want you for sex?'

He frowned. 'But you understand, don't you? It's not just cos I'm tired. I just don't feel like it anymore. How can you put up with it?'

She rested her finger across his lips. 'I love you,' she said. 'It doesn't matter to me if you make love to me or cuddle me as long as I know you love me.'

'I do,' he said.

'I know it's only the dialysis doing it. You'll be better soon.'

Sean gripped her hands now and his eyes filled up and started dripping onto the plate.

'Oh, Jen,' he said. 'Christ knows what I'd do without you. If it wasn't for you . . .' His voice stumbled on the tears and he couldn't continue.

She got up and sat beside him and took him in her arms. 'Shush, baby,' she said.

'Do you still love me?' he said.

'Sean! Look at me!' She held up his head so he could see her. 'Don't you ever dare to think I don't love you. I'll love you forever, you know that. Now come on, finish your sandwiches.'

I turned up at Monica's with a few beers. Everyone else was there. Lesley was there, you remember, she shares with Jenny.

'Have you done this before, Toys?' Monica asked me as if she'd known me forever and we were best buddies.

'No,' I said. 'I'm a ouija board virgin!'

'Well, don't worry,' she said. 'It's not dangerous.'

My mouth fell open. I half expected her to pat my hand and reassure me. It really makes me retch, these fucking overconfident pseudo-clairvoyant little Madames. It's not just that, not just this situation, I remember when my girl cousins were growing up and they seemed to be constantly prancing about in high heels and flowery pansy frocks 'like Mummy' acting so grown up and talking to you like you were retarded or something.

So Monica made us all a cuppa and said, 'Now, you've all got to promise not to move the glass. Don't piss about cos it really does work.'

I put my fingers in my mouth and made sick noises. She didn't follow. I'm sorry but just saying *piss* doesn't redeem her.

'Does the glass really move, then?' asked Lesley.

'Yeah.'

'You have to touch the glass,' Jenny said. 'But it's the spirit that moves it.'

'You done this, then?' I said to Jenny.

'Yeah. We did it at college a few times. It's really amazing.'

'Come on, then,' I said. 'Let's get going, I wanna see this glass move. Spooky!' And I laughed, waving my hands over the table like a slightly unhinged person.

'Do you have to believe in it for it to work?' asked Lesley, looking sideways at me.

'Don't look at me,' I said still laughing but everyone ignored me.

'Not really,' said Monica, looking for help from Jenny.

'I don't think everybody has to,' she said. 'But me and Monica do, so that's probably enough.'

On the shiny hardwood table top, Monica had arranged the letters in a circle with YES and NO cards facing one another. They were just biro on plain paper. It occurred to me that numbers would be a good idea. But I burst out laughing.

'Hey, you ought to have special characters,' I said. 'Commas, full-stops. Asterisks and everything! What about curly brackets and a copyright symbol? You never know, we might get an awkward bastard for grammar!'

Surprisingly no one took any notice.

'Put the lights out,' said Jenny.

Lesley shrieked. 'No! Leave them on!'

'I've got candles,' said Monica. 'Is that OK?'

She still looked scared.

'Come on, you pansy,' I said. 'It's only a laugh.'

'OK, but I'm sitting here by the lightswitch.'

Monica lit the candles and put them on the sideboard. Then the lights went out and I could see Lesley's face, tight and nervous, in the faint glow.

'Right,' Monica said. 'I want everyone to breathe into the glass to put your spirit into it.'

We passed it round and I looked across to Sean and grinned. I wondered what he wanted from this. To find out if he was gonna get better?

Monica put the glass upside down in the centre and said, 'OK, rest one finger on it lightly. Don't rest your hand on it or it won't move.'

We sat there for a second in the flickering candlelight, fingers on the wide base of the glass and I could tell my arm was going to ache in no time.

'Everyone relax,' Monica said. 'And no moving the glass. Let it go.'

We looked at her and she closed her eyes. This was it, the seance was beginning.

Monica spoke first.

'If there is a spirit in this room, move the glass to YES . . . '

The glass shook almost immediately. My heart nearly stopped, my breathing *did* stop. Just a little rocking movement then it began to glide across the table to the letter *R*.

The glass was actually pulling my arm across the table. I could have lifted off my finger and I'm sure it would've kept going.

'R,' said Jenny.

Then the glass slid back just as surely to the centre and stopped.

'R,' Jenny said again, looking up at our faces. She sounded like Long John Silver.

My mouth had dropped and I shut it up quickly. 'Fuck me,' I said. 'Was anybody pushing that?'

Their faces were solemn and each one shook, still looking at the glass. Bollocks, I thought and I grinned to myself.

Monica spoke again.

'If there is a spirit in this room, move the glass to YES . . . '

This time the glass went straight to the letter *I*.

As soon as it was back in the middle I saw Monica open her mouth to speak but the glass hadn't finished. It moved back to the *I* card and then spelled out D-I-E-D-F-R-O-M-Y-I-F-J-T-J-F-R . . .

But it stopped making sense. It was swinging into the middle then back out to any old letter and back, just going faster and faster.

'Stop it!' shouted Lesley and she snatched her finger back.

We all took our fingers off and the glass actually slid to a halt next to the letter *R*.

'It's OK,' said Monica. 'It does that sometimes. I call it swinging.'

'It's fucking uncanny,' I said. 'Spooky!'

'What was it?' said Sean. 'I DIED FROM JIFJT-something?'

'No, it was YIFJT something, with a *Y*,' said Monica.

'Oh, well, *that's* different – that makes more sense!' I said with as much sarcasm as I could muster.

'Put your fingers on again,' said Monica.

Hesitantly we put our fingers back on the glass.

'If there is . . . ' Monica began but the glass was off again.

I-D-I-E-D-F-R-O-M-E-T-M-E-H . . . then back to the *I*. Back to the centre and then to the *I*. And again. It was stuck on *I*. It was swinging again, faster.

Lesley gasped and took back her hand and we all followed.

Again the glass slid to a standstill under its own power. Christ, it was possessed by the spirits! It almost had a silvery glow around it.

Possessed! We'd all be possessed before the night was out. I wondered if I could get it to improve my boxing!

'Come on,' said Monica and she put her finger back.

One by one we rested our fingers on the glass hoping it wouldn't move.   'Repeat the last word,' said Monica.

Nothing happened. We sat there, relieved.

'Did you die naturally?' Monica asked.

I could see Lesley getting scared again. There was no movement from the glass.

'Were you murdered?' Monica asked.

Then it moved. Over to the NO card and back to the centre.

Jenny spoke. 'Was your death an accident?'

The glass moved to YES.

She was on a roll. 'Did you die before your time?' Jenny said.

YES again.

'Was it a car accident?'

I thought Monica was going to say 'Look, Jenny! I'm asking the questions, OK?' But she didn't.

The glass didn't move.

'Do you know what a car is?' Monica asked smugly.

NO, it said.

'Did you die this century?'

NO.

'Nineteenth century?'

NO.

'Eighteenth?'

NO.

'Seventeenth?'

NO.

'Sixteenth?'

NO.

I wondered when she'd shut up. 'Did you die in AD?' I put in.

NO.

Wow, I thought! A spirit spoke to me! Christ, that was something to tell Marco. Mind you it would have been easier for Monica just to turn and tell me the answer rather than mess about with this glass business.

But I was enjoying the game. 'Did you die earlier than a thousand BC?' I said.

NO.

'Spell out the number BC' Monica said.

E-I-G-H-T-E-E-N.

'We need numbers,' I said. 'I told you.'

'Did you have a name?' asked Monica.

YES.

'What is your name?'

It went E-M . . . then to either M or N, I couldn't tell . . . Y-Y-E-E-E-. Then the glass stopped.

'Is your name E-M-M-Y?'

NO.

'Are you male?'

NO.

'Are you English?' That was Lesley. The first time she'd spoken since she squealed. Monica smiled reassuringly at her and Lesley's mouth broadened into an embarrassed grin.

Now it moved and Lesley jumped in shock. Her face paled.

NO.

'Could you repeat your name please?' asked Jenny.

E-M-M-I-E.

'I was nearly right!' said Monica.

'Is that all of it?' asked Jenny.

YES.

'Are you willing to talk to us?' Jenny said.

YES.

'Will any harm come to us?' Lesley checked.

NO.

'Are you sure?' Jenny asked.

YES.

There was a dirty swirling line of smoke rising from the candle and the flame seemed to be suspended from it and swinging. The intense patch of light was hypnotising me and making my eyes hurt. I was getting eyestrain. And the girls were getting real pally with Emmie. Asking about her ethnic background, kids – did they die an' all that. I thought this was getting a bit insensitive.

Anyway, Monica asked her some question or other an' she reckoned one of us was descended from her.

'One of us five?' asked Jenny.

YES.

'Is it Jenny?' asked Monica.

NO.

'Sean?'

YES.

'The descendant of your line is Sean?'

YES

'Have you a message for him?' said Jenny excitedly.

YES.

'Could you spell the message out please?'

L-O-V-E-I-S-L-I-F-E.

'Will this help Sean in his illness?' asked Jenny.

YES.

'What's gonna happen at the end of the world?' I said suddenly.

Lesley gasped and dragged her hand away. Before the glass had a chance to move so did Monica and Jenny.

I looked across at Sean. Only him and me left.

'Come on, *move*,' I said to the glass.

'Don't ask things like that!' Monica said.

Lesley stared at me with frightened eyes.

'Why not?' I said.

The glass clearly wasn't going anywhere.

'Why won't it move?' I said to Monica.

'It never works with two,' she said.

I wanted to say *it never works without you on it, you mean*.

'Shall we carry on?' Sean said.

'As long as Toys shuts up,' Lesley said.

'OK,' I said. 'We'll forget it.'

The fingers went slowly back on.

'Please disregard the Armageddon question,' Monica said.

The glass gave a jerk and almost took off from under our fingers. I could feel it gliding away and everyone else's fingers just seemed to be resting on it incredibly lightly. You can usually see white nails when there's pressure but no . . .

The message came from nowhere I-D-I-E-D-F-R-O-M-F-I-R-E. Completely unexpected.

Out of the blue, it was so moving. That's what she was trying to say right back at the start. It was the first thing she tried to say to us.

It all went wild after that. They were asking questions I didn't understand about people I didn't know. One question overlapped another, rapid fire but each was answered. It had become like an exclusive Knightsbridge soirée . . .

Does Daniel care? Does he love me? Do love charms work?

What's the name of the bookshop assistant? What's his surname? Will Sean have any children? Alain what? Please spell his surname. Do you think this is pointless? But fun? Don't you want to talk about your own love? Did the world frighten you? Should I contact Daniel? Where is he? Is he still in Avon? Will I get married? Is he working at the theatre? Do malign spirits come to the board?

'Do you have a specific different message for any of us?' asked Jenny.

NO.

Fine.

'Do you mind if we leave now?' asked Monica.

NO.

'Do you mind if we contact you again?' asked Jenny.

NO.

'Will you be pleased?' she said.

YES.

'Can we contact you at any time?'

YES.

'Will it be safe?' asked Lesley.

YES.

Monica had to step in and finish things off.

'Please move the glass to the letter G and then leave.'

The glass slid off to G and stopped.

The room felt suddenly empty. The glass stood lifeless. The first time it hadn't returned to the centre. The spirit had left. If it had been a spirit.

Jenny wanted to stay and talk about it all night but Sean managed to drag her away. I was piss bored with it all and I wanted to get down the pub.

'What did you reckon?' Sean said to me outside.

'I reckon I should have taken more beers.'

I did have a laugh that night, though. There was a tramp on the way home with his dog.

'Give us a couple of pence for something to eat, willya?'

'Why don't you eat your dog?' I said under my breath.

I said goodbye to Sean and Jenny and dashed off for my train. Monica had put me on edge. She was a weird bird. Anyway I'd make last orders.

I got the train. There was a woman sitting next to me, reading her letter. Then I farted. A quiet one but I could smell it right away.

Oh shit, I thought, she's gonna say something. If she does I'll say *I wasn't reading your letter so you shouldn't have been smelling my fart!*

It was quite sunny these days.

I was over the common one time and these two little girls came walking past.

The little one in a white cardigan said, 'Run, and I'll chase you.'

The other looked at her friend. Or her sister. As if she didn't understand.

'Go on, run! I'll give you till that flower.'

She started to run, a little hesitantly. 'Which flower?'

'Just keep running! Run! Run! Go!'

Her mother called. 'This way, girls.' She was heading for the road.

'That way, that way!' called the bossy sister.

The other girl stopped again and looked back.

'Which flower?' she said.

It was how I used to feel with Sean. He used to be totally dense.

Strange. Now he's so different. So alive. He's still quiet, but his eyes shine now. And you know he's taking in what's going on and he's thinking, he's got opinions. If you asked him something you know he'd have a proper reply instead of a dumb shake of the head.

He used to remind me of the Biology textbook we had at school. There was a section on genetic diseases and a bit on cretins, with pictures. I expected to see a picture of Sean. He was a cretin.

That same day in the park I saw these two little boys on three-wheelers and one said, 'Look, a policeman on a bike!'

I was sitting close by and I said, 'I know him, he's called Mr Pig. Go an' say hello to him.'

They rode off and I saw the little lad's eyes look up to the copper who looked back and the kid's mouth opened to speak. I was off!

'Did you hear about that Turkish bloke today?' Jenny asked.

'Yeah. *I'd* pay three thousand quid for a kidney. I tell you!' Sean was scared, you could hear it in his voice.

'Oh, babe, I'd pay a million pounds to have you well again even if it meant me paying it back for the rest of my life!'

He held her close.

'I'm definitely on call,' he said. 'I asked about it today. They said keep a bag packed but I'm so close you could bring any stuff round I needed.'

'I hope it's soon, babe. How often does a kidney come up?'

'Dunno. When someone dies.'

She frowned. 'Oh Sean . . .'

'There's a shortage, you know, Jen. There just aren't enough to go around.'

'I thought you could have a kidney from someone you know. Have they mentioned that?'

'No. I think it has to be a relative though.'

'You could have one of mine,' Jenny said though it scared her to say it.

'No, baby. I wouldn't take one of yours. I want you whole.' He managed a smile.

I think he was taking it well. He was taking it like the boys take a bruising down the gym.

But right now I think the fascination has left me. The attraction of punching someone's face in with a laced-up padded claret glove. And all at the expense of whooshing in your ears and a rush of excitement when you just pull back centimetres from a swinging fist. It's like when you enter a huge junction with amber lights fading into red and you can see the cars to each side revving and by the time you're over it they're moving and that's the feeling I'm talking about.

Heart almost beating stars into your eyes and your veins all alive with adrenalin – phew!

But I think I'm past all that now, I really do. Course I wasn't then. And I used to drag Sean down sometimes to play cards or just sit in the gym after hours and drink and talk with the boys. He never came down when the fighting was on. Never smelt the sweat and the fatigue or saw the blood and the eyes of a man and, if his face is broken, fat cushions of red puffed flesh under the eyes and black, almost hollowed bloodshot whites.

It was nothing to the boys. If they got a bloody nose or a busted eye they laughed cos in a couple of weeks it'd be gone. They knew that all the good food and exercise made it so their bodies repaired pretty quickly.

But it wasn't a place to take Sean. He needs love and comfort right now and relaxation and affection and good times.

Jenny the bitch! Listen to this – I was gonna take Sean out on Saturday night, right? She said she was going home to see her Mum so I thought right, we'll go out like we used to an' see some of the boys – well, he said he wanted to see McGurk and Al Irving and Ravensknowle and some other boys down one of the clubs in Islington – Paradise or somewhere. Then of course she says, 'I've changed my mind, babe. I want to stay with *you* this weekend.' What a fucking kid!

'Have you told your Mum?' he said. This was Friday night.

'Oh, I'll ring her later.' She simpers up to him and I can almost feel the revulsion I imagine is slithering up his throat. I wait for him to push her away and be sick.

He puts an arm round her small back and brushes thin blonde hair away from her mouth and kisses her forehead.

'Go on, ring her, Jen. You'd better – it's only fair.'

So I'm there, an' all. I was there cos I thought she'd have gone by now. It was Friday night and she's still there. Christ, I was so mad!

She waddled off to the kitchen in her flat shoes and started tapping at the plastic buttons on the phone, the St Helens dialling code blipping out across miles of cable to the exchange.

'Sean,' I started and frowning lines began across my forehead and I cast glances at her then back at him. His face said *what?*

'What's this, is she staying or what? I thought we was going dancing.'

'Yeah, I know, mate. Jenny can come an' all. It's alright.'

I reached forward and grabbed his knee and my eyes locked into his. 'I've heard it before,' I said slowly. 'She won't come. She won't even let you go, you know that. She don't want you seeing them guys. She thinks they're a bunch of fucking fruits!'

'Toys, they *are*—'

'I know!' I interrupted. 'But to her . . . ' I sat back and breathed out slowly. 'They're a bunch of fucking fruits.'

I was just weak with disappointment. You know how you feel sometimes you work so hard at something and just as it's about to come off someone craps it up. Makes you feel sick. In fact I remember seeing a bird on the common one day in the summer and she was there in her bikini, on her front, and she'd undone her top. Her back was bare and, where the two ends of the straps sprawled on the blanketed grass, her breasts squeezed out beneath her weight. So anyway a bit later on she tried to refasten the straps and I watched her for a while. It seemed such an effort for her to contort her arms right behind her and fiddle with the fastening for a minute or so then she'd flop back down, exhausted and rest for a while before trying again.

Almost like a beetle on its back she had no chance. It soon became obvious to the giggling blokes not far off that she didn't have a prayer. Was this the first time she'd tried this? I think they were waiting for her to give in and she'd have to stand up and flash her tits. Wankers!

Well, I helped her in the end but I was a bit embarrassed. Anyway, that's the sort of despair and frustration that really saps your will.

And I remember something else, one time when my Dad lived with us and I was in the kitchen. It was black outside and the windows were steamy from the cooking. If I stood on my tiptoes I could stare at the misty glass just over the windowsill. There was a tiny dead fly in the dust on the sill and I traced my finger over the rough bits that must have been that plastic wood stuff filling in a countersunk nail hole. Then all painted white matt emulsion.

My Mum said *Don't be long, Doug, I'm dishing up in a minute* and my Dad slipped out to the offy which in those days was about four doors down so he should have been back in seconds.

And when he did turn up finally, after throwing-out time, my Mum was grey and disappointed but calm.

'I waited till it got cold, Doug,' she said.

My Dad stood there with a week's curly beard. Pissed. No remorse, just an ignorant grin. She'd waited till the meal got cold before she'd eaten it. Did you see that? Christ, how disappointing can you get?

So Jenny came back from the phone with a little hurt scowl.

'OK?' asked Sean.

'Oh, she's never happy. She really gets on my nerves.'

I shook my head inwardly. What an arsehole bird.

'You going then or not?' he said.

'Home? No, I said I wasn't.'

'Right, we're off dancing,' Sean announced.

'Where to?' she said.

'Islington. Paradise or somewhere.'

Jenny's lips tightened. Then she opened her mouth to speak.

'With the fruits,' I put in.

'Oh, no,' she said. 'No, Sean I thought you said you weren't messing round with them lot again.'

'I didn't say that. They're my mates.'

'The clubs I mean. You said you'd—'

'Yeah, I know.' He hesitated, trying to think of something reasonable to say. 'Well, it don't matter. Anyway you said you were going away, didn't you? – I've already had it arranged.'

'That's not the point, Sean. What else do you get up to when I'm away?'

I wanted to tell her to can it, or maybe I wanted to throw something at her.

'Do you always do what she says?' I sneered. 'I told you she wouldn't let you go out.'

'Toys, do you *mind*?' Her eyes were cold. 'I don't remember including you in this conversation.' There was a pause as she stared me down. 'There's plenty of other clubs we can go to, but you said you weren't going *there* again.'

'Oh yeah, but that was ages ago, when I was still on the edge. I dunno, kind of vulnerable. I reckon I could go now alright.'

She stared at him now and he backed down. 'OK, we'll go, er . . .'

'Let's go to the World's End,' Jenny said.

'That ain't a club,' I grinned.

'I know that,' said Jenny hiding her impatience.

'Well, I thought we were talking about clubs. Christ, let's go to the British Museum, is that a club?'

Sean cut in. 'If we're going to Camden, might as well try the Palace or Dome or something.'

'Nah,' I said, holding my head. 'Not the Dome. It's too fucking loud. Full of young kids and the music's bollocks.'

'Well, you don't have to come then,' said Jenny. I knew I'd made a mistake – I knew where her vote was going.

I picked up my coat and left.

'I'll ring you tomorrow,' Sean said. 'Let you know where we'll be, alright?'

I said *yeah* and walked back to the station but a darkness had suddenly fallen over me. I was remembering that time when I woke up at Sean's alone. We'd been drinking locally and he'd let me stay at his place while he slept with Jenny. I mean he was at Jenny's.

And for years these old photos had been gathering dust and loneliness at his Mum's but Jenny made him go and collect them and take them to his place. Old photos. The family photos of the baby Sean and then Sean as a kid and a teenager and all sorts.

There weren't many. Perhaps the old man was rarely sober enough to operate a camera or the two of them were rarely sentimental enough to want to record their kid's progress. But anyway I woke up alone that day and made breakfast and I was sitting up on the bed listening to Capital and drinking my tea. There's an old hinged box, more like a chest, with the top painted, copied from a tapestry or a rug or something. I'd seen Jenny sometimes sitting on the floor in front of this box and flicking through the loose photos and smiling.

So I looked. I took out all the pictures and went through them feeling almost voyeuristic and violating his trust. Illegal and furtive I examined them like a schoolboy would the underwear pages in the Grattan catalogue. But soon I was heavy inside and my throat hurt. Because he didn't smile. In *any* of them. These were the days the little boy had no smile and it made my eyes shiver and I had to clench back the tears.

My gaze bolted and searched out the windows for relief and I gasped almost wondering where he was right now. I was still so afraid he was as unhappy as then and my selfishness stabbed me. I so much wanted him with me, only me, but guilty it all came home to me then how much I loved him that it didn't matter who cared for him now, who it was that made him forget those times as long as someone did. And he'd chosen Jenny and that should be enough. But selfishness is a hard habit to break.

And in those family shots – Christmas with the uncles and cousins and aunts and Sean dressed up and glass of lemonade, sideboard with pale black and white flowers and cards and the bleak hard chairs and best behaviour, I felt like I'd lost someone because this was a different person – it wasn't Sean anymore and I cried for him and for me.

And I'm crying now, guilty again that I'd had a childhood and he hadn't. That I wasn't there to save him and even if I was there I could do nothing. Even through my hate for his father I can see that a part of him was a part of us all – nature and instinct had driven me to use Sean just as the old man had done. But my abuse was tempered with tenderness and at least afterwards, though sickened at both of us, I knew how I felt, knew how much I wanted him still. But didn't the old man suffer afterwards? He must have done.

It's at times like these you consider every word or thing that passed and you measure up the bad things you said and pile them together and torture yourself. Why did I *say* that? why was I so mean? I didn't intend to hurt so much. He's so sensitive but . . . No, he was never sensitive until recently and now he's hurt me more.

I adored that face, that image for days in the space of a morning. The soft young flesh and my mind conjures another, a bristly face leering in at the camera close behind him, grabbing his arse with one hand, beer can in the other. But the old man appeared in none of the pictures. Jenny's perfume lingered always in the air there in that room, Sean's young eyes teased me from the print, saying that they loved me but they lied.

I could hear the telly from next door but they couldn't hear me. Yellow and orange freesia petals lay at the foot of a vase on the table beside the window and I heard ticking from some clock or other, I didn't bother to find out. It was pretty grim that morning, can't say I enjoyed it, but I do remember searching in the kitchen cupboards for a lager. I didn't find any cos of course he didn't keep it anymore. He didn't have any alcohol at all. So I kicked my way down the roads to the station hating the world generally and thinking *how many times have I walked this way and how many times will I do it again and isn't it about time I changed my life or something? Do I want to do this forever or what?*

So I remembered that day. The photo day. That depressing session looking over Sean's past, if you can call it that. And I went home with similar feelings. Didn't really do much, I just waited for Sean's call the following day.

An' he phoned about ten past five from Victoria.

'Toys, I'm with Simon. How long will it take you to get to Victoria station?'

'Fucking ages, mate. Victoria's a pissy place to get to from here. Where you going to?'

'We got to pick up Al at Regent's Park. Can you be here at six? The Quicksnack, alright?'

'I'm not going to Victoria, Sean. Not a chance! Do you know how many changes I have to make to get there? I have to go all over the shop, it's a pissing joke!'

'Yeah, alright. Regent's Park then?'

'No! Tell him to meet you at the pub! Christ, who's organising this, fucking Phileas Fogg? Regent's Park is so far out of your way it's unbelievable. Look, are we going to Camden or what?'

I heard him mumbling to the others. Then, 'Yeah' he said. 'Camden Town to the End of the World – I mean the World's End. That's where Jenny wants to go.'

'She's with you, yeah?'

'Yeah.'

'Look, ring Irving and tell him to meet you there at about seven. That should give him plenty of time. You guys go for something to eat, have a few beers or something and I'll see you at the pub same time, about seven. OK?'

'It's a big place,' Sean said.

'We'll find you. Wear a red carnation or something.'

I laughed to myself and hung up.

Tubes again. Christ, Victoria! Did he realise what a crappy place, how difficult it is – oh, forget it. Some guy was playing that *take five* or whatever it's called thing on his sax – that five/four time thing like swing jazz or whatever at London Bridge tube and I got the northern line to Camden Town. Kingston Town. Didn't need my passport. Didn't need to wear a condom to enter Camden Town. But fifteen minutes later the place was swarming with uniforms and two flashing fire tenders were outside. Ask 'em what they think of *London's Burning*, I thought. Is it realistic? Is it representative? Ask 'em what they think of *Twin Peaks*. Some crazy writing or what!

I lit a fag out of the station but I didn't enjoy it. No. Went to Burger King and got a bacon double cheeseburger type thing. I asked for my game piece – why didn't she volunteer it? I had to *ask* for it. What's going on? Bleeding tight bastards. One eighty-five and they don't even offer you a game piece. I got the Lone Ranger. Should I buy another BK Double and see if I get Tonto? Nah!

So I'm in the World's End, looking out for Sean and the fruits and everywhere there's these huge bastards with duvets up their shirts or something – bouncers with earphones and microphones like Madonna's. Tits bigger than Madonna's some of 'em. They are big. These guys are big and I mean *big*.

A black woman with a handpiece walkie-talkie type thing, and I say, 'What's the half-time score?' laughing. But she's miserable – 'Stop that, you!' she says and women keep pushing past me to the bogs. My hearing is dodgy, I feel nearly sick on Foster's and it's past seven. They should be here by now so I walk around. To the other bar and past the dining-room area where there's a sign saying something like THIS AREA IS RESERVED FOR DINERS but it's full of people who look like they're more drinking than eating. And just there are four girls with spangly tights on their legs and sweet short skirts so I hang around and lean on the wall with a fag in my mouth and hands in pockets. My beer is on the shelf and I dangle the cigarette beneath my smarting eyes – smoke in my eyes – can't help it but I figure I must look cool without touching my fag, just drawing and inhaling and blowing out, look no hands!

So the ash grows long and I wish I'd put a paper clip all folded out long into my fag, slid it deep into the fag so the ash stays unfalling, someone once said that. And I hope as I stand and stare I don't give the impression I'm pissed. They swim past – all slim waists and breasts designed to lie cleaved within tight tops. And why did I decide to be gay this time round?

Fuck, I hardly notice, hardly realise that they're here now. Sean and Jenny and the boys all merging into one buying me beers and someone playing the goddamn fruit machine like Jenny thinks we all are and she's right. She has stockings around her legs and seams surgically sharp but I'm not looking into her drawers tonight. This evening I mean, not tonight. Sean's got her tonight. He really had us fooled. I wonder if the others are thinking that too.

It's all chords almost a synthy heaven and I can't really get a grip on my thoughts do you know that feeling when the beers seem to swell into your throat and up into your brain and it hits your heart when the music reaches a song you like it seems like anyone you ever knew or loved could appear like a dream and say those things that were always your fantasy you always wanted them to say. Or something. But I remember looking into Jenny's face that evening she seems to have such an expanse of cheek – the bit under her eyes that reaches to her delicate little nose. What was it, the girl in her made me feel like a father or what? But remember I said her voice sounded like a grown woman laughing? That was it.

And I couldn't help admiring her skirt and stockings again but it was a silent type of thing. My throat began to play tricks – it happens when the fear rises and tears announce their intentions. Call me, I dunno, what you like but she really has big eyes and did it come home to me just how attractive I could see she was to Sean? That girl has big eyes. She can love, I know. She can be hurt I know, but there seems always to be something defiant about her as if the fact that she is in love has nothing to do with anyone but herself. That *is* frightening.

The most frightening thing about a girl – but *I* don't care cos I don't love women really but you know what it is, don't you? – that a girl really does choose who to love. She *chooses* and there's nothing you can do about it! It seems like a considered choice so scary the way the dice fall. And me who's excluded gets little comfort from the whole other population who's also excluded because that rejection is painful and cold and empty and so mercifully quick and mercilessly endless.

You have to be able to let go if you're going to fall in love and you have to let go again when it's over. It kind of makes you think *is it all worth it?* Why not stay out of it all along? All alone.

Some girls were staring at the balloons high up in the ceiling and we decided to push off up to Tufnell Park. The fire engines were gone so two stops and we're out. There's a pub next to the Dome club and in it a band play country music and old light rock 'n roll type things. There's a girl singing and the guitarist really knows what he's doing.

'Christ,' I said. 'No one's clapping or anything. What a bunch of boring bastards. Let's give the band some support or what!'

So we started clapping and whistling and the girl smiled shyly, embarrassed. We were enjoying it and I think they appreciated it. Then I found myself shouting 'You've lost that loving feeling!' over and over and the guitarist, never once looking up, considered something for a moment then announced the song as if it was his idea.

It was great, us lot singing along and really filling out the sound and I had a real sense of showing up the dull tossers that were just sitting there and taking this all in and not contributing a thing.

I think it struck someone that time was escaping intangibly and we found ourselves outside the Dome though whose idea it was to go there I have no idea unless it was Jenny's. And after paying and dropping our coats off for fifty pence we were inside by the bar. Even here the music is loud.

I wandered onto the dance floor and began to move in time with the other dancers. Their bodies writhed and arms swung like streamers. If that was the way you did it then hell, I thought, I'll try anything. There seemed to be a lot of wild head movement and hair, long hair, whipped and flashed. Three girls headbanged, one with a white woollen string sweater, and perspiration fell in almost clairvoyant patterns on the dirty floor. Screens hung above and all around. On one I saw a skull-type image and on others huge daisy shapes bold like poster art. And from two sides were they lasers? No, but a pair of spotlights were split into hundreds of beams and changing colour they blinded and absorbed the spirit of the beat and reproduced it in painful bright beams that made me wild, my body taking on the madness that seemed to pervade the tribal forms that surrounded me.

I looked aside and there, sharp against the darkness that hid everything except what I was looking at (because how could anything hide that), were Sean and Jenny and their gaze invaded one another's eyes. They stood far and long away and touch was all I could feel as they moved in so completely alone and kissed. Was I aware that I'd stopped moving? I thought I was so absorbed in the beat of the music. How wrong. They were there, over there and that seemed to be the only place to be. Absorbed – was that the word, was that the sentiment? It's what I was.

I later watched them dance. I watched the night pass into early morning and it doesn't sound it but it was a long night. Longer for having to watch them out there where I'd aped so madly and they now writhe together and reach out touching. He holds her waist, hand, cheek and they dip low with legs bent and hips grinding, their bellies pressed together.

We began to leave. I went to the bog and at the door I saw Sean's face straighten, that look of trapped desperation I've never seen before. There were two boys I didn't recognise but *he* did. It hurt and they began to speak, well, shout really and for a while I didn't hear but he heard. He felt it all. I was thinking about the coats but he was struggling with these guys and soon it all started to make sense.

Oh, Christ!

I heard the word *bender* and these weren't long-haired kids like the others, they were round-headed and wore close clothes, they didn't really look like they should have been here. Anyway it seemed they knew Sean from his previous existence and they were keen to remind him of it.

They said it again somewhere in amongst the taunts and strikes; they were pulling him and slapping his face. 'It's him. That bender!'

It all seemed so unlikely and out of order. Did he want their brother again? they wanted to know. What!

'This is the pansy Ray fucked!' one of them said to a third bloke who'd swaggered up.

'Wanna fuck me? Queer!' Yes, you could see why they were mates.

Go on, Sean, answer them! Did he want to fuck them? Seemed like a peculiar question, I know, but . . .

I hit one in the mouth as hard as my elbow could hit and I'm sure I saw teeth. They were too fast for me to get a good second punch in so I let them floor me and then I allowed my ribs and head to be booted till I forgot where I was. I remember thinking at least I haven't damaged my fists so I'll not miss any boxing.

So of course the bouncers jumped on us and we were outside in seconds. I sat in the gutter, rubbing at the side of my eye where it burnt and swelled. I looked around for the fighters. I was drowsy like you feel sometimes in the hot summer weekend afternoons when you drop off and wake sweaty and guilty with a start and at first you don't know where you are.

I was dazed and Sean stood over me asking for my cloakroom ticket. I looked for the bastards but they were gone.

Jenny appeared with some of the coats.

'Toys, where's your ticket?' she said.

I fiddled in my pocket and handed over the crumpled wet ticket. I grinned at Sean. 'You alright, mate?'

He nodded.

'I think,' I said and swallowed painfully. 'I think I took a few teeth out of one of 'em.'

'Yeah,' Sean said. 'Come on, we'll get a taxi.'

I touched my sides tenderly and smiled as Jenny appeared and pushed my coat towards me.

I giggled in a little sick way. 'I think they took some shit out of me,' I said to Sean.

We wandered up to Camden Taxis beside the road bridge over

the railway and I don't think I looked too bad. No one said anything about it. And if my face was broken it was politely ignored. If my face was broken I just laughed cos I knew it'd be fine in a few weeks.

That ouija board session was so weird. I was telling it to the guys down the gym one time. I'd invited Sean over one evening and we all met up in the gym after hours for cards. I said bring beers.

'Brag, OK?' said Marco. He was the card-sharp.

'Do you know this?' I said to Sean.

'Yeah. Three card brag?'

I nodded.

'Sure, they used to play it at school.'

'You played it at school?' asked Marco.

'No, I used to watch.'

I suddenly felt embarrassed. I remembered those games, I remembered our first painful gasps of fags at school and how dirty they tasted. And Sean standing dumbly and watching. His hair was untidy and his trousers were always worn at the knees even at his age just before leaving school.

We played brag near the boiler building always imagining it would blow up any second. Other kids would follow us, mostly younger ones and we'd tell 'em to piss off. They swore at us and threatened to grass us up. And no one ever told Sean he couldn't play but it was obvious he wasn't wanted. The usual prejudices kids have. He smelt, he was stupid and ugly. Anyway he just used to stand and watch. As if there was something somehow clever about what we did there.

We weren't about to break the smooth cold by inviting him to play. No, we wouldn't let him play. But now. How things are different when you're a stupid ignorant kid.

Marco was shuffling and cutting the cards.

'Anyway,' he said. 'So what happened about this bookshop guy?'

'Oh, yeah,' I said. 'Well, she went to talk to him, Lesley, and it turns out it had got his name right. The *I* in the right place and everything.'

'What, Alain Parrett?'

'No, Alain something. But guess what? He *trains parrots*! Jesus, I couldn't believe it, it's amazing, innit!'

'I *don't* believe it,' said Marco. 'She probably knew him before.'

'Course she did,' I laughed. 'What else?'

'What's he train parrots to do?' asked Chris.

'Yeah,' Marco said. 'She was bluffing.'

'Anyway,' said Chris. 'Shut up and deal. Start on five pence stakes an' fifty pence maximum blind, alright?'

'Blind's when you don't look at your cards, yeah?' asked Sean. I nodded.

'Five pence blind, you mean?' asked Big Jim.

'Yeah. Ten seen.'

'What about sets, how much? Two pence?'

'Nah,' said Marco. 'We don't have sets. Fingers down who's in.'

Marco dealt to the fingers then sat back, his cards still face down in front of him. He toyed with his towers of coins, straightening 'em with his fingers.

'It's on you, Jim,' he said.

'Stacking,' said Big Jim and he threw his cards face down next to Marco. Marco put the cards under the pack.

'Ten seen,' I said, sliding the coin across to the centre.

'Five blind,' Sean said and his five pence joined my coin.

Chris slid his cards under the pack. 'Fuck that,' he said.

'Five blind,' said Marco with his best Goldfinger scowl.

'Ten seen.' I had to slide in a fifty this time. 'Owes me forty,' I said.

Sean picked up his cards and smiled ever so slightly into them. Just curled up the corner of his mouth then eased it back again. It was just enough along with his confident 'Ten seen,' to make Marco pick up.

Marco stared at Sean and back at his hand. He must've had some shit, five high or something cos he quickly shoved it under the pack and looked up trying not to look flustered.

Just me and Sean now.

I slid in a ten pence bit. 'I'll see you,' I said, turning over my pair of queens.

'It's yours,' Sean said and reached across for the pack, sliding his hand under it and taking my pair and the ten and slotting them under there too.

I scooped the winnings back to my bank.

'What did you have?' Marco asked.

'Not that,' Sean said coolly. 'You deal,' he said handing the pack to Jim.

Jim's big fingers struggled with the cards and he finally had them all back in line and cut them.

He put the pack on the table. 'You wanna cut, Marco?'

'No. Just deal.'

'Did you hear about Stuey stacking his car on the M25?' I said.

No, what happened?' Chris asked.

'He was in the fast lane,' I said. 'And he reckons he turned off the engine and coasted for a bit just for the hell of it. Anyway, it wouldn't start again and he was trying to steer over to the hard shoulder when this Granada came up behind him in the middle lane and pushed him over into a van. Totally stacked it.'

'He's alright, though?'

'Oh yeah. Bit pissed off!'

'Twat!' said Marco.

'I got lost on a roundabout once,' said Chris. 'My girlfriend was giving me a blow job and I came off at the wrong exit!'

He pissed himself. We just looked at one another.

The cards came round again. It was serious blind betting all over the shop, then we started to look and the cards began going under the pack.

Sean had seen. Only him and Marco, still blind, kept throwing the money in.

Almost before he'd bet, another two tens from Sean. 'Twenty seen.'

'Ten blind.'

'Twenty seen.'

'Ten blind.'

'Twenty seen.'

It was becoming a race to get their money in the centre quickest. I could see the sweat on Marco's forehead now. This was great, it was better than a Clint Eastwood film.

But he wasn't giving in. 'Ten blind,' Marco said.

'Twenty seen.'

Marco stared down at his cards frantically. He'd have given anything to know what was under there. Christ, how long could he keep this up!

He picked up his cards and held them close to his chest. We all sighed.

He looked up, his face strangled. His eyes were bulging and I'm sure he'd stopped breathing. I could feel his agony and my legs were jumping about excitedly under the table. I felt like something wound up about to blow.

Marco bet his twenty then Sean raised.

'*Fifty* seen.' He slid that huge thick slab of metal into the centre and it could have been a thousand pounds for the thrill it gave me.

I was grinning uncontrollably and I darted back to Marco.

Jim leaned round to see Marco's hand. 'Let's have a look,' he said.

Marco pulled away. 'No,' he said coldly.

Sean rattled his pile of quids and waited for the bet. Marco slid in another fifty.

'A quid,' from Sean. Marco followed. Then Sean said, 'You wanna go higher? A fiver?'

Marco stared with a cold face. He looked so hostile. It's amazing what this game does to you. He didn't answer.

Sean pulled his folding out of his back pocket and peeled off a wrinkled fiver and threw it in.

'Fiver seen.'

'I thought a quid was the limit,' Big Jim said.

'Stack it!' Chris said to Marco.

'It's alright,' Marco said. 'I'll see you.'

Sean looked back. 'Let's see your money.'

Marco slipped out a fiver from his breast pocket and put it in. 'Go on,' he said.

Sean laid down his cards. Three sevens.

Marco looked so angry. His ears were steaming.

'Fucking hell,' said Jim. 'Beat that!'

Marco stuck his hand under the pack but it didn't have the same effect as when Sean had done it. That was it. Sean had won!

He raked back his money.

He looked around to the door. 'Well, I'd better be going now,' he joked with a massive grin.

I cracked up and watched him pile up his quid coins and stuff the tenner back into his pocket.

'OK, my deal,' I smiled. 'Everyone in?'

They all nodded. Sean shook his head, still grinning. I laughed and started dealing.

The phone started ringing in Ron's office.

'That'll be . . . ' started Jim.

'The phone,' I said.

Marco dashed off to answer it.

'You heard about that place in Streatham where they have blokes fighting dogs?' Chris said.

'Yeah, it was in the paper. They fight Rotters don't they?'

'Yeah. You can get two grand for it. Fancy it?'

'No, not really,' I said. 'How're you supposed to box a Rotter?'

Marco came back. 'It was Ron,' he said. 'We've got to turn on the alarm when we leave.'

'Deal again, Toys,' Marco said.

'I've just dealt! Don't you trust me?' I said.

'Not really. Go on, deal.'

I dealt.

'Put your can on the floor, Jim.'

'Why?'

'You'll knock it over in a minute.'

'Chris,' I said and he looked. I held the flame under his cigarette and he sat back and exhaled, brushing something from his sleeve.

'You alright, Sean?' He was rubbing his chest and frowning.

'Yeah, it's just a little pain.'

'You wanna stop?'

'Nah, I'm OK.'

I counted my money then looked over at the fridge, working out how many cans I had left. Shame the tape deck weren't working. I could do with some music. Them lot probably wouldn't want it on, though. My cards were gone – everyone but Sean had stacked.

Marco picked his cards up. He wasn't falling for it again.

'Ten seen,' he said.

Sean giggled and threw his cards in. 'Eight high!' he laughed.

Marco looked around and realised he was the only one left.

'Fuck!' he said and turned over his cards without thinking. He had a flush!

Chris pissed himself laughing and I could hear Sean choking beside me.

'You didn't get much mileage out of that one, Marco!' I was laughing. 'What's that, seventy-five pence!'

I looked at Jim but his face was white and shocked. He was staring at Sean.

Christ! He *was* choking! Sweet Jesus, his face was going black and he was fighting for air, I could see the fear in his poor eyes and his throat bulging.

He was clutching his chest and all I could think was *God Almighty, he's gonna die, he's really gonna die this time!* There's nothing I can do for him now, he's having a heart attack and he's gonna die on me!

And for the first time I thought of Jenny. I thought why couldn't she be here to be with him at the end. And I thought well maybe, just maybe, she does love him more than I do. Perhaps it's not fair that she shouldn't be here, cos she should be.

And I found myself screaming at Marco. 'Phone an ambulance, for Christ's sake! Fucking phone an ambulance!'

He ran into Ron's office faster than I've ever seen anyone move before.

'Open the door!' I shouted at Jim. 'Get some air in here! Chris, help me get his neck undone!'

We clawed at his buttons and relieved the pressure on his throat.

I was saying, 'It's OK, Sean, there's an ambulance coming, mate. Just hold on. Think about Jenny, she's waiting for you. Hold on, mate, don't go to sleep, just keep thinking about Jenny, eh?'

It was absolute hell, those minutes waiting for the ambulance. Everyone seemed to be talking at once and talking shit.

'Can't we do anything?' said Chris. 'Mouth to mouth or something?'

'You wanna try?' I snapped.

He backed off, shaking his head.

'Isn't it too cold now?' said Jim.

Marco rushed back in. 'A couple of minutes!'

Sean was writhing, his back arching as he gasped for air. His forehead was creased in pain and he still clutched at his chest.

'I'm with you, mate,' I said and held his hand. 'Hold on, Sean. I know it hurts, but we're all with you.'

I couldn't hold on anymore and I collapsed into tears, heaving and dribbling from my mouth like a baby. I just emptied it out. All the fear and hurt I had in me for Sean, for the injustice of it all and I cried and cried, my tears spattering onto Sean's T-shirt.

'We're with you, mate,' I gasped. 'I love you, baby,' I cried and buried my wet eyes onto his hand and moaned there. 'Hold on, for God's sake. Just think of Jenny. Think of Jenny and me. We both love you! Oh God, we love you, Sean!'

The ambulance men found me there and they took him away.

'No, you'd better not,' they said when I asked to ride with him. 'He'll be alright now. Get a taxi to Guy's Hospital, you'll find him easy enough.'

I nodded bleakly, my eyes still wet.

'Guy's Hospital, OK?' he said again.

I nodded. 'Yeah.'

And nearly two hours later found me still sitting in the waiting room with Marco. He'd stayed with me. I told Jim and Chris to go home. They were no fucking good.

It was after midnight. We were in Bostock House, the prefab dialysis unit. In the nurses' room with the microwave and the coffee stuff. I'd been here before to see Sean hook up to the machine but I'd never been so scared as I was then.

Jenny was in there with him. And the nurses and the doctor and the wires they had in him, hooked up to a machine that sent arcade sounds echoing round the bare scrubbed walls.

'Have they told you what it is?' Jenny asked.

She was sitting beside him nursing his hand in her lap like a little lame bird.

'Pericarditis,' he managed to say. 'They're dialysing the crystals away.'

His face was still a little dark and he was so weak.

'That's what they told me. Your heart's poorly now, darling. It's the blood pressure I think they said, I couldn't really take it in.'

He didn't even have the energy to nod. Jenny wanted to cry for him until she died, to take away all this pain and have it for herself if she could. She was making pacts with God – *If he can just get better, take me, I want to die, not him!*

'Is that what the pains were?' she said. 'You've had 'em for weeks, haven't you, why didn't you tell me?'

He stared at her little face screwed up with concern and his eyes seemed glazed.

'You're faint,' he said. 'I can't see you very well.'

'Oh, babe,' she said and squeezed his hand. It hurt her so much to see him like this.

He smiled. 'They said I can have the very next kidney that

comes along, Jen.' He'd have been excited if he'd had the energy. 'That's great, isn't it? I'm gonna be OK.'

The nurse came back. 'Shall we let him get a little sleep now, love?' she said. 'He'll be finished in about three hours. He can go back to the ward then.'

Jenny just burst into tears. She leaned over and kissed him.

'Goodbye, babe,' she said. 'I'll be here tomorrow.'

And the nurse put her arm around Jenny as she walked away, dripping tears onto the shining tiles.

'You'd better go home, Toys.'

Jenny came past the waiting room and stuck her head in. Streaked with tear lines.

I was too tired to argue and too upset. 'Yeah, OK,' I said.

There was a sticker in the door window that said *Nurses are beautiful people*. Like I said I was too tired to argue.

Marco stood up and looked at me with big sad doggy eyes. He could see how I was hurting. I think we all were. We were just kids really, this was all far too big for us to handle.

That's the way I felt that night going home. I had thought I was so adult and cool. Thought I knew the world, thought I could handle anything. But this – tonight I felt three years old and I broke down telling the story to my Mum.

She held me like she hasn't done for fifteen years and whispered things to me, stroking my head and I cried like a baby – a little, confused, broken-hearted baby.

I remember the last thing I saw as I crawled up the stairs to bed, still sobbing, was Skelly sitting in front of the telly with his cans and his poor confused, embarrassed face looking at me. He was concerned and he didn't know what was going on. Poor bastard.

I think Jenny must've slept at the hospital that night. Anyway she was there when the morning broke bright in those Vim-scrubbed halls. I dunno what she did, wandered round the maze of neat signs, stared out the high windows, watched trolleys rattle past, little kidney bowls and shiny scalpels and rubber gloves and sterilised water and blood bag units.

Did she hear them talking in the early hours, their medical voices shining off the bright metal scalpel textbooks, their concern drowned in professional attention?

'It's very faint.' The doctor was tuning into his stethoscope, the pickup on Sean's heart. 'I think he's bleeding – it looks like tamponade.'

'The blood pressure's falling—'

'I know! I'm getting tachycardia.'

The doctor's hand shot out pointing between the nurse's eyes. 'Get adrenalin and for Christ's sake get Denis!'

Sean's poor chest was heaving up and down twenty to the dozen – deep breaths sucked in desperately, and straight out ready for the next.

But they knew what they were doing. Everything would be alright when Denis arrived. And they worked through the dark until the sun rose and Jenny wandered about among the pale nurses.

Them nurses are always thin and tired. They give so much of themselves, one hundred per cent so that they drain the very life out of their bodies and give it to the sick. Life saving, comforting, loving, gorgeous people. Sacrificing – Christ, it's incredible how anyone could do that. Nurses are beautiful people like the sticker said.

Jenny, I dunno what she did until she phoned me. Probably ambled round in a helpless daze and cried as much as she could, then when she realised she didn't feel any better she phoned me.

'Hello?' I said.

'He's dead, Toys.'

They were the coldest words I have ever heard, I tell you. Almost funny. I nearly laughed, I really did. What else could I do? Christ, I knew I'd never be able to cry enough!

It was just . . . not fair. Not fair. Nothing else – I just can't put it into . . .

So I met her in the pub and we talked for hours. I know it's a cliché, but I thought she'd get totally pissed. But she didn't. She hardly drank anything, just a couple of Cokes.

And she sat there with a quiet weak voice and her hands buried between her knees like little dead fish.

I stared at the fire and the wallpaper and the copper pans hanging by the bar. And I actually wanted a shit all that time. I sat there but hardly noticed. There was another pain. And I could feel it in Jenny's heart, too.

At last we were together in something. Together. And yet we'd never felt so alone.

So here I am. She said it today. I heard it this morning just before lunch.
He's dead, Toys.

He's dead.
Here I am in our house. My Mum's out and I need her so much tonight. I want her to hold me like she did last night but she's not here.

I'm more relaxed now than I've been all day.
I've got that secure, washed-out feeling you get after a hangover leaves you late in the evening.
The headache's gone, the sick feeling's faded and you're just left tired and sighing.
Jenny said to me, 'You're afraid to write, aren't you? Afraid you'll create something that'll outlive you!'
Well, she's wrong, look. I wanna say it better than *she* could. It's the only thing I can do for Sean
The poems are hers but the rest is *mine*. And I give it to Sean along with all the pain it's caused me this afternoon and all the past years to write it down.
I give it all to Sean. My best mate. Ever.

That ouija board thing said Sean and Jenny would get married. It was wrong there.

I don't think he'd have thought much of this last poem if he'd read it anyway. Jenny put it on the back of a postcard with a picture of a chair on it. The chair's a tubular steel frame with the seat made of loads of leather straps.
Looks perverted to me.
She says she wrote it in the early morning. When Sean's heart was stopping.

EMPTY CHAIR

A chair waiting, lonely.
Waiting for someone to fill the space
Where someone should be.
Just as I sit here, waiting, lonely,
For you sitting, together, with me.

Love you.
Come and fill my empty space
without you.

If ever I need you I need you now
To hold me, to want me,
To love me, to kiss me.

Jenny

XXXXX

You know what happened to Fitzsimons? The old pervert from Wimbledon.

He got into rebirthing. Got the rebirthing bug up his arse and he won't stop talking about it now, it's all he ever goes on about.

I wonder if Jenny's gonna see him again. Or if she'll go back to Grant at the club. Will she go back and sit next to scatty Natassia again, and that fit French bird?

Nah, *she's* back in Paris.

I was talking to Monica and the girls recently about abortion.

They were arguing about when life begins.

'Life begins at the moment of conception,' Monica said.

'Nah, there ain't no *moment* of conception – it's a continuous process,' said Lesley.

'Anyway,' I said. 'They reckon life begins at forty. So you should be able to abort your kid any time before they reach forty!'

I think it's cuppa time. And a biscuit. Then I'm off to bed, I can't be arsed waiting for my Mum now. Doubt if I'll be able to sleep though.